Readers love the THIRDS series by CHARLIE COCHET

Catch a Tiger by the Tail

"I love the THIRDS series. It's fun, action-packed, and hella sexy."

—Just Love: Romance Novel Reviews

Smoke & Mirrors

"If you aren't reading this series, well, you absolutely should be. And I, for one, have no qualms about recommending it to you."

—Joyfully Jay

Thick & Thin

"This series has always amazed me and the amazement continued when reading this one…"

—Three Books Over the Rainbow

Darkest Hour Before Dawn

"The briskly paced novel is packed with exciting action, steamy sex scenes, melodramatic passion, and tender moments of romance."

—Foreword Reviews

Gummy Bears & Grenades

"*Gummy Bears & Grenades* was pure fun."

—Birdie Bookworm

By Charlie Cochet

LOCKE AND KEYES AGENCY
Kept in the Dark

THIRDS
Hell & High Water
Blood & Thunder
Rack & Ruin
Rise & Fall
Against the Grain
Catch a Tiger by the Tail
Manga: Hell & High Water

Published by Dreamspinner Press
www.dreamspinnerpress.com

KEPT IN THE DARK

CHARLIE COCHET

Published by
DREAMSPINNER PRESS

5032 Capital Circle SW, Suite 2, PMB# 279,
Tallahassee, FL 32305-7886 USA
www.dreamspinnerpress.com

This is a work of fiction. Names, characters, places, and incidents either are the product of author imagination or are used fictitiously, and any resemblance to actual persons, living or dead, business establishments, events, or locales is entirely coincidental.

Cover content is for illustrative purposes only and any person depicted on the cover is a model.

Mass Market Paperback ISBN: 978-1-64108-166-5
Mass Market Paperback published February 2020
v. 1.0

Printed in the United States of America

This paper meets the requirements of
ANSI/NISO Z39.48-1992 (Permanence of Paper).

Chapter One

"MY GOD, you're amazing."

Jerry stumbled through the darkened living room, nearly tripping over his own feet as he toed off his Italian loafers. He fumbled with the buttons of his designer shirt, attempting to undress himself without tearing his mouth away from the curvy brunet wearing the snug black cocktail dress. Giving up on the buttons, he stepped back and tugged at his shirt, pulled it over his head, and tossed it somewhere behind him.

"I'm going to make this a night you'll never forget," Jerry promised, hands sliding up her body to cup her breasts, his breath labored.

"That's because he intends to strangle you to death." D's gruff voice carried through the shadows, and he grinned at Jerry's startled red panda impression. D loved those little guys. He'd never seen a more overly dramatic animal. Except for Jerry here. Red pandas were adorable, unlike Jerry, who didn't deserve the air he breathed.

"Fuck!" Jerry jerked the brunet in front of him, using her as a shield.

"Real classy, Jerry." D shook his head and emerged from the darkness, gloved hand raised, his trusty SIG P320 with suppressor aimed at the monster standing in the living room of the multimillion-dollar South Florida mansion. Jerry's eyes went comically wide from behind the brunet, who gasped, terror filling her big brown eyes. "It's okay, sweetheart," D assured her, keeping his tone soft. "I'm not here for you. I'm here for the guy who was planning on killing you during sex and then having his goons dump your body where no one would find it. Just another Saturday night for our psychopathic friend here. Isn't that right, Jerry?"

She choked on air and darted away from Jerry, arms wrapped around herself as she started to tremble. Poor girl. She had no idea how close she'd come to becoming a tragic statistic. As it was, D hated he was too late to save the others, but how could he stop something he hadn't known was happening?

Now he knew.

Jerry attempted to move, and D shot him in the leg, ignoring Jerry's howl as he hit the tiled floor.

"It's just a flesh wound, Jerry. Stop being such a baby." D rolled his eyes. Really? The guy dragged himself dramatically across the floor like he was a WWI soldier who'd been shot in no-man's-land. "You can use your left leg, you know. There's nothing wrong with your left leg." Jerry ignored him, grunting and groaning as he pulled himself, smearing a trail of blood along the way. *Idiot.* D approached the young woman, hands up in front of him. "I'm not going to hurt you."

Not that he expected her to believe him, what with the gun still in his hand.

"Please." Tears streamed down her cheeks as she slowly backed away.

"What's your name?" D asked gently.

"M-Miranda."

"Miranda, there's a driver waiting out front, ready to take you wherever you want to go, but I can call you a Lyft if you prefer. You're safe, okay? No one is going to hurt you." He offered her a warm smile. "I know that's hard to believe coming from a guy who just shot someone, but trust me, he deserves it."

"Was he really going to kill me?" Miranda asked, chin wobbling and voice breaking. Her eyes went to Jerry, and D glanced behind him, releasing a heavy sigh. He stopped beside Jerry and pressed a booted foot to his wrist, stopping him from picking up the cell phone he'd pulled out from the pocket of his discarded suit jacket.

"Jerry was planning on making you victim number twelve."

"*Twelve*?" Miranda gasped, her hand flying to her red lips.

"He's been doing it for years, and Daddy's been helping him cover it up." D crouched down, grinning broadly at Jerry. "I'm afraid dear old Dad won't be in the race for governor next election. What with him facing prison time for helping you keep your dirty little secret."

"You have no proof," Jerry spat out.

D reached into the inner pocket of his leather jacket and pulled out the photos tucked inside. He tossed them in Jerry's face. "I think the bodies of the eleven young women you raped and murdered is proof enough, wouldn't you say?"

Jerry stared down at the photos. "How… how did you get these?"

"Exposing secrets is my business, Jerry, and I'm very good at my job." He also had an entire agency and team of professionals behind him, but Jerry didn't need to know that. It's how he'd found Jerry's little trophy stash.

A screech pierced the silence, and D jumped to his feet. One second Miranda was standing on the other side of the room all quiet and scared, the next she was kicking the shit out of Jerry. D cringed when Miranda stabbed her stiletto into Jerry's back. *Ouch.* That had to hurt. Judging by Jerry's wail, D gathered it hurt *a lot.* Should he do something? Maybe he should do something. In a minute.

"You sick motherfucker!" Miranda kicked Jerry in the balls so hard, D felt it. He sucked in a sharp breath and cupped himself. *Holy shit.*

"Okay. Time to go," D prompted, wrapping an arm around a cursing and spitting Miranda. He lifted her and put her on her feet by the door. "Go home. Take care of yourself, and if anyone asks, you never saw me."

Miranda nodded, her brown eyes almost black as she glared at Jerry, no doubt wishing him a long and painful demise. "Just promise me you're going to make that hijo de puta pay."

"Him and everyone else involved," D promised. He'd knocked over the first domino in a very long line of depraved and corrupt pieces. They had no idea what was about to hit them.

Miranda gave him a curt nod, then disappeared.

"When my father finds out about this, you're dead!"

D chuckled at the threat.

"What's so fucking funny?"

In reality, nothing. If the average person saw even a flicker of the horrors he'd witnessed, it'd break them. D didn't break. It was why he could do what he did, or at least what he used to do. The term *compartmentalize* had been created with people like him in mind. He'd come across the most putrid, dehumanized filth the world had to offer, and locked it away behind closed doors, the keys of which he'd tossed into the ocean of his mind to be forever lost. Then he would do his job. Jerry wasn't the worst he'd seen. Not even close. Which was why D found the man amusing.

D crouched down in front of Jerry. "Can't kill a guy who's already dead, Jer."

Being dead had its advantages. For one, people who'd been out to kill him were no longer looking to do so, and those who wanted him dead now were chasing a ghost. Dying wasn't fun. It had hurt like a son of a bitch, and then came all the misery of leaving people he cared about behind, people he'd never be able to talk to again, but he'd brooded over that enough.

His death had not been peaceful, and he sure as shit hadn't gone quietly into the night. Bitter betrayal and a bullet to the chest tended to do that to a guy. No, his last breath had been coupled with blind fury.

"You don't look dead to me," Jerry spat, eyes narrowed.

Wow. Sharp as a whip, this guy.

Clearly he wasn't *actually* dead, but he *had* died. When Alpha found him, he'd expelled his last breath. They'd revived him and placed him in a medically induced coma. No one came to visit him. Not that anyone would have been able to find him had they known. His funeral had been lovely, or so he'd been told.

Two years later, here he was, in possession of a new name, a new life, and a new purpose. Today's purpose was currently glaring at him in the hopes D would explode into human confetti.

Sweat trickled down the side of Jerry's face, his soulless eyes studying D's face, as if trying to figure out an angle he could exploit. His lips spread into a satisfied grin, and the hairs on the back of D's neck stood on end.

Click. D sprang into action, darting toward a large leather sofa and diving behind it as a spray of bullets turned the once quiet living room into a war zone. D removed his second SIG from the shoulder holster beneath his jacket, followed by the suppressor tucked into the slim pocket beside it. Fucking Jerry. He'd clearly pushed some kind of panic button while D had been dealing with Miranda.

Where the hell had these guys come from? He'd knocked out all the guards in the small command center behind the house as well as the half dozen patrolling the property. He'd done surveillance on the place before making his move. Always did. He tapped the tiny earpiece in his right ear.

"Alpha, I've got unexpected company. I need eyes on the new guests."

"I'm on it," his boss's digitally altered voice replied. "Accessing security feed. Six heavily armed hostiles, more on the way. Three near the sliding glass doors, two near the front door, and one with the target. Police have been notified of an intruder, and officers have been dispatched. ETA fifteen minutes."

"I'll be done in ten."

"I thought you took care of security."

"I did," he said through his teeth, rolling onto his stomach, preparing to make a move.

"I'll look into it."

D waited for a pause in the gunfire before darting out from behind the couch and shooting two of the goons by the glass doors—clean shots to the legs. Once upon a time, he would have aimed much higher and taken them out of the equation, but that wasn't him anymore. That wasn't his job. These weren't targets. They were stupid men who'd picked the wrong employer. D landed behind the loveseat, his pulse steady. Two down, four to go.

Alpha's voice came over the line. "Target had a panic button built into his belt buckle. Extra security came from a van parked down the street."

"For when he killed Miranda." Maybe they hadn't picked the wrong employer after all. Still. He had his mission, and he *never* deviated from the mission.

"Five minutes," Alpha stated.

"Got it." D ducked behind a pillar, grateful for the open-plan layout of Jerry's ridiculous, modern two-story mansion. "Police are on their way, Jerry. It's over."

"Please," Jerry scoffed from somewhere across the room. "My dad has the police in his pocket. Not that it matters. All you've done is put me in a position to garner sympathy from the public, which will only serve to boost my father's campaign." The shooting stopped while Jerry fed his ego. "Just think about it. He'll appeal to them as a parent, promising to do something about the crime and corruption. How crime in South Florida is out of control, his own son a victim of a violent and ruthless criminal who broke into his home and shot him."

"All the while Daddy continues to bury the bodies of the innocent women you rape and kill."

"What else are those whores good for?"

D stepped out from behind the pillar. One, two, three, four. The bodies crumpled to the floor. Jerry stood, stunned stupid. He gaped at D before throwing his hands up.

"Please."

Sirens sounded in the distance, and D ignored them, stalking to Jerry who tried to hop away, his back coming up against the bar. The men Jerry had hired were too busy trying to save themselves to bother with their employer. Hire scum, get scum service. D put the muzzle of his suppressor under Jerry's chin. "I should save the taxpayers their money and go straight to the execution."

D's earpiece crackled. "Delta, killing the target is not the objective."

D gritted his teeth, his jaw muscles clenched so tight his face hurt. "Those women didn't deserve what they got, but you…." D moved the suppressor of his second gun to Jerry's crotch. "You deserve to be in the ground."

"Please. I'll give you whatever you want."

"Police vehicles approaching," Alpha informed him. "Get out now."

D's finger twitched over his trigger. He'd killed for so much less. "Those women deserve justice."

Jerry's bottom lip trembled, but D wasn't talking to him.

"And they'll get it," Alpha assured him. "Story's breaking now."

An evil grin spread across D's face. He punched Jerry in the balls for good measure before securing one of his SIGs into the waistband of his jeans, then turned to swipe the TV remote off the couch. The blue-and-red lights from the small army of police cruisers pulling into the expansive driveway sent streaks of color swirling through the many open windows and glass doors, reflecting off the various mirrors and white walls, making the room look like a seedy nightclub.

D turned on the TV, a special news bulletin blaring through the surround-sound system, Jerry's face plastered on the screen along with images of his victims, followed by news of his father's involvement. D smiled as he headed for the side door, calling out over his shoulder.

"Have fun in prison, Jerry. Hey, maybe you and your dad will be cellmates. That'll be real swell." D slipped out into the darkness of the garden as a *boom* resounded and the shouts of SWAT officers echoed. He moved silently among the lush greenery, removing the suppressors from his SIGs and returning them to his jacket's inside pockets before tucking his SIGs into his shoulder holster. Officers flooded into the mansion, and he crossed the street, strolling onto the dock, where a small speedboat waited for him.

"Good job," Alpha said, and D smiled as he steered the boat away from the crumbling empire behind him. "How do you feel?" The electronic voice had taken some getting used to, not to mention the fact he had no idea who it belonged to. He'd stopped trying to figure out the identity of his mysterious employer a year ago. Whoever they were, they'd saved him, given him a reason to get up in the morning.

"One less monster in the world," D replied, loving the smell of the ocean, the salty wind whipping in his face.

"Good. Report to the agency."

"You got it."

Music filled the air, and the colorful lights of Bayside Marketplace danced on the water's dark surface as he approached the marina, steering past a small party boat filled with women and a handful of men. Salsa music blared from the boat's speakers as everyone aboard danced and cheered. When they saw him, they clamored over to the railing, waved, and catcalled.

"Oye, guapo!"

A perky blond wearing a satin sash stating she was the bride leaned over the rail, her ample assets on display for him. "Hey, baby, come join us! It's my last night as a single woman!"

He slowed down and grinned up at her. Beside her, a tall dark-haired drink of water licked his lips, and D blew him a kiss. The bride-to-be's mouth formed a perfect little O before she threw her arm around her companion.

"He's single too!"

"I'll take a dance from both of you," D yelled up, laughing at the delighted shrieks. Boat secured, he climbed up the rope ladder hanging off the side, and jumped over the railing, the crowd of pretty people losing their minds, a sea of tipsy and drunk men and women up for anything as they helped their friend celebrate her upcoming nuptials. The bride took his hand along with the hand of her friend and led them to the center of the dance floor. D spun her around, smiling at her laugh before he pulled her against him, her friend stepping in behind him.

"Fuck, you're gorgeous. Come home with me," the handsome man begged in his ear, his hard erection grinding into D's ass. D wrapped one arm around the bride as he danced with her, his free hand finding his male dance partner's neck. He turned his head, responding to the plea with a deep kiss, the taste of beer swirling around his tongue.

The music pulsed, colored spotlights casting a wave of sparkling rainbow diamonds across the dance floor. He danced and kissed his way through the crowd, men and women grabbing fistfuls of his shirt, fingers trailing through his hair, hands sliding over his biceps and tracing his spine. Handsome returned, and he'd brought a friend, a cute blond twink with pouty pink lips.

"Well, hello, boys."

Handsome pulled him toward the end of the boat, and D happily followed, twink in tow as he was led to a storage closet just big enough for the three of them. The door had barely closed when he had mouths and hands all over him. His belt was unfastened, his jeans and underwear jerked down to his thighs.

Handsome shoved his tongue into D's mouth, his fingers closing over fistfuls of D's hair as wet heat swallowed D's cock. He lost his pleasured groan inside the mouth of the man dry humping his leg. D unfastened the man's slacks with one hand before slipping his hand inside his underwear and using his precome to aid in jerking him off.

Blondie popped off him, slapped a condom at D's chest before lubing D up.

"So efficient," D purred in approval. "Let's kick things up a notch, shall we?"

Blondie's pupils were blown, and he pushed his pants down as he turned and braced his hands on the wall. D pulled a condom and packet of lube from his pocket and put them in Handsome's hand. He motioned to Blondie. "I'll be right behind you. Literally."

"Fuck." Handsome didn't waste any time. He sheathed himself up, slathered on some lube, and by the time he was balls-deep inside Blondie, D was pushing his slicked up, sheathed cock inside Handsome. His first hard, deep thrust had both men crying out, and a shiver ran through D. He pumped himself inside tall, dark, and handsome, while the man he fucked drove himself inside the blond beauty.

"That's it," D breathed, the tiny room filled with their panting and cursing. "Oh fuck." He doubled his efforts, the sound of flesh smacking against flesh wonderfully obscene. He wrapped a hand around Handsome's neck, turning his face so he could shove his tongue down the man's throat as best he could from behind. His hips lost their rhythm as he drove himself in fast and hard, his orgasm barreling through him, his shout muffled by Handsome's mouth as he filled the condom.

Blondie shouted his release, followed closely by the filling in their little sex sandwich. A quick kiss, and D removed his condom, tied it up, and wrapped it in a baggie he found on the supply closet shelf behind him. He shoved it into his pocket while the other two were busy cleaning up. No leaving DNA behind for someone to find. It would put a damper on his whole being dead thing. Though with forensics being what it was today, someone really determined to find traces of him could do so—still, no sense in making it *that* easy for them.

Pulling away from the two very hot and still horny guys, D smiled apologetically and blew them a kiss as he walked out to more cheering. *Time to go.* They begged him to stay, asked for his number, his name. With a wink he climbed over the railing.

"Congratulations, Wendy!" To the rest, he shook a finger at them. "Don't do anything I wouldn't do, which is pretty much nothing, come to think of it. Just don't get caught!"

They cheered, and he climbed down the ladder and hopped down into his boat. With a wave, he took off. Time to head home. Life couldn't get any better than this.

Chapter Two

Seven hours earlier.

LIFE COULDN'T possibly get any worse.

Caiden's printer ground to a crushing halt, the clicking and grunting loud enough to be heard from HQS.

Who was he kidding? Of course it could get worse. Served him right for volunteering to run these damn reports on a Saturday.

The silence that followed the death of Satan's printer was interrupted by the thud of Caiden's head thumping against his desk. First he'd run out of toner and had to make a mad dash to the store—because his backup toner had sprung a leak and ruined a whole ream of paper along with it—where he was forced to all but give up a kidney in exchange because apparently toner was milked from the teat of Zeus's magical fucking cow.

Then he got home only to discover that in his haste, he'd grabbed the wrong cartridge. Returning yet again to the store, and after being judged by a kid who looked like he'd yet to hit puberty, Caiden returned home, where his laptop decided it wasn't going to recognize said satanic printer, forcing him to turn his apartment upside down to find the damned USB cable. Two hours, three cups of coffee, and a step closer to inhaling a Xanax later, he was ready to print out his report. That's when Beelzebub's printer decided to fuck off and die.

Caiden breathed in deep through his nose and let the breath out through his mouth. He hit Print once more, and several prompts popped up on his screen, the gist of them telling him he was basically screwed. He stood, picked up the printer—now an overpriced doorstop—walked to the window, and sighed. The sky was cloudy and dismal, his view consisting of the parking lot and the gray-and-white apartment complex that reminded him of a nuclear facility he'd seen during his travels abroad.

After opening the window, he peeked out, checked the coast was clear, and tossed the printer. It plummeted eight floors down to the sidewalk before it met a spectacular demise, much like his career. And much like his career, he quickly found himself picking up the broken pieces and tossing them into the black trash bag. He shoved the bag into the communal trash container, then headed back to the door, where he came across a piece he'd missed. He stared down at the tiny shard of plastic, the words *Made in America* printed in faded white. The irony was not lost on him. He crushed the plastic beneath his sneaker and kicked it for good measure.

On his way up to his apartment, his phone buzzed in his pocket. He frowned at the blank screen, swiped to take the call, and put it to his ear. The smooth, husky voice made him smile.

"Did you murder your printer, or did it decide to put itself out of its misery?" Savannah Moore asked, her voice filled with amusement.

"Both? It felt like a fitting end to its life." How did she know about the printer?

"Wow. Feeling sorry for ourselves, are we?"

"You have no idea," he muttered. "But it's nice to hear your voice." Savannah hadn't just been his case officer; she was his friend. When the shit had hit the fan, she'd been one of two people who'd fought tooth and nail for him. He could never repay her and Gibson enough for saving his life, for getting him out.

"How about a few rounds at the gym?"

Caiden straightened. "My gym?"

"Yep."

He'd wondered how she'd known about the printer, but his initial thought had been her checking up on him, not that she was in the country. What was she doing in town? Not that he could ask her that over the phone. Though he doubted she'd be able to tell him much anyway. "Okay. I'll see you in fifteen." After hanging up, he hurried to his tiny apartment and his even smaller bedroom.

When he'd been assigned the place, he hadn't cared how small it was because he would barely be there. His legend—his carefully fabricated identity—at the time as a fledgling global business consultant meant he traveled a lot. For the last two years, however, it had been his home. All five hundred square feet of it. The brown carpet was hideous, the walls stained in some parts from leaks, the kitchen barely big enough for one person, and both his AC and heating had paved the path of self-destruction that every other piece of equipment and appliance seemed determined to follow.

He grabbed his gym bag and stuffed a change of clothes, fresh towel, and his toiletry bag before quickly changing into his workout clothes. He headed for the kitchen, got his water bottle, then his jacket from the hook behind the front door. He needed to find a new place and soon—one where the ceilings didn't feel like they were going to crush him at any moment—though that was hard to do when he didn't know what the hell he was doing with his life.

Screw this. He refused to think about it. For now, he'd meet his former CO and figure out what was going on. He hurried down Fleetwood Road to his local gym, the November air nipping at his skin. It was still in the fifties, but he'd have to get the heating fixed before the cold winter nights arrived. How had he gone from exciting vistas and thrilling missions to this?

At the gym, he greeted some of the regulars on his way to the locker room. He probably spent more time here than he did at home. Hell, he spent more time anywhere than he did at home. Once he put his stuff away, he filled up his water bottle and made his way to the freestanding punching bags.

At this time of day, the gym was pretty empty, and everyone else was at the treadmills or doing weights. He put down his water bottle, then grabbed one of the wraps and first wrapped his right hand and then his left before he started his warm-up. Savannah would join him when she was good and ready. He still couldn't believe she was in the US, much less in Virginia. He hadn't seen her since the clusterfuck that was his arrival back on US soil after his cover was blown and he was accused of being a terrorist during an assignment in

Vienna. She'd been the only familiar face, a small comfort after a nearly seven-hour full lifestyle polygraph. *Fucking pricks.* Rolling his shoulders, he closed his eyes and did his best to block out the endless questions, meetings, debriefings, and investigations that had followed. Two years later and he was no closer to finding out how the hell it happened.

Finished stretching his leg muscles, he bounced in front of the punching bag and delivered a fierce right hook. This wasn't how it was supposed to go. Yes, he'd been cleared of any wrongdoing, was still cleared Top Secret/Sensitive Compartmented Intelligence, but the damage was done. His life as an operations officer for the Directorate of Operations was over. His superiors informed him he should be grateful. He still had a career with the DO, was still a vital asset—his job as an intelligence collection analyst was important. They weren't wrong, but it wasn't his heart, what he'd been trained to do, and in some instances what he believed he'd been *born* to do.

As a kid, while his friends all wanted to be astronauts, race car drivers, and helicopter pilots, he'd wanted to be a spy. At home he'd sneak around the house wearing ridiculous toy disguises he bought from the corner store with his allowance. His parents were the only parents on their block wishing their kid would spend his money on candy instead. When he wasn't driving them crazy with his disguises, he'd be playing hide-and-seek, his favorite game. He'd been an expert at it too. His spy activities drove his family bonkers, especially when the school principal called to inform them he kept hiding from the teachers, then popping out of nowhere and scaring the life out of them. By high school his path was even clearer.

Twelve years of his life. Of living his dream. Gone.

Caiden growled, unleashing his anger on the punching bag. Right, left, right, left, right. Roundhouse kick. He beat the shit out of the bag until sweat ran down his face toward his eyes. Forced to stop, he wiped his face with his shirt, smiling when he sensed someone behind him. He spun around, grabbed Savannah's arm, and swept a leg out, but she was quick, avoiding his sweep and retaliating with a spin of her own, taking him with her. He used the momentum to his advantage, throwing his legs around her torso, bringing her crashing to the mat with him.

She laughed and tapped his flank. "I see you haven't lost your touch."

"It hasn't been that long," he said with a chuckle. After getting up, he helped her to her feet.

"Ink's still fresh on the paperwork," she agreed.

Caiden groaned. "Please don't talk to me about ink."

"Oh, right. Your evil nemesis." She waggled her eyebrows, and he laughed. At nearly six feet tall, she was a stunning woman with flawless dark skin and the most alluring gold-green eyes he'd ever seen, and a terrifying mind made her one of the youngest COs the Company had ever had. She'd spent years molding him into the agent he was now.

"Stop," she ordered, snapping him to attention.

"What?"

"Stop feeling sorry for yourself." She took a stance, and he sighed. "This isn't the end, Caiden. You know that better than anyone."

"I know." He nodded. "You're right."

"Of course I'm right." She motioned for him to advance. "I'm always right, remember?"

"Mm, not always."

She cringed, and he let out a bark of laughter. "Oh my God, remember Matzner Park?" Their dead drop had become compromised, leading to a swift detour through the park, where Caiden had wanted to go down one path and Savannah had insisted on the other. They'd briskly walked down her path until they ran into trouble in the form of an evil dachshund duo who'd escaped their person.

"How the hell does something with such short legs run that fast!"

Caiden doubled over with laughter, tears in his eyes. Oh shit, he couldn't breathe. Her face reflected the same horror it had seconds before they'd taken off in the opposite direction, running like they were being chased by armed mercenaries and not a couple of stubby-legged puff pillows with razor-sharp teeth and bad tempers. Caiden wiped at his eyes, his smile warm.

"It was always better when you were there."

"I miss you too," she said, motioning for him to advance. "Let's go. We wouldn't want you to lose your edge."

"We're in a public space." Like she of all people needed reminding.

"I'll try not to look like such a badass," she teased, though he knew exactly how much of a badass she actually was.

"Fine." They were two and a half miles away from HQS, and with his identity compromised by foreign agents, who the hell knew what would happen. He lived in a constant state of awareness, and although it had been ingrained into him since his days at the Farm, at times it was exhausting. It was either that or his lack of sleep.

"You waiting for an invite from POTUS?"

"It's been a while since someone's given me a good workout," he said, taking his stance.

She arched a perfectly shaped eyebrow at him. "Sounds to me like someone needs to get a little action between the sheets. When's the last time you got some hot man action?"

Caiden snorted out a laugh before charging. "Too long ago. Way too long." His brain conjured up images of a certain hot man with pitch-black hair and a delicious, full-body golden tan. Damn it, he thought he'd purged the guy from his system ages ago. He did *not* need to be thinking about that bastard.

Moving in close, Caiden curled in on his stomach, keeping elbows tucked in to protect his head and ribs. Savannah might be slender, but she could easily take a man twice her size and weight out. She was quick on her feet, dodging his blows, ducking under his hooks, and sidestepping his jabs.

Caiden picked up his speed, throwing one punch after the other, his muscles straining as she put him through his paces. She used his bent leg for leverage and swung her light frame up, throwing her legs around his neck and using the momentum to spin him off his feet, bringing them both crashing to the ground. He grabbed her arm, and had she been an enemy, he would have broken it. Instead he tapped her thigh.

"You need to find your joy, Caiden."

"I'm trying," he grumbled, wincing as she tightened her hold on his neck. "Come on, Sav."

"You were my best," she said sadly before a determined look came into her eyes, and she smacked him.

"Ow! What did you do that for?"

"Get your shit together, Cade. You're too good for this moping bullshit. Yes, what happened sucked.

But it's nothing that hasn't happened before to others. You knew the risks going in. We both know how things could have turned out."

Caiden sighed. "I know, and I don't know how I'm going to repay you for what you did."

"You want to repay me?" She released him, swung around, and sat facing him, her eyes soft. "Find a new purpose. Start again. Be happy." Standing, she held out her hand to him. "Move out of that shithole apartment, get a dog, a new man, I don't know, just…."

Caiden took her hand and stood.

"You're walking around like a ghost, Cade. Live."

Caiden swallowed hard and nodded. She was right. He'd been walking around like his life was over when it wasn't. He was only thirty-five, for fuck's sake. So maybe he didn't have his dream. Did that mean he couldn't find a new dream? He squeezed her hand and smiled.

"Thanks, Sav."

She patted his cheek. "You're welcome. Now come on. Let's go to that little bakery down the street and stuff our faces with sugar."

He practically melted into a puddle of goo. "Oh God yes. Their Not-your-average Lemon Bars are *amazing*. Going to shower real quick and change. Meet you outside the locker room." He left for the showers, feeling better than he had in a long time. Maybe after he found himself a new place, he'd get out more, make some friends, find a hot guy and have some sex, *lots* of sex.

After a quick shower and change into jeans and a henley, he pulled on his jacket and joined Savannah. The bakery was tiny, only a two-minute walk from the gym.

"I miss the cafés," he murmured softly, wrinkling his nose at the cold, industrial-looking buildings around them. Even the café was hidden away, seemingly swallowed up by the black steel structure with pitch-black windows, the bakery's black-and-pink awning with cute cheerful logos a stark contrast.

"Remember Café Landtmann?"

Caiden groaned. "Don't. I still dream about their Erdbeer-Schoko Sacher." With all the decadent chocolate and pastries in Vienna, it was amazing he hadn't gained a ridiculous amount of weight, what with his sweet tooth.

"For me it's their Schwarzwälder Kirsch Törtchen. Chocolate and cherries. I will take that over sex any day of the week."

Caiden chuckled as he opened the door to the bakery for her. They approached the counter and each ordered one of the delectable lemon bars and a coffee. Taking a seat at one of the tiny tables in the far corner, they reminisced while they ate and laughed. Caiden took a sip of his coffee and leaned in.

"As happy as I am to spend time with you, Sav, why are you here?"

She shrugged. "Taking a little R and R."

"You?" He blinked at her. "The same woman who took down a drug trafficking ring while she was supposed to be on vacation seven years ago?"

"What? It just fell into my lap."

Caiden pursed his lips. "Mm-hm."

Her laugh made him smile. It was warm and genuine, reaching her eyes. He gave her a pointed look, and she sighed. "Things are tough right now. Hard to know who to trust inside your own government. I'm thinking of retiring."

Had she said she was taking on a legend requiring her to don a habit and start singing with a choir of nuns, he would have been less surprised. "Retire?"

"I've been doing this a long time."

"You're barely sixty, and you look amazing, by the way."

She tilted her head in approval. "I knew there was a reason you were my favorite." She dropped her gaze to her fingers. "Forty years is a hell of a long time in this business."

"No doubt. You should have been COS by now. Gibson got the job for being in Vienna longer, but we all know that was a BS reason. You've been in the field longer in a dozen places. Bahler recommended him when he retired. And we know what a real hardass Bahler was. Being a chief of station is a huge responsibility, but I never agreed with his methods. We were all just glad to be rid of him, and Gibson was a hell of a lot easier to work with."

"You and Ryan made a good team," Savannah said, a wicked gleam in her eyes.

"Yeah. I miss him. We still talk on the phone, but it's not the same."

Ryan Gibson had been his Chief of Station in Vienna, a good man who always had Caiden's back. He was tough as nails, gruff, and fucking hilarious—he never meant to be, but his dry humor and facial expression used to have Caiden in stitches all the time. Whenever Caiden was in a tough spot, or if he just needed guidance, Gibson had been there. The man had been present in Caiden's life more than his own father.

"Gibson never said anything, but I knew he was worried about me, especially the closer I got to unraveling the clusterfuck of political corruption and electoral fraud. I was going to ask for more resources after I talked to my asset." Which of course never happened. Had someone else taken over his case? Not that he could ask. It was out of his hands now. Had been for the last two years. Months and months of work, gone. "Anyway, yeah. You should have been COS."

"Yeah, well. You know how much of a boy's club it's been until recent years."

Caiden grimaced. She didn't have to tell him twice. His being a gay man was something that had been used to the Company's advantage. Over the years, several of his assets and targets had been gay men, most of them in the closet. He'd been used as a honey trap more than once. After all, it was naive to think all the agents, assets, and everyone in between that the Company dealt with were straight. And yeah, he caught shit from his colleagues, but when he was on assignment abroad, it was a nonissue, mostly because if he was caught in a country where being gay meant death, being a spy would be the least of his worries.

Despite all that, Caiden still had it easier than Savannah, because gay or not, he was a man and white. His father might have been Spanish, but Caiden had inherited his mother's looks. German born, his mother had passed on the same fair skin, blond hair, and green eyes.

"The truth is, I'm getting married."

Caiden's face could barely contain his huge smile. "Oh my God, that's amazing! Congratulations!" Then he realized what she was saying. Just another thing she was going to get more shit for.

"I know there have been other female agents who've done it," she whispered, her eyes filled with turmoil. "But that's not me. For the first time, I've met someone who I can spend the rest of my life with, who adores me and doesn't get pissed off that I'm independent. He's so damned proud of the fact I'm a self-employed business consultant, and that's not even what I do. I don't want to spend my marriage lying to the man I love."

Caiden understood. He'd never had that problem. The job had always come first, mostly because he never met anyone he could see himself giving up his career for. Every day agents lived double lives, lying to their coworkers, friends, and families, hiding the truth of who they were and what they did. Caiden didn't have a problem with the lying, because what he did kept those he cared about safe. His parents still didn't know who he really worked for. Would he still be able to lie if he met *the one*? One thing was for certain….

"You're the bravest woman I have ever known," Caiden said, taking her hands in his and meeting her gaze. "You deserve to be happy too, Sav. You've always followed your gut, and it's never steered you wrong. Fuck them. No matter what you do, someone's always going to have something to say about it. Someone's always going to judge you without even knowing you. You've given everything for your job, the Company, this country. Maybe it's time to think about *you*."

Savannah squeezed his hands. "See? My favorite."

He laughed, glad she'd come to see him. Maybe what he'd done for her wasn't on par with her saving his ass, but the smile lighting up her beautiful face was enough. She stood and kissed his cheek.

"I'll keep you posted. Thanks for this. It was nice."

"Stay safe," he said, hugging her tight.

"You too." She walked with him out the bakery and into the crisp late afternoon, the sun breaking through the clouds. "Oh, and Caiden?"

"Yeah?"

She shoved her hands into her jacket pockets and smiled. "Trust your gut. You might just find what you didn't know you were looking for."

Frowning, he opened his mouth to ask her what she was going on about when his pocket buzzed. He fished out his phone, glancing up to find Savannah nowhere in sight. He shook his head with a chuckle. His caller ID was blank, and as he walked up Elm Street toward Fleetwood Road, he swiped the answer button and held the phone to his ear. Maybe it was Gibson calling from another undisclosed location.

"Hello?"

"Caiden Cardosa."

The distorted voice stilled Caiden. "Who is this?" Definitely not Gibson.

"Someone who can give you what you've been searching for."

Caiden remained unmoving, the breeze ruffling his hair on the quiet street lined with manicured lawns, pristine redbrick businesses, and parked cars. The hairs on the back of his neck pricked up, and he discreetly scanned the area. The street was empty. Not that whoever was calling had to be anywhere near him to make the call. He started walking again, subtly checking inside parked cars, but they were empty.

"And what have I been searching for?" he asked quietly.

"The truth. You want to know what happened in Vienna."

Caiden froze, a chill traveling up his spine. "What do you know about it?" Glancing around, he swiftly turned onto the small empty road between the gym and the Mars building. He ducked behind the trees near the gym, the shadows concealing him. "Answer me."

"I know you were taken into custody by local authorities after a phone call reported a suspicious man staying at Hotel Bristol. You were supposed to be meeting an asset at the Vienna State Opera that night. Good job hiding your EDC. The hotel still hasn't found your little stash."

"What? You thought I was an amateur?" The first thing he'd done when he checked into his room was find the perfect hiding spot for his everyday carry—his guns, cash, burner phone, and everything else he might need while he made contact with his asset. When the police pounded on his door, everything was safely hidden in the hole he'd carefully created behind the baseboard in his suite.

"On the contrary, Mr. Cardosa. I believe you're a very smart, skilled operative."

"Yeah? What else do you know?"

"I know you were released by the police, only to have them informed you were a terrorist. You were arrested and managed to escape before you could be transported for questioning where you would most likely have been killed. Someone put a price on your head, forcing you to flee the country. I know your clandestine career was over before you even stepped foot back on US soil. Your dream is over."

Caiden swallowed hard. "Who the hell are you, and how do you know so much about me?"

"You can call me Alpha."

"Well, that explains… absolutely nothing."

"Like I said. I'm someone who can give you what you've been searching for. If you're interested, be on that flight. You'll receive further instruction upon arrival."

"What? Wait, what flight?" Before he could ask any more questions, the line went dead, and the screen flashed back to his home screen, showing he had a new email. Tapping the little envelope, he found a plane ticket for a flight to Tampa, getting in late that evening. He stared at the flight itinerary. What the hell was going on?

Savannah's words echoed in his head. *"Trust your gut. You might just find what you didn't know you were looking for."*

Had she known about this?

Making sure the coast was clear, he quickly headed home, his heart pounding in his ears when he reached his front door. Checking the lock, he cursed himself for not having his Glock on him. He never left the house without it, especially these days. Goddamn it. How could he have been so careless? Had he learned nothing in his twelve years of covert operations? *Too busy wallowing in my own fucking misery. Dumbass.*

Silently he unlocked his front door and slipped inside, listening for any movement. Nothing. Inching up to the kitchen, he took a quick peek. Unless someone was in the fridge, and a contortionist, there was nowhere for them to hide. From there, a quick glance around allowed him to clear the small living room and bedroom areas before he checked the bathroom. He looked under the bed and in the two tiny closets. Empty.

After years of listening to his instincts, he relaxed. At least as much as someone in his line of work could relax. Man, he could use a beer.

He walked into the kitchen and froze. From his angle when he'd looked in earlier, he hadn't been able to see the corner of the counter. A cheerfully wrapped gift basket sat on the counter. The thick yellow ribbon around it said *Welcome to Florida.*

Picking up a mango, he studied it. He pulled out his phone and checked the weather down in Tampa. Clear sunny skies and seventy-eight degrees. Maybe it was time to take that tropical vacation he'd always wanted.

"Guess I'm going to Florida."

Chapter Three

WHAT A beautiful night.

D took the elevator up to the top floor of the eighteen-story building on First Avenue N in downtown St. Petersburg. He loved November in Florida. The weather was perfect—sunny but cool, with a perfect breeze. He could wear his leather jacket without feeling like the heat was trying to fuse the material to his body. The stylish lobby was empty, but then it always was. He ran a hand through his hair and smoothed down his clothes before heading to the sleek reception desk.

The Locke and Keyes Agency was a business solutions company offering all manner of business-type services to a long list of clients, everything from consultation to data analysis and advertising. It was also a front.

On paper, Locke and Keyes appeared to be a legitimate business owned and operated by David Locke and his wife, Becky Keyes, with several employees on staff. In truth, it was a cover for a black op codenamed

Alpha Orion, created by Orion and run by their boss, Alpha. Neither of whom anyone in the office had met in person. D stopped asking questions long ago. His job was to take orders from Alpha. End of story.

Reaching the sleek white desk, he leaned against it, his smile wide for the pretty, petite blond who reminded him of Sandy Olsson from *Grease*, all rosy cheeks and bouncy ponytail, big blue eyes and pink cashmere sweater with a white Peter Pan collar.

His teasing her about her choice of wardrobe was the only reason he knew what the hell a Peter Pan collar was. That nugget of useless information had come just before he discovered the scale used to measure what kind of day she was having, because unlike most people who conveyed their anger or annoyance through visible tells, Becky was always smiling. It was her nail polish that gave her away.

"Hi, Becky."

Becky scrunched up her delicate little nose as she continued to paint her nails. Today's color was a blush pink that matched her sweater. She was in a good mood despite the very late hour.

"You smell like sex."

"At least I remembered to get rid of the condom *before* I got to the office."

She shook her head at him like he was too much—a daily occurrence—before motioning to the hall. "Meeting room A."

"Sweetie, is this invoice correct? I could have sworn I ordered twenty of the Nighthawk Fire Hawks. This says twenty-four." David walked out from his office, pushing his glasses up his nose. When he saw D, he smiled big. "Hey, D. Nice work on tonight's job. How's the new suppressor working out for you?"

"Like a dream, David. Thanks."

"Great! The new SIG Sauer P220 Combat comes in next week. I'll let you know when it arrives so you can give it a test run."

D saluted him and winked at Becky before spinning on his heels and heading for the meeting room, leaving Becky to her husband. The sound of a kiss made him smile. Those two were ridiculously sweet; it made his teeth hurt.

"I upped the order, honey bear. Zed added two more guys to his team, remember?"

"Oh, dang it. That's right. Also, I had to order another coffee machine. How is it Si can hack his way into the Pentagon, but he can't work a darn coffee machine? All he has to do is look at it and the thing goes up in smoke."

Becky giggled. "I'll talk to him, snookums."

"Thank you, love bunny."

D shook his head as he entered the swanky, high-tech meeting room. In the time he'd been here, he never once heard Becky or her husband raise their voices, much less curse. Becky was the agency's receptionist, and David the accountant, not much of a stretch from their true roles. Becky was sort of what they termed a "cut-out," an intermediary between Alpha and the agency's "assets." All information came through Becky from Alpha and was distributed to the appropriate parties. David was the money man. Whatever D needed, David could get it, no questions asked.

The Locke and Keyes Agency reminded D of how the CIA operated. Could there be a connection between them and Alpha? In many ways, Alpha was like the spymaster, while D and the rest of the guys were the agents. Except they weren't spies sent around the globe. They operated on US soil, often going after their own. They had one goal, one purpose. Expose the truth.

D took a seat around the touch-screen conference table in the center, angling his seat to face the end of the room and the three large flat-screens on the wall. Becky walked in, her slim-fitting pants a lighter pink than her sweater, while her ballet flats were a darker shade. She should have looked like a flamingo, but somehow, she managed to pull it off. Her outfits were always cute and colorful. Come to think of it, she was the only pop of color against the office's stark black-and-white decor.

Instead of getting to it, she simply took a seat in the chair opposite him, her pink lips pulled into a sweet smile.

D eyed her. "What are we waiting for?"

"Not what. Who?"

Someone was going to be joining them. That was new. Not unheard of, but not common. He tended to work alone. Occasionally an expert was called in if a talent was needed for something he wasn't proficient in. He couldn't be an expert in *all* areas, no matter how much he liked to think he was. Alpha brought in contractors all the time, but usually once they agreed to the mission, D met them in a secure location, never at the office.

"Are they cute?" he asked her, wiggling his eyebrows.

"Behave yourself."

Like she didn't know him.

The door opened, and the smile fell off his face. His heart lurched at the familiar green eyes staring at him, his breath hitching as images of strong hands and scorching lips assaulted his mind, until the man opened his mouth.

"What the hell—you're dead."

A fierce growl tore through Caiden as he marched over, grabbed D's jacket, and jerked him out of his seat. He slammed D against the wall, fingers curled around D's neck.

Looked like D's beautiful night had just gone to shit.

"IF YOU had anything to do with what happened, you're a dead man! For real this time," Caiden snarled, voice rough, bile stuck in his throat at the possible betrayal.

It hit him harder than expected. What a fucking idiot he'd been. He should have known better than to trust this asshole with his big whiskey-colored eyes, gorgeous face, and stupidly coiffed black hair. Screw him and his bad-boy looks.

"What?" D wrapped his hands around Caiden's wrists, his brows drawn together as he searched Caiden's gaze. D's full lips twisted in a grimace, as if he had no idea what Caiden was so pissed off about. No way was Caiden letting the guy fool him a second time. Caiden jerked D forward, then slammed him against the wall once more.

"Were you in on it?"

"What the hell are you talking about?" D narrowed his eyes, his next words spoken through gritted teeth. "You have two seconds to get your hands off me."

"Answer the damn question."

"Fine." D slid his hand up Caiden's arms, his lips curling up in the corner at Caiden's subtle flinch before D slipped those long fingers behind Caiden's neck. He brought his knee up sharply, but Caiden anticipated the move, dodging the blow but making sure to swiftly retaliate with a right hook to D's ribs. "Fuck!"

Spinning away from Caiden, D came after him, giving as good as he got, his moves precise and without hesitation. Caiden didn't hold back, his frustration ratcheting up with every punch D blocked. Something pink moved from the corner of Caiden's eye, but he ignored it, too focused on the blast from his past trying to cause him serious damage, as if the betrayal hadn't been enough.

"Boys, stop it right now."

"Tell me," Caiden demanded, faking a right and coming in left, catching D in the shoulder, earning himself a chance to grab D and kick his legs out from under him. "How long did you wait before you made the call?" Had it been a setup? A honey trap with him as the target? D went down, but not without taking Caiden with him, both of them slamming into the pristine carpet.

"Are you kidding me with this bullshit?" D growled, wrapping his legs around Caiden's waist.

Now *this* brought back memories. For all Caiden knew, those memories were fake. It shouldn't bother him like it did. He'd slept with countless men across several continents while on assignment. It was one night. The setup? That was a whole other matter. Caiden had to give the guy credit. He sure as hell was convincing playing the part of innocent lover.

"You fuck me, take off while I'm in the goddamn bathroom—but then what else should I expect from an egotistical bastard like you—and when I do hear about you, it's that you're dead, and now here you are, very much alive, telling me you had nothing to do with what happened to me? Fuck you, Montero!"

"It's D."

"What?"

D threw an arm around Caiden's neck, pulling him into a headlock. "D. Montero is dead."

If D didn't let go of him, and soon, Caiden's traitorous body was going to forget he hated the guy.

"D. That's it?" With gritted teeth, Caiden dug his fingers into D's left thigh, ignoring D's sharp intake of breath or the way the black of his pupils spread into the pools of whiskey.

"It's short for Delta."

No. Nope. He wasn't doing this. He'd ignore the man's panting breath, the flush of his cheeks, and the strength of his thighs as he squeezed Caiden.

"You know what else starts with D?" Caiden spat out, smacking D's cheek, *hard.*

"Ow, fuck!"

"Deceitful, detestable, *dick*."

"Give it a rest, will you?"

Caiden narrowed his eyes, and he smacked D again. "Detached. Deplorable."

"Stop hitting me in the face! It was one night! I didn't realize I was supposed to ask you to fucking marry me!"

"Disreputable, distrusting, *dickhead*!"

They struggled on the floor, each of them getting a jab in before something wet hit D's face.

"What the fuck?" They both stilled, and D turned his head, his wide eyes going to the little plastic spray bottle in Becky's hand. "Did you…? Did you just mist me in the face like I was your cat? What the hell, Becky?"

"No, my cat is more refined."

"Really? You gonna ride my ass too?"

Caiden let out a snort. He shoved away from D. "Make sure you wait until he's in the bathroom, then disappear. See how he likes it." Pushing himself to his feet, he gave D a shove as he got up, for the hell of it, taking pleasure in D's flailing before he managed to regain his balance.

The "I hope you burn in the fiery pits of hell" glare D gave him was impressive.

"Why is he here? Other than to make my life miserable."

Becky motioned for D to sit. "Alpha never mentioned anything regarding you two having slept together."

"Oh, there was no sleeping," Caiden scoffed, smoothing down his tie. "Someone would have had to stick around long enough for that." He hated that the sting of D walking out on him was as fierce now as the night it happened, especially now knowing there was a good chance D hadn't betrayed him but chose to fuck off anyway.

"For the love of—" D held his hands up in front of himself, as if he were summoning patience, before running his fingers through his hair. Caiden resumed his seat. "Why is he here?"

"Alpha has a job for you two."

D let out a bark of laughter.

"Something funny?" she asked, one blond eyebrow raised.

"Holy shit." D wiped a tear from the corner of his eye. "That's hysterical."

"Not really."

"Whatever the offer is, you can forget it," Caiden said smoothly, heading for the door. "You couldn't pay me enough to be in the same state as him. Now if you'll excuse me, I'm going to go back to my hotel room, take a scalding shower, and pretend he's still dead."

D flipped him off.

"You're going to want this job," Becky assured Caiden. "You both are."

Not happening. Caiden shook his head. "I'm not working with him." The verdict on whether D had ruined his life was still out, but that didn't change the one declaring D an asshole.

"Ditto," D replied. "What's more, you don't want him. What good is a spook who can't keep his cover?"

Caiden returned D's friendly gesture. "Fuck off and die, Montero. Again."

"It involves the man who betrayed you," she told Caiden, who stopped in his tracks at the words. Caiden let his head hang. Great. No way he wasn't going to do the job now. How many times had he told himself that given the chance to take down the bastard who'd ended him, he'd take it in a heartbeat? Part of him had given up hope he'd ever get the chance, and now here it was, a once-in-a-lifetime opportunity. What any of this had to do with D, he had no idea.

As if reading his thoughts, Becky turned to meet D's gaze. "It so happens that the man who ended Caiden's clandestine career is the same man who ordered the hit on you."

Well, damn. Caiden hadn't expected *that*. Someone *had* tried to kill D, and from the rumors of his death, had succeeded. Caiden had seen the death certificate with his own eyes. How was D alive?

D slowly sat up. "Say that again?"

"Your cases are connected," Becky said, snapping him out of his thoughts.

Caiden marched over and slammed his hands on the table beside Becky. "Who was it?"

"Back the fuck up," D snarled, standing and getting in Caiden's face. "She didn't have anything to do with it. So. Back. Up."

A growl rumbled out of Caiden, but he moved away. He paced near the end of the table, fingers flexing open and closed.

"I don't know who it is. What I do know is that he's been using his position for years to sabotage and eliminate agents and officers who get in the way of his illegal business transactions with foreign governments. A third party seems to have gathered evidence against him and is keeping it in a secret location, a sort of insurance policy. My guess is the two have had business in the past. Whoever is responsible for betraying you both, there's someone even more dangerous keeping your guy under their thumb."

Caiden took a seat in the chair beside D. "Do you think whoever screwed us over is being blackmailed?"

"It's possible." Becky tapped at the table, and it came to life, a rectangular section in front of her displaying a secure log-in screen. She typed away at the digital keyboard, and the three flat-screens on the wall turned on, the middle screen showing an image of a fair-haired man in a designer suit. "This is Kenneth Graves, otherwise known as the Steward."

D appeared unimpressed. "Really? Are we part of the fall TV lineup now?" He thrust a thumb in Caiden's direction. "Is he my sassy new sidekick who provides zingy one-liners and acts as a foil to my grumpy but profound character?"

Caiden appreciated Becky's indelicate snort.

"What? I read."

"More like binge-watches TV shows," Caiden muttered.

Becky's pink lips twitched at the corners like she was trying not to laugh. "As I was saying, this is Kenneth Graves, aka the Steward. Graves is part of a new generation of criminal. Over the years, he's acquired quite the client list. His global connections range from high-ranking military and government officials to organized crime members. If you're a client and you need something, Graves will get it for you or connect you with someone who can. We're talking drugs, arms deals, racketeering, blackmail, and prostitution rings, to name a few. Heck, if you need a new nanny or dog walker, Graves will find you the perfect fit."

"How have the feds not caught on to him?" Caiden asked, studying the man on the screen.

"He's extremely smart and careful. He's a wealthy, successful businessman in his own right, with legitimate businesses. One of the most profitable is Kenneth Graves Financial, which offers diversified financial services, everything from wealth management to market insights. He keeps his two lives separate, and none of his criminal clients have any connections to his legitimate businesses.

"Graves is forty-six years old, married, with no children and has no pets. He pays his taxes, attends church every Sunday, dotes on his wife, and visits his mother on the weekends at a luxury retirement villa that he pays for. His wife runs a children's charity, one among several charities they're both involved in. A pillar of the community."

"And Graves has the evidence against the bastard who betrayed us," D confirmed.

Becky nodded. "One of the many services the Steward offers. If you need to hide evidence or have it destroyed, he'll take care of it." She tapped the table's surface, and an image of a beautiful woman with long dark hair and near-black eyes appeared on the right screen.

"This is Isabella Graves, his wife. She's mob royalty, connected to the biggest, most powerful crime family in New York. However, not wanting to be part of that life, she moved to Florida to get away from it all. Several very protective 'uncles' who have connections to the family but are now retired, followed her when she moved. They mostly serve as counselors and advisers."

"Does she know who her husband is?" Caiden asked.

Becky shook her head, her blond ponytail bouncing with the movement. "No. Graves is exceptionally careful. The whole reason Isabella left New York was to get away from that life. My guess is she married for love, he married for the connections. That makes him very possessive. Whatever her family knows about Graves, they've kept it from her." She pressed the button again, and Isabella's image was replaced by a huge European-style villa surrounded by lush greenery and palm trees, the ocean behind the mansion, and a different body of water with a dock at the front.

"This is the Graves mansion. It's over twenty-four and a half thousand square feet on two and a quarter acres of property located in Lake Worth, Palm Beach. It has eight bedrooms, eleven bathrooms, eight half bathrooms, a library, formal dining room, living room, billiard room, kitchen, butler's pantry, staff quarters, among other rooms, and every inch of it is about to be renovated. Which is where you two come in.

"Alpha believes the key to the evidence you're looking for is somewhere in the house. Caiden, you'll be posing as the personal assistant to elite interior designer Jacqueline Draper. She owes Alpha a favor. And D, you'll be posing as one of the carpenters working alongside Tobias Hicks, the interior foreman, who also happens to owe Alpha a favor."

D leaned forward. "Wait a second. So the gringo gets to be the designer assistant while the Cuban guy's manual labor? What the hell, Becky? That's stereotyping."

Caiden raked his gaze over D, making him shift in his seat. Interesting. "Yes, because nothing says 'interior design and great customer service' like a guy whose biceps are trying to burst through his jacket and a scowl that could freeze your balls off. Tell me, can you even get through a whole sentence without cursing?"

"Fuck you. Of course I can."

Caiden lifted a perfectly shaped brow at him before turning to Becky. "Well, I'm convinced. How about you?"

"Caiden, would you excuse us for a moment?"

Was he really going to do this? Just because D hadn't betrayed him, didn't mean he wasn't an asshole. The guy had fucked him and snuck out while Caiden was in the bathroom. Who did that? And now Becky wanted them to work together? Christ. Could his life *be* any more of a train wreck? Guess he was about to find out.

UNBELIEVABLE. NO. Scratch that. Totally believable. During his military years, his CO accused him of being a trouble magnet and personally responsible for the man's high blood pressure. This hadn't changed after leaving the military. Becky often commented on his love for trouble. D was starting to think maybe there was something to that. What else could explain Caiden Cardosa being back in his life?

"Of course." Caiden stood, his movements fluid. He moved toward the door, his suit hiding long legs and perfectly sculpted muscles, along with what D knew to be a spectacular pert ass filling those slacks. Damn Caiden and his stupid sleekness. He was the perfect package with his expressive green eyes, handsome face, and pretty blond hair, but what had enraptured D, snagging his attention among the splendor that was Café Central in Vienna, had been the man's smile.

The glowing historic chandeliers had nothing on Caiden's smile. When his plump lips parted, the angels sang, and his husky laugh had forced D to subtly adjust himself. In that instant, D had to have the beautiful man.

Caiden was charming, skilled, and at this very moment, D wanted to punch him in his pretty face. "I don't appreciate this, Becky."

"D, the reason you made a great assassin wasn't just because of your ability to detach yourself from the target, but because no one believed the six foot two, two-hundred-and-thirty-pound wall of muscle could possibly be the guy coming to take them out. You're the guy who sits at the bar to watch the game, orders chicken wings, and flirts with the waitress."

"And waiters. I'm an equal opportunity flirt. Also, liking chicken wings doesn't make me a stereotype."

"You're not listening. You're everyone's bro. The guy who likes a good beer and bar food. You're not the trained assassin sent to kill someone. You're the guy they never see coming because they *can* see you coming. You wear biker boots, jeans, a T-shirt, and a leather jacket on the job, disarm them with that crooked smile of yours, and make them laugh before they end up dead. I need you to be that guy. To be you."

"You need me to be the muscle, and you're right. They never see me coming, which is why I can take on any role you put me in. This isn't my first covert assignment, you know. You want me to stare at paint swatches and pretend I give a fuck? I can do that."

Becky dropped a hefty brick of a book onto the table, and for a second D worried the thing was going to go straight through. He'd seen encyclopedias that were thinner. "This is the *Interior Design Reference Manual*. It's six hundred and fifty-six pages of design concepts, elements, principles, programming, site analysis, information analysis and synthesis. And that's one of the six sections."

"Let me see that." D flipped to the introduction and started reading. What was she trying to say? That he was incapable of reading a damned reference book? He was more than muscle. He was smart as a fucking whip. Shit, he lost his place. Didn't matter. D rubbed his eyes. "Like I said. I can do this."

"Really? Is that why you fell asleep?"

"What?"

"You literally fell asleep."

"*Pfft*. No, I didn't."

"You did. You even snored."

"I don't snore."

"You breathed loudly. You fell asleep and breathed loudly while sitting up."

D rolled his eyes. "I'm trained to make myself fall asleep pretty much anywhere at any time."

"And you what? Decided now was a good time to take a nap? How exactly is that supposed to convince me?"

"Shit. Okay. Fine." D sat back and crossed his arms over his chest. "Nerd Boy can be the designer, not because I can't do the job, but because he can do prissy better than I can. If a paint can accidentally ends up hitting him in the head or he breaks something tripping over a tarp that happens to be on the floor, it's not my fault. Just sayin'."

"Face it. The only reason you want it so bad is because you'd be taking it away from Caiden, and that delights you."

"Not gonna lie. It does. Seeing the way his lips make that sad little upside-down smile brings my heart great joy. Like my abuelita's arroz con leche and puppies."

"You know, if that bullet hadn't gone through your chest, I might have wondered."

D scowled at her.

"Too soon?"

Smartass.

Becky's expression softened, and he was done. No way could he deny her anything when she gave him those sad doe eyes. "D, this is your first real lead. You can find the man who killed you. Don't you want to know why?"

D's sigh went down to his bones. "You know I do."

"So don't lose sight of the mission. Work with Caiden. He has as much invested in this as you do. He's an exceptionally skilled spy, compromised or not."

Fuck. He was going to regret this. "Fine."

Becky clapped her hands with glee. What the hell was she so excited about? D peered at her as she hurried over to the door and invited Caiden back in. Great. Just what he needed. To be stuck doing a job with the CIA's poster boy. Well, ex–poster boy, he supposed. Nope. He wasn't going to feel bad for the guy. If Caiden fucked up and blew his cover, that was on him.

"Alpha's providing you with everything you need for this op," Becky said, sliding a couple of smartphones across the desk. "Your legends have already been created, along with all the necessary credentials and IDs. Graves's security firm is doing a background check on you both as we speak. The man is very thorough. Laptops are—"

"Wait." D held up a hand. "How is Graves having a background check done if we only—" Heavy sigh. "Alpha knew we'd accept."

Becky smiled sweetly. "Of course. Alpha knows everything. Including your little detour in Bayside." She frowned in disapproval.

D shrugged. "I was letting off a little steam after a mission." He put a hand to his chest, his bottom lip jutted out pathetically. "I was shot at, Becky."

Becky didn't look convinced. "You're always shot at."

"That's not.... Okay, that's probably true."

"As I was saying, laptops are in the supply closet. Submit your stationery order to David, and he'll make sure it's all at the safe house by the time you arrive."

"Ooh, safe house in Palm Beach." D couldn't hide his excitement. "Tell me you got me a condo on the beach."

Becky wrinkled her nose. "Of course I did."

"Yes!" D jumped to his feet, took hold of her hand, and kissed it. "You're the best, Becky."

She rolled her eyes at him again and waved him off, but her lips twitched with her amusement. “Behave yourself,” she called out after him.

“Always do,” he promised, leaving the room with Caiden on his heels. He leaned over to stage whisper at him, “I never do.”

Chapter Four

WEIRD PLACE to keep computer equipment.

Caiden stood to one side of the supply closet, his curiosity piqued when "D"—what kind of a name was Delta, anyway?—slid the printed sign reading Office Supplies to one side, revealing some kind of scanner. What the—

"Alpha has the best toys," D said, his face lit up like a little kid who was about to be given free rein of the toy store. He stood close to the scanner as retina identification software scanned his eye.

D waggled his eyebrows, and Caiden ignored him. How had he found this man irresistible? Keyword being *had.* D stepped to one side, sweeping his arm dramatically as he bent at the waist, bidding Caiden to enter. Rolling his eyes, Caiden stepped into the room, the lights flickering to life inside the tiny closet barely big enough for the two of them.

"That was… anticlimactic," Caiden muttered, looking around. "Where are the laptops?"

"In here." D turned to face Caiden, their bodies so close they were almost touching. He reached over Caiden's shoulder, and Caiden cursed his traitorous body for the way it jumped to awareness at D's proximity, especially since the little smirk that appeared on D's face said he knew exactly what kind of effect his nearness was causing. "Just reaching to press something on this shelf here," D murmured as he leaned in, his hot breath ghosting Caiden's skin below his ear. A shiver went through Caiden, and he closed his eyes. Damn the bastard. Something clicked behind him, and he turned toward the metal bookcase stacked with boxes of Post-Its, paper clips, tape, pens, and other office supplies. D put his hands to Caiden's waist, and Caiden's eyes nearly popped out of their sockets.

"What are you doing?"

"Moving you," D replied, his lips tugged in a sinful smile. "We need to switch positions."

Caiden snorted. "Always need to be on top, do you?"

"I'm actually very versatile, but in this instance yes. I need to be on top."

The man was going to kill him.

Caiden shifted positions, curious when D pushed on the bookcase and it slid into the wall, then opened, revealing a doorway. Now *that* was impressive. Again, D motioned for Caiden to enter first.

"Such a gentleman," Caiden teased.

"I can be charming."

Didn't Caiden know it. He smartly chose to ignore that remark and walked inside, setting off some kind of motion sensor that had the lights turning on. Caiden stopped abruptly. Nope. He'd been wrong. *This* was impressive.

"Holy shit."

"This is the supply closet," D said, moving Caiden out of the way so the door could close behind them. The man really needed to stop putting his hands on Caiden. It wasn't so much the touching—though that was a problem too—it was the familiarity of his touch. As if they were intimately acquainted, lovers, instead of a couple of guys who'd fucked that one time.

The so-called supply closet was a mini warehouse, flawlessly organized and packed to the brim with all manner of weapons and equipment, an armory housing everything one might need for any number of ops. A quick scan showed handguns, rifles, tech gadgets, surveillance equipment, radios, and a host of other items Caiden couldn't make out from where he stood.

"Whatever you need, Alpha can get it," D explained. "If you need something that's not here, you put in what we call a 'stationery order,' and David will get it for you."

"How?" Caiden asked, following D to a steel table near the center of the room containing several laptops. "How does no one know this is here? How does Alpha get all this?" *Who* was Alpha? Were they a person or a group of people? An organization? Normally Caiden would have used his TS/SCI clearance at HQS to look into Alpha, but he couldn't. Not if he didn't want to bring the Company down on them, which led to another question. Why would Alpha trust him?

As far as the CIA was concerned, Caiden was taking a much-needed leave of absence. They'd been trying to get him to take some time off since his return. He hadn't even called in sick once. For years, he'd lied for the job, but this was the first time he'd lied to his bosses, stating it was all catching up to him and he was taking a vacation to Florida. His request had been swiftly approved.

"I have no idea who Alpha is," D replied, opening one of the laptops and signing in when prompted. "And no one knows this is here because this room isn't on any of the floor plans of this building. My guess is Alpha had the plans altered."

Caiden's gaze landed on the longest wall, lined with weapons storage lockers. The wall to his right had built-in drawers of various depths, a good number of them pulled out to reveal smaller equipment such as scanners, signal scramblers, burner phones, and a few other gadgets. The bottom deeper drawers contained bags, backpacks, duffel bags, laptop bags, and suitcases.

"I've seen countries with less firepower." Caiden peeked inside one of the weapons lockers. "How does Alpha get all this? How much do you know about Alpha?" He certainly hadn't come across any intel pertaining to Alpha or Orion, but then he didn't exactly get clearance to every black op. In the movies, they made it seem like CIA agents had access to all information. A tap of a few keystrokes and they could access any and all intel. The thought was terrifying. Intelligence was compartmentalized and often required varying levels of security clearance. "Need to Know" ran firm and true. Caiden only ever knew what he needed to know to do his job; everything else was irrelevant.

D removed a black duffel bag from one of the bottom drawers, then carried it over to an empty table. "I know as much as I need to. Sound familiar?"

"Except I work for the United States government. You don't even know who the hell you're working for!" Caiden stepped up close, his voice low. "What if Alpha isn't who you think they are?"

How could D be so blasé about it? Then again, this was a man who was paid to kill people for a living. Not that Caiden was judging. Maybe he was judging a little. He'd been assigned SEALs from the SAD—Special Activities Division—during covert operations, and he respected what they did, knowing if they were compromised during a mission that the government might deny all knowledge. Then there were soldiers from special military forces who were sheep-dipped, working under the CIA, who years later didn't return to the military. Was that what happened to D? Caiden definitely got a military vibe from him. The way he stood, like he was always ready to spring into action. The set of his jaw, the precision in which he checked the firearms.

"And you think they're what?" D asked, snapping Caiden's attention back to their current conversation. "You think Alpha's part of a secret terrorist organization that's recruiting people like me and then sending them off to expose rapists, murderers, arms dealers, sex traffickers, and the rest of the scumbags who think they can get away with it, simply to bide their time before they attack? Play the saint to hide the sinner? Is that what you think?"

Maybe coming here was a mistake. Caiden rubbed a hand over his jaw. "So they're doing this out of the goodness of their hearts? This all has to cost money, D. Who's footing the bill?"

D turned to face Caiden. "Do you know how many people have seen this room?"

"I don't know. How many people does Alpha have working for him? Her? Whoever."

"Five."

Caiden squinted at him. "Five what? Hundred? Thousand? Hundred-thousand?" Exactly how big was this operation? If this room had anything to go by, pretty fucking big.

D held up five fingers. "Five. Becky, David, me, and two other guys like me."

That couldn't be right. You couldn't run a black op of this size with five people, two of them civilians. "Like you, how? Contract killers?"

"Nope, but they did work for the government, and they were both killed for it, same as me. We've done missions together. Good guys who didn't deserve to end up with a bullet in them. Well, Si was shot, Zed was blown up. We're the only ones on the payroll, so to speak. We run the ops. Everyone else is vetted and contracted in by Alpha, then they go on their merry way, but we stay."

Caiden side-eyed him. "Alpha Orion is the op, right?" Becky had briefed him when he'd first arrived—or at least as much as she was permitted to—before the meeting with D.

"Yeah. So what?"

"The op was created by someone codenamed Orion, and Alpha Orion is your boss. You're Delta. Let me guess, Si is short for Epsilon, and Zed is Zeta."

"I'm not sure where you're going with this," D said, his body rigid and his expression wary. "What's with the smugness all of a sudden?"

"It's cute."

"What is?"

Caiden leaned against the table, his arms crossed over his chest. "Orion has seven main stars, three of which are Orion's Belt. Delta Orion, Epsilon Orion, and Zeta Orion." He held up three fingers. "That leaves Beta Orion, Gamma Orion, and Kappa Orion. Don't suppose you know who they are?"

"What the fuck? You an astrologist now?"

"Astronomer." Caiden held back a laugh at D's startled expression. It was cute. *No.* It was not cute. Not in the slightest. Contract killer, remember? Nowhere near cute.

"That's what I said."

"No, an astronomer is a scientist who studies the earth, stars, and galaxies. An astrologist can tell you your horoscope. What month and day were you born?"

D squinted at him. "November 6. Why?"

"Ah, Scorpio. That explains *so* much." Caiden headed for the drawers D had pulled his bag from, smiling to himself when D growled after him.

"What the hell is that supposed to mean?" He stomped over to Caiden, beefy arms crossed over his expansive chest.

Good God, the man's biceps were huge. Seriously. How did he not tear through his clothes like the Hulk? Every inch of him was bulging, but not in an unattractive over-the-top way—more in a sinful, curvy, "want to lick him all over" kind of way. It didn't help that Caiden had managed to get a thorough taste of D before the guy had fucked off, leaving him craving more. Yep, this was definitely a big mistake.

"What does it mean?"

Caiden shrugged before pulling out a messenger bag. "Just fascinating, that's all."

"Whatever. Like I care." D spun around, ignoring Caiden's laugh as he stormed off to one of the weapons lockers, jerking two rifles out.

Intense. That was one way to describe the fiery Cuban. In the few hours they'd been together, Caiden had managed to get that much out of him. Mostly because D had cursed in Spanish while they fucked and it had been the sexiest thing Caiden ever heard, prompting him to beg—Jesus how he'd begged—D to talk to him in Spanish. D obliged, and Caiden came so hard he thought he'd pass out.

Time to get his head in the game. Whatever happened between them was done, left behind in Vienna two years ago. The sooner they got this over with, the sooner Caiden could start his new life, leaving D in the past with the rest of the painful memories. They'd had one night together. One night was hardly the foundation for any kind of relationship, whether a professional working one or—

Not going there. One job. That's it. One job, and D would be out of his life for good, the last remaining piece of the shattered life he'd discarded much like his smashed demon printer. Until then, he'd keep his distance and focus on the job.

In order to do that, it meant he'd have to maybe, possibly, begrudgingly cooperate with D. Stifling a groan, he carried the messenger bag, burner phone, and a couple of other pieces of small equipment he'd grabbed from the top drawer, and joined D at the table. Were they heading into some kind of battle he wasn't aware of?

"I thought we were going undercover?" Caiden asked, looking between his near-empty messenger bag and the full arsenal D was stuffing into the huge duffel bag.

"I like to be prepared."

"For what? A hostile government takeover? The Graves mansion is in Palm Beach, right?"

"Grab what you need and shut up. The quicker we get this done, the quicker you can fuck off back to Langley to your shit coffee and 401K."

Caiden turned back to his bag with a sniff. "Nothing wrong with the coffee there, and everyone should have a retirement plan."

D stopped to stare at him. "I don't know what the hell I was thinking hooking up with you."

"The feeling is mutual," Caiden snapped, pissed with himself for letting D's words sting him. "A momentary lapse of judgment for sure." He shoved gear into his bag, doing his best to ignore the jackass grumbling to himself beside him.

Was he really going to do this? Go out on a mission with a former—what? One night of hot sex did not a lover make. Why was he even so hung up on this guy? Jesus. He'd had plenty of one-night stands and trysts with guys all over the world, and in much worse places than a gorgeous luxury hotel. Not once had he thought about any of those men afterward. He couldn't even remember what they looked like. But D? He hadn't forgotten one damn thing about the guy. Not his silky black hair, gorgeous tanned skin, or delicious—

Fuck! Come on, man!

If his bosses got wind of what he was up to, his career with the Company *would* be over. For good this time. Hell, his *life* would be over. Something told him if they came after Alpha, they wouldn't find a thing, and where would that leave Caiden, other than picking up the pieces of his shattered life? Again. But what if he *could* find the asshole who betrayed him? Who'd ruined his life. Who knew how many more lives the bastard had ruined? Whoever it was, they were a traitor to their country. It was time they paid for their crimes. Alpha could help with that, even if Caiden was trusting the word of a mysterious voice and a man he barely knew.

Let it go. Just let it go. Screw it, he couldn't let it go. Wasn't it obvious he couldn't let it go? "I don't understand how you can blindly follow someone you know nothing about." The way he was following D? The irony was not lost on him.

"You know, you're very judgmental for a guy who lies for a living."

"That's different." Caiden glanced between D's bulging duffel and his own much slighter, slimmer bag. Maybe he should get a bigger bag? Was his masculinity being slighted? D faced him, a couple of grenades in his large hand. Overcompensating much?

"Why, because you do it to protect your country? Newsflash, so do I."

Caiden shook his head. "It's not the same thing."

"You spooks think you're so much better than the rest of us. So clever. So damn righteous. You operate on a need-to-know basis just like we do. Innocent people get caught in the crossfire the same for you as for us. We're the ones who get blood on our hands so you can stay righteous." He closed his mouth, then opened it to say something else but hesitated. A heartbeat later, he spoke up. "You don't know me, so maybe you shouldn't be so quick to judge."

D's tone gave Caiden pause. Was that what he'd been about to say earlier? Caiden went back to the drawer and grabbed a duffel bag. It wasn't as big as D's, but he'd never been a size-queen. Not that he didn't appreciate D's size. The man was big all over. All. Over. Why was he even trying? Seriously? It's like his brain had given control over to his dick.

"So how'd your cover get blown?" D asked, organizing the small arsenal in his bag.

"I'm not discussing that with you," Caiden sniped.

D held his hands up in surrender. "Okay. Touchy subject. Sorry."

"What I *am* willing to discuss is how you went from being a contract killer for the Company to this?" Caiden asked, motioning around them.

"I never worked for the Company."

Caiden's chuckle was humorless. "Right. Executive Order 12333, Part 2, Section 2.11. I'm well aware. It also states *political assassination* but whatever. How'd you go from being employed by a certain private military company holding a contract with the CIA to this?"

D cast him a rueful smile. "I died."

"And yet here you are."

"How do you know who I worked for?" D narrowed his gaze. "I never told you that."

"Becky did." He shrugged. "I guess it was relevant for some reason. When she briefed me, she said if I accepted the mission, I'd be working with a skilled contractor and former employee of said Company. I read between the lines. So how did you end up here?"

"I don't know how they found me, and I never asked. I was shot in the chest. My heart had stopped, but they managed to bring me back to life. I was in a medically induced coma for months. When I came to, Becky and David were there. Good call on Alpha's part, sending in the most nonthreatening-looking people ever. I reacted with confusion rather than the urge to take them out.

"They took care of me, helped me heal. When I was well enough, David set up a meeting with Alpha. As much of a meeting as you can have with a black screen and a digitized voice." He finished checking the extra magazines and packed them neatly into his bag.

"Alpha explained how I was one of countless victims sacrificed to keep some corrupt asshole's secret. I was dead. My family believed I'd been killed on the job. They had a funeral for me while I was in my coma. I couldn't return to my old life, so Alpha offered me a new one with the Locke and Keyes Agency. A black op created to expose corrupt individuals in positions of power who've killed and hurt innocent people to keep their dirty secrets."

"You're hardly innocent," Caiden pointed out. "Neither am I."

D nodded. "You're right, and I wasn't interested in redemption, in being the hero or the good guy. I'd been fine doing what I did before. I wanted revenge. Pure and simple. Alpha would give me a new name, a new life, an endless supply of funds, firepower, equipment, whatever I needed. I'd use the opportunity I was being presented to get my revenge and then ghost."

Caiden studied D, aware of the muscles in his jaw working, the neatly trimmed beard, and the scar in his thick black eyebrows. He was a man adept at hiding his thoughts, his emotions, but he wasn't now. Why? "Something changed your mind."

"My first mission. I was to expose a corrupt sheriff connected to a prostitution ring. I did what I'd been trained to do. Conducted surveillance, gathered intel, studied the players, analyzed, put together a plan of action, and went undercover. I told myself it was nothing I hadn't seen before. Whatever I faced, I'd seen so much worse." D stopped packing his bag and stared down into the blackness of it, his jaw clenched tight like he was recalling a terrible memory.

"I was hired as muscle and earned their trust. One of their 'perks' was a free pass to sample the goods whenever I wanted, provided I didn't leave any visible marks. I was taken to the warehouse where they kept the *merchandise*. A real shithole. One of the guys took me to one of dozens of rooms, and inside were two drugged-out girls and a boy. He told me to have fun and left me to it. The oldest girl couldn't have been any more than fifteen. The youngest…." He shook his head, his hands balled into fists. "They were kids. All of them."

"Jesus." Caiden ran a hand over his face. The amount of putrid humanity in the world somehow still managed to surprise him. "What did you do?" Did he even want to know? The steel that came into D's eyes was unsettling, and Caiden braced himself.

"The kids were so out of it, they didn't know what was happening, so I had them lie down and told them to go to sleep. I sat there for several minutes fighting every instinct to go out there and put a bullet in each and every one of those motherfuckers. When enough time had passed, I left, joking with the asshole who'd shown me to the kids, pretending I'd—" D cleared his throat.

"Anyway, I left the warehouse, walked behind it, and threw up until I couldn't see straight. When I had the evidence I needed, I went to the warehouse one morning because they'd all be sleeping off their hangovers, chained all the doors except for my exit, got the kids out, and burned the place to the ground with all those sick fucks in it."

Caiden sucked in a sharp breath. Whatever he'd been expecting, it wasn't that. "You burned them alive?"

D met Caiden's gaze, and Caiden hated that he took a step back. He'd come across cold-hearted killers before, mercenaries who'd do anything if paid enough, and monsters who did unspeakable things like the ones who kidnapped and sold those children into sex slavery, but at this moment, the most terrifying man he'd ever faced stood in front of him, eyes so hard and black they appeared almost not human.

"They weren't worth the bullets."

Caiden swallowed and nodded, unable to find the right words, or any words for that matter. Yes, the men from that warehouse deserved to be punished, but to be burned alive? Then again, after everything he'd seen, had he been there would he have stopped D? Had he witnessed the horror with his own eyes? Would he have written those men off as casualties of war? Would he even be giving it a second thought had they been a part of one of his missions somewhere else in the world?

D continued packing. "Alpha wasn't a fan of my methods either, but couldn't argue those sons of bitches didn't deserve it. If I was going to do this, I'd do it my way. The sheriff was killed in prison the night he was transferred in."

"And your personal revenge?"

"I'd get it someday. Alpha calls it justice. I call it vengeance. The victims might not be able to get theirs, so I'll get it for them."

"So you just go around killing the bad guys? An avenging angel with a gun?"

D rolled his eyes. "No. I admit, I had a few anger issues to work out in the beginning, but I'm past that now."

Caiden's giggle-snort was unexpected, for both of them apparently.

D stared at him. "Really?"

"I'm sorry."

"No, you're not."

"You're right. I'm not. No more anger issues, huh? Got that all worked out? Alpha provide a shrink along with all these guns?" He couldn't help his laugh at D's uninspiring expression.

"Come on, smartass."

Caiden held back a smile as he followed D. He remembered Becky saying David would make sure everything was delivered to the safe house. Made sense. Not like they could walk out of the building into the middle of downtown St. Petersburg with duffel bags full of weapons even at this late hour. When they reached the lobby, D smiled brightly at Becky and winked at her.

"Call you when we get there."

Becky waved cheerfully. She moved her big blue eyes to Caiden before motioning to D. "Make sure he doesn't get into too much trouble."

The elevator doors opened, and D's grin turned wicked, his dark eyes filled with heat as he raked his gaze over every inch of Caiden. "Don't let the three-piece suit fool you, Becky. Caiden here is more of a troublemaker than you think. Good thing I have experience in handling him."

Yeah, this wasn't going to be a clusterfuck of epic proportions *at all*.

Chapter Five

WHEN D said condo on the beach, Caiden expected a small apartment of some kind, not a multimillion-dollar Palm Beach townhouse.

The property was stunning, and the view? Jesus, it was beautiful. A far cry from the dreary parking-lot vista at his apartment. What would it be like to wake up to this view every morning? The sun's rays cast a blanket of glittering diamonds across the ocean's dazzling blue surface, the breeze ruffling the greenery near the private sandy beach, not a soul in sight. Caiden had traveled to Florida on more than one occasion, but always for work, never able to enjoy the views or the beach. It reminded him of how long it had been since he'd taken a vacation. Not that he was on vacation now, but he might be able to sneak in a few hours at the pool—or the beach, considering it was in their backyard.

After leaving the Locke and Keyes Agency, D had handed Caiden a burner phone and instructed him to go to his hotel room and await further instructions. In that time, Caiden was to get familiar with his cover and the op. How he was supposed to do that, he had no idea, considering he'd left everything behind in the supply closet for delivery. When he arrived at his hotel room, a *Welcome* gift basket filled with fruit, wine, and snacks sat on the dresser beside a large gift box. Becky seemed to have a thing for gift baskets. It was cute.

The gift box contained everything he needed to get started, including the *Interior Design Reference Manual* and a laptop. Within seconds of opening the laptop, he received a call on his burner phone from Becky with log-in details, and after a cheerful "we'll talk soon," she hung up, and he logged in to find encrypted files on everything and everyone, from floor plans of the Graves mansion to profiles on Kenneth Graves, his wife, and everyone associated with them, including the very handsome house manager, Harrison Caveley, who lived in the guest house on the property.

For the next three days while Isabella met with Jacqueline Draper to discuss design concepts for the house, sign contracts, and meet with the interior foreman, Tobias Hicks, Caiden readied himself for his performance. Then this morning he received an address, and here he stood in the two-story townhouse with four bedrooms, six bathrooms, numerous gilded mirrors, elegant crystal chandeliers, gleaming marble floors, and ornate crown molding. All that was missing was his partner in crime.

Caiden checked his watch. They were supposed to be having a meeting with Becky in ten minutes. The heavy footfalls thumping up the stairs could only belong to one man, and Caiden rolled his eyes.

"Cutting it close aren't w—" Oh God, he almost swallowed his tongue. Swiftly schooling his expression, he focused on his breathing and not the porn star D was expertly channeling. "Where's the rest of your clothes?"

D's thick brows drew together, his plump lips twisting in a grimace as he looked down at himself. "What the hell are you talking about?"

Caiden took in the sight before him. D's thick thighs and heavily muscled legs were encased in snug denim, and a heavy tool belt matching his work boots hung from his tapered waist. The white T-shirt he wore barely contained his impossibly wide chest and broad shoulders. His beard was neatly trimmed, and his tanned skin appeared even more golden against the stark white of his shirt. To top it off, D's silky black hair was a mess, falling over his brow.

"Whatever," D huffed. "I'm going to drop my shit off in my room." He walked away, giving Caiden a perfect view of his tight round ass cupped lovingly inside his jeans.

"Christ." Caiden rubbed a hand over his face. If he didn't rein it in, he was going to be in serious need of a cold shower.

"You okay?"

Becky's voice snapped him out of it, and he cleared his throat, grateful for the chair between him and the open laptop sitting on the dining room table. Becky didn't need to see the way his shameful dick was reaching out for D, like it was a fucking dowsing rod and D's ass was thirst-quenching water.

The most frustrating part of this whole experience was how very obviously one-sided this attraction was. D had moved on from him, not given him so much as a second thought, so why couldn't Caiden do the same? It wasn't like D was the only attractive man in existence, and really, Caiden would be *far* better off finding someone—*anyone*—else.

Caiden quickly took a seat at the table, leaning in toward Becky, who looked far too amused for her own good.

"Can you please make him wear some clothes?"

"He didn't show up naked again, did he?"

"No—wait, what? What do you mean *again*?"

Becky shook her head. "Never mind. What's wrong?"

"Are you sure he understood carpenter and not stripper? Because he's dressed like he's ready to have a bunch of dollar bills shoved down his pants." If anyone could even get their hands in there, considering how snug they were.

"Oh, that." Becky waved a hand in dismissal. "Isabella may adore her husband, but she's a notorious flirt and loves a bit of eye candy. Should you need a distraction where Isabella is concerned, D will provide it."

"What else will he provide?" Caiden asked snidely before realizing how petty he sounded. Time to get his shit together. "I mean, good thinking. It may come in handy."

"What will come in handy?" D asked, joining them in the dining room. He stopped next to Caiden's chair, leaning his hip against it, one large hand placed on the backrest.

Really? Seven other chairs, and he had to stand—no, *lean*—against Caiden? *How else is Becky supposed to see you both?* Well, if his brain was going to be all logical about it.... *Fine.*

A whiff of something familiar and pleasant caught his attention. "What's that scent?"

"Sandalwood and eucalyptus. It's a new essential oils bodywash."

Caiden stared up at him. "Essential oils bodywash?"

"What?" D cast him a wary glance. "You have a problem with bodywash?"

"No, I just didn't figure you for an essential oils type of guy."

"There's that stereotyping again."

Caiden sighed. "I meant—never mind. It smells nice."

D hummed but didn't reply, like he didn't believe Caiden.

"I mean it. It smells really good." Combined with how he was dressed, how could Isabella *not* be distracted by him? How could anyone not be distracted?

"Okay," Becky chirped. "You have everything you need for your mission. The items from the supply closet have been delivered and are secured in the master bedroom. You're both scheduled to arrive at the house at 2:00 p.m. Kenneth is at the office, and Isabella will be at her weekly spa appointment. You'll have two hours to insert the necessary surveillance devices and do a cursory search before she returns. Alpha will be in your ear should you need assistance. Good luck." She waved cheerfully before the screen went blank.

Caiden pushed his chair back, and D moved away. "Time for Avery Ashwood to get dressed," Caiden said, standing.

D planted his hands on his tool belt, his lips quirked into a smug grin. "I see what's going on."

"Really? And here I thought your vision was permanently obstructed by your massive ego."

"Cute. You don't want to share me."

Caiden snorted out a laugh. "Wow. I didn't think it was possible for that ego to grow any bigger, but I was wrong. Amazing. Tell me, how do you not topple over?" He put his hands to the sides of his head and moved them far out. "Must take quite a balancing act to maneuver something *that* huge."

D dropped his gaze to his crotch. "Yes, I have been blessed in many ways, but I give thanks by sharing my gifts with others."

Caiden opened his mouth only to have D interrupt.

"No, it's okay. I get it. Once you've had a taste of this, it's hard to move on."

"Fascinating. It walks and talks, and yet there seems to be no brain function." Caiden ignored D's amused snicker.

"What can I say? Lorenzo Rivas is a sensual beast."

"He's something all right," Caiden muttered, walking into his bedroom.

Concentrate on the mission. That's all he had to do. He opened the closet and removed a tailored blue-with-white-pinstripe three-piece suit, blue tie, crisp white button-down shirt, and brown Italian leather brogues. The material was designer, expensive, and felt so damned good against his skin. *Never underestimate the power of a well-fitted suit.*

On top of the dresser sat a little black velvet box containing a pair of silver cufflinks. The left cufflink concealed a USB drive capable of turning any internet-connected computer into a Wi-Fi hotspot, and the right hid a micro SD card. D was right about one thing. Alpha certainly had the best toys.

Caiden's shoes housed an array of nifty gadgets beneath the insole, from a GPS tracking device to a tiny camera with video and night vision capabilities, and the shoelaces were made of Kevlar. His tie clip concealed a pinhole camera, and his watch did far more than tell time.

Cufflinks in, he went into the bathroom and spruced up his hair, adding enough product to tame the short waves neatly parted to one side. Despite readying himself for a mission where he had no idea what the outcome would be or what kind of backup he'd have other than a smug, foul-mouthed former hitman, he'd slept like the dead the past two nights, and the dark circles around his eyes, along with the huge bags, had disappeared.

The cologne bottle on the marble sink was a brand he wasn't familiar with but looked expensive. Avery Ashwood had money to burn, far more than Caiden Cardosa did. He hadn't joined the CIA for the money, that was for damn sure. He'd make more money filing people's taxes.

Rounding his shoulders, he lifted his chin and walked out of the room, ready to play his role. D was in the kitchen looking for something in one of the cabinets.

"Ready when you are, Mr. Rivas."

D turned, and Caiden cringed when D smacked into the kitchen cabinet door. "Motherfucker!"

"Jesus, D, you okay?" He hurried over and tried to move D's hand away from his forehead. "Let me see."

"I'm fine," D growled, slapping Caiden's hand away. "Go over there."

"What?" Caiden frowned.

"Go over there, please. Away from me."

"Fine," Caiden snapped, spinning on his heels and storming off into the living room. That's what he got for being concerned for the asshole. Why was he even bothering? Clearly he was nothing but a nuisance as far as D was concerned. "Let's get this over with." He grabbed his—or rather *Avery's*—messenger bag, then headed for the door.

"Caiden, wait. I'm—"

"I'll see you at the house." Caiden left in a hurry, knowing D wouldn't follow him. Lesson learned. They weren't friends. This was good. A reminder of where Caiden stood in the scheme of things. Time to get to work.

Inside the two-car garage, he climbed behind the wheel of Avery's sleek black Audi A3 Cabriolet and slid on his Ray-Ban aviator sunglasses. At this time on a weekday afternoon, few people were about, and in a neighborhood lined with multimillion-dollar homes and mansions, his car was nothing of interest. He made a left onto Sloans Curve Drive since the road was a cul-de-sac with one exit.

After turning right onto A1A, Caiden drove the three minutes it took to reach the Graves mansion. No one on the property would suspect a thing, considering a small forest of trees, bushes, and state road separated the Graves mansion from the pocket of residencies of Sloans Curve Drive, but just in case, both Caiden and D would take the scenic route when leaving the Graves mansion before heading back to the safe house.

Arriving at the mansion, he made a left onto the brick drive and drove up to the gate. He lowered his window, the white speaker perched on the white pole coming to life. Caiden smiled for the camera, knowing he could be seen by the three guards in the guard house.

"Can I help you?"

"Yes. I'm Avery Ashwood, Ms. Draper's assistant."

"Hold your ID up to the camera, please."

"Of course." Caiden opened his messenger bag, removed the expertly fabricated driver's license from the leather wallet, and held it up to the camera.

"Thank you, Mr. Ashwood. Please park at the end of the drive near the guest house. Mr. Caveley, the house manager, will meet you there."

"Thank you."

The iron gate slowly opened, and Caiden drove between the stone pillars, subtly taking note of everything and everyone, from the lawn service truck to the guards walking the property. He parked at the end as instructed, noting the private dock on Lake Worth Lagoon just a short walk across the pristine lawn. Taking his bag, he exited the car, smiling at the tall, handsome man with salt-and-pepper hair who approached.

Harrison Caveley was in his mid to late forties and even more handsome in person. He was a former Marine, and it was evident in the set of his shoulders and the way he walked. His pink polo shirt stretched across his wide, muscular chest, and the tan slacks pulled snug in all the right places.

Considering what Caiden knew about Kenneth and how possessive he was of his wife, it was puzzling that Kenneth had hired such a gorgeous man to live on his property. Then Mr. Caveley's stoic expression melted into rapt attention as he not-so-subtly checked out Caiden. The man even licked his lips. Perhaps that explained it.

"Mr. Ashwood?" Caveley asked, his voice deep and husky.

"Please, call me Avery," Caiden insisted, taking the man's offered hand and allowing Caveley to hold on to it longer than necessary. It would seem D wasn't the only one capable of distracting, should the need arise.

"Then I insist you call me Harrison." He covered Caiden's hand with his other hand, his smile wide, reaching the corners of his gray eyes. Caiden had to be careful *he* didn't get distracted.

"Shall we go inside?"

"Of course! I'm so sorry." Harrison let out a deep rumbling laugh. "Forgive me. I'm not usually distracted by pretty things."

"Oh, well, thank you?"

Harrison smiled ruefully before motioning for Caiden to walk with him. "Too forward?"

"Refreshingly forward," Caiden said with a chuckle.

Harrison laughed, a deep booming sound pleasing to Caiden's ears. Shame Harrison was off-limits. Had Caiden met the man under different circumstances, he would have certainly been interested. They walked up a set of stone steps to an exceptionally ornate stone archway, the vintage iron-and-glass door matching the two faded blue lanterns secured to the wall on both sides of the archway.

"I believe we're expecting a Mr. Rivas shortly as well," Harrison said as he opened the door for Caiden.

"Thank you." Caiden walked inside, feeling Harrison's eyes on his ass. "Yes, he's one of Mr. Hicks's carpenters. He'll be helping me with my schematics. I'll be developing the furniture layout and space planning, creating rough sketches, preliminary finishing, that sort of thing. Mr. Rivas will be starting the construction documentation so we can begin providing Mrs. Graves with cost estimates." He stopped inside the lobby and managed not to cringe. "Well, this is… interesting."

"It's hideous," Harrison murmured, leaning in. "Wait until you see the rest of the house. This is nothing."

Caiden quirked a smile. "Not a fan, are we?"

"Isabella has been wanting to redecorate for months, but all the top designers she wanted were booked solid. Thank goodness Ms. Draper had a last-minute cancellation. Shall we go upstairs?" Just as he said the words, Harrison's phone went off. "Excuse me one second."

"Sure."

"Yes? Oh."

That was a disappointed "oh."

"Yes, we're expecting him. Let him in." He hung up and quickly smiled. "It looks like Mr. Rivas has arrived. Would you mind waiting here a moment while I get him?"

"Please. Go ahead."

Harrison excused himself and went off to fetch D. Meanwhile, Caiden busied himself studying the lobby. It was black-and-white checkered marble tiles, the smooth stone walls giving the place a very castle-like feel. At the end of the room was a marble staircase with ironwork railings. The modern blue painting on the wall didn't match the odd rust-colored full armor standing by the set of glass doors.

"I'm back," Harrison declared cheerfully as he made straight for Caiden, his hand coming to rest between Caiden's shoulder blades as he leaned in to whisper in his ear, "Tell me. Is everyone who Ms. Draper works with as gorgeous as you?"

Caiden cleared his throat. He turned and held a hand out to D, who looked from Caiden to Harrison and back, his eyes narrowing.

"Mr. Rivas. Good to meet you."

D took Caiden's hand, his grip firm. "Yeah. Good to meet you too. Call me Lorenzo."

"Well, in that case, Avery."

Harrison turned Caiden away from D, forcing them to let go. He smiled wide, his hand sliding down Caiden's spine to just above his ass. "Shall we go upstairs, Avery?"

Before Caiden could reply, Harrison's phone went off again. With a sigh, he held a finger up and answered. "Yes? Can't you handle it? Very well. I'll be right there." His smile was apologetic. "I'm afraid I'm going to have to leave you, but I'll return soon. Please go on ahead upstairs, and if you need anything at all, call me. You have my number, correct?"

"Yes. Thank you, Harrison. I truly appreciate it." Caiden watched the man leave, admiring the view, but then D stepped in front of him, hissing quietly.

"What the hell are you doing?"

"What are you talking about?"

D motioned to the door, where Harrison had left. "Grabby Hands McGee."

"Oh, right. He said he wasn't usually 'distracted by pretty things.'" Caiden's heart did a little flip at D's murderous glare. *Hmm. Interesting.*

"And you just let him put his hands all over you? We're here for a reason."

"I know," Caiden said, heading for the stairs. "I can handle him."

"That so?" D caught up; his eyes narrowed.

"Yep." They reached the top of the landing, which led into a long hallway, the checkered marble floor gleaming as it stretched out ahead between Venetian-style pillars, intricately detailed white stone arches, and coffered ceilings above their heads. Tall stone vases with small palms lined the hall along with marble plinths displaying blue-and-white porcelain Chinese vases.

"You need to be careful," D advised as he followed Caiden. According to the floor plan Caiden had memorized, the first room on the left would be the sitting room.

"Not my first rodeo."

Next to Caiden, D jumped like a startled cat. "Holy fuck!"

"What? What's wrong?"

"Sorry. I, uh, I wasn't expecting my vision to be assaulted by… by *that*." D swept his arm in the direction of the ceiling, and Caiden followed the movement, pressing his lips together to keep from laughing.

Was it the horror on D's face that amused him or the cause of said horror? Somehow D's expression managed to convey both fascination and revulsion at the same time. Wait, *amusing*? No, D was *not* amusing. He was an asshole. "What's wrong with it?"

D gaped at him. "Are you serious? There's naked flying babies on the ceiling."

"You mean the *cherubs*?"

"I don't care what you call them. They're naked flying babies. Why the hell would someone think that's a good idea? Someone actually stood right here, looked up, and thought 'Yep, this would be a perfect place for a bunch of naked flying babies.'"

Caiden took the two steps up to the raised sitting room, past two large pillars. The high ceiling was coffered, with a black ironwork chandelier hanging from the center. Two bookcases were built into the walls, with arches above and pillars to each side. Two sets of mismatched couches sat on opposite sides, one set solid colors, the other set floral that matched the curtains on the three double doors at the end of the room. "I'm supposed to be the designer."

"You don't need to be a designer to know how *not* to decorate your house," D said, scowling at the vintage floral love seat across from the blue velvet couch. "I think my grandmother had a couch like that. Except it was vacuum sealed in plastic. Nothing like sitting on a plastic-lined couch in the summer with no AC."

Caiden gasped. "Wait, you had a grandmother?"

"Have. Yes."

"Which means you had a mother."

"*Have* a mother. Yes." D squinted at him. "Where are you going with this?"

"Well, damn."

"What?"

Caiden shrugged. "I was under the impression you emerged from the darkness below. Clawing yourself out from the dirt, like a zombie or a great evil that's come back to life after a misguided loved one buried you in Stephen King's *Pet Sematary*."

D didn't appear impressed. "Funny."

"What does the Dark Lord look like?" Caiden asked, moving to inspect one of the pillars between two bookcases. "Was he like Tim Curry in *Legend* or sexy and British like Tom Ellis in *Lucifer*?"

"He was your height, blondish hair, with green eyes. A mouthy motherfucker who never shut up because he was a smart little shit who thought he knew everything."

"Wow. That's pretty specific." Caiden nodded, removing his tablet from inside his messenger bag. "A mouthy motherfucker *and* a smart little shit. Sounds like an interesting guy."

"Sounds like a certain pain in my ass," D hissed from behind him.

"Well, it can't be me because I was never *in* your ass." Caiden opened his tablet case and removed a pin-hole camera from the hidden compartment. "What with you taking off like you did." D's exasperated sigh was rather over the top, in Caiden's opinion.

"Fuck my life."

"I don't think fucking is the problem. I think it's what comes after."

"Would you shut up and get on with it, please?"

Caiden cringed and put a hand up. "Sorry, shit. I forgot. You're not used to conversation, just the sound of grunting followed by the ping of the elevator as you haul ass out of there the moment you've come."

"Look, I'm sorry, okay? Is that what you want to hear? I'm sorry I was an asshole and bailed."

Caiden met D's eyes. "*Are* you sorry?"

D squinted at him.

"Are you kidding me? Fuck you." Caiden whirled around when D caught his arm.

"Where are you going?"

"To inspect the other rooms."

D searched Caiden's gaze, for what, Caiden couldn't fathom. He released a heavy sigh.

"Just… stay alert."

Caiden jerked his arm out of D's grasp and left the sitting room before he ended up punching the guy. What an arrogant, stubborn, infuriating asshole! Was it really so hard for D to apologize? Why did Caiden even care, anyway? How many times did he have to remind himself it had been one night? One night—and two years since he'd seen the man.

It was ridiculous that he was still upset about it, and even more outrageous that it bothered him to begin with. Like he hadn't sneaked out of other guys' rooms himself. He'd had plenty of one-night stands, quick and dirty fucks with men while on assignment, as part of assignments, and in his personal life. He didn't do attachments. Not in his line of work. Well, in his previous line of work. Had D stuck around, Caiden would have been the one leaving him. At least that's what he told himself.

Enough of this. He had more important things to worry about than some jerk he'd picked up while on a mission. His lips quirked at the memory, though. Of him sitting at his table, sipping coffee and reading the newspaper.

He'd spotted the handsome Cuban man the moment D walked in. Their eyes met across the café, and D's smile had sparked something inside Caiden. It was stupid. Like something out of one of those romantic movies. Then D asked if he could join Caiden, and that deep timbre of his gruff voice, those full lips and big hands, stole Caiden's thoughts, his brain, his power of speech. He'd nodded dumbly, his breath hitching when D leaned in to wipe the corner of Caiden's mouth. *"You had a crumb,"* D had said, motioning down to the half-eaten slice of cake in front of Caiden that he'd completely forgotten about because something far more decadent had taken its place.

Caiden shook his head to clear the memory. Something had to give. He couldn't keep going on like this. After two years of wondering who had betrayed him, he finally had a chance to get some answers. He was *not* going to jeopardize that for a man who wanted nothing to do with him and never had. Álvaro Montero was dead, and one way or another, whatever Caiden felt for him would die too. For good.

Chapter Six

WHY WAS every room in this house an insult to good taste? No wonder Isabella wanted the whole thing redone.

D stood in the middle of the billiard room, trying to decide what was more hideous, the purple-green-and-orange-striped velvet couches or the mustard-yellow floral curtains with pom-pom trim.

The couches. Definitely the couches.

They reminded him of those horrible Christmas candy puffs his abuelita used to keep in a crystal dish in her living room. Checking the coast was clear, he stuck one of the pinhole cameras into the wood paneling in the corner of the room.

"Jesus. The nineteen thirties called. They want their wallpaper back."

One more room down. Time to check in with Caid-en. He went to tap the Bluetooth earpiece with a secure connection, but then laughter caught his ear. Discreetly peeking out of the room, he balled his hands into fists and his jaw muscles clenched tight. That son of a bitch Harrison was flirting with Caiden again. Not that D was jealous, because he wasn't. What they were doing was too important to jeopardize.

How the hell was Caiden supposed to get any work done with Harrison hovering over him? Did the man not know the meaning of personal space? He was all up in Caiden's face, smiling down at him, using any excuse to touch Caiden. Harrison said something, and Caiden laughed, a genuine laugh that reached his green eyes and formed little wrinkles at the corners.

When Caiden had come out of his room that morning in that tailored suit, D's brain had short-circuited. He'd felt like an idiot, smacking himself with the cabinet door, but he'd been stunned stupid. Not a good sign, considering he'd seen the man in a suit before—not to mention naked.

Caiden was a suit man. It was pretty much all he wore. Except those suits hadn't been tailor-made to hug his sleek, toned body, from his long legs to his slim waist and broad shoulders. Caiden was the same height as D, over six feet tall, but D was wider, bulkier, heavier, a contrast to Caiden in every way, from D's pitch-black hair and dark eyes, to his darker tanned skin. Caiden was graceful, lithe, and quick to smile. His pink lips and bright eyes were distracting, his long fingers and creamy fair skin a reminder of the hours D had spent acquainting himself with Caiden's body.

How was it possible for one man to turn his entire world upside down? From the instant D met Caiden, he'd known Caiden was going to fuck things up in his life, and after the night they spent together, he'd been positive, which was why he left. That and what had possibly been the worst moment of his life—dying not included. He tried to push the memories of that night out of his mind.

When D recovered and started working for Alpha, he'd busied himself with his missions, refusing to give Caiden another thought, but the man had continued to crawl into his head, into his dreams, refusing to leave him alone.

During a particularly pathetic bout of vulnerability, D looked Caiden up, surprised to find him back in the US, no longer out in the field as an operations officer. After some digging around, D discovered Caiden's cover had been blown during his last mission, benching him, where he'd been forced to make the move to analyst. The details of what happened were out of D's reach, and although he could have gotten the information out of Alpha, D respected Caiden and his privacy. Knowing Caiden was back in the US for good didn't help.

What D assumed was a one-time hookup with a sexy guy turned into so much more, an instant connection and odd sense of familiarity, despite the fact they'd never met before that day at the café in Vienna. Talking to Caiden had been so easy. Everything with Caiden had been easy. D had never experienced anything like it. The encounter had been dangerous, because in those few minutes when D sat with Caiden, drinking coffee and laughing, D lost himself. He forgot who he was and why he was in Vienna in the first place. He'd been distracted, completely smitten by Caiden's beautiful face and warm smile. Much like now. Damn it. This couldn't continue. But first things first.

D removed his phone from his pocket and called Caiden, the jingle of his phone echoing through the empty hallway.

"Shit. I'm sorry. I need to take this."

Harrison held his hands up and took a step away from Caiden. "No, I'm sorry. You're here to work, and I'm distracting you. Would you like a coffee? Our chef makes one hell of a cappuccino."

"I would love one, Harry. Thank you."

Harry?

"I'll be back in a few minutes. Don't get lost." With a wink, Harrison continued down the hall in the opposite direction.

"I won't," Caiden promised, his voice almost a purr.

What the fuck?

When Harrison was out of earshot, Caiden's smile vanished, and he growled into the phone. "What do you want?"

"*Harry*?"

"Are you spying on me?"

"Was that a joke?"

Caiden sighed. "Why are you calling me?"

"Because we're in the middle of a job, or have you forgotten? Too busy thinking with your dick?"

Caiden glared down at his phone before tapping the screen and walking off.

"What? Oh no. That motherfucker did not just hang up on me." D pocketed his phone and marched out of the room. Taking a quick look around before catching up to Caiden, D grabbed his arm and dragged him into the first open doorway. He slammed Caiden up against the wall.

"Don't you *ever* hang up on me again," he hissed. "You hear me?"

"Get the fuck off me." Caiden pushed at D's chest, but D didn't budge. "What the hell, man?"

"Are you out of your mind? We're in the middle of an op, and you're flirting?"

"What do you care, D?"

"I don't. What I do care about is this mission, and I don't want you fucking it up because you can't keep it in your pants."

Caiden let out a harsh laugh D wasn't fond of. "Oh, that's rich coming from you."

"What is that supposed to mean?"

"Nothing. You're right. There's nothing more important than the mission. That's why I accepted Harrison's invite to drinks Friday night." Caiden's green eyes were hard, his gaze challenging. "It's a great opportunity to get some intel. Harrison knows this household and everyone in it inside and out. He could be useful."

D wasn't convinced. His gaze dropped to Caiden's lips, and he cursed himself, realizing how close he was to Caiden. They were all but pressed up against each other, reminding D of that night in Vienna. He slid his hand up Caiden's arm to his neck, his thumb stroking the soft skin above his collar. Fuck, what was he doing? Caiden's idea was sound. They had an opportunity to get intel from Harrison. It was a good move. Any agent worth his salt would exploit the opportunity given to them. And yet….

"Caiden, I—"

"It's fine, D. You're right. I've been an idiot. We had one night. It was one hell of a night, but that's all it was. It didn't mean anything."

D flinched at Caiden's soft-spoken words. He let Caiden push past him, the warmth leaving with him. This was good. D should take the out Caiden was offering. His gut squeezed in response to Caiden standing by the window, the lines of his back enticing, his striking figure calling to D.

"I'm back," Harrison called out in a singsong voice as he entered the room carrying a silver drink tray. "Did you miss me?"

D cleared his throat, and Harrison frowned before he expertly schooled his expression, plastering on a fake smile. "Oh, Mr. Rivas. I forgot you were here."

How very pleasant.

"There's coffee in the kitchen. Why don't you help yourself?" It wasn't so much a suggestion as a not-so-subtle hint. In other words, get the fuck out of here and leave me alone with the hot blond.

Harrison turned his attention back to Caiden, his smile growing wide and genuine. "I wasn't sure how sweet you liked it." Harrison's husky tone suggested he was talking about more than coffee. He placed the tray on a table by the balcony doors. Only then did D notice they were in one of the guest bedrooms. *Fucking perfect.*

Caiden returned Harrison's smile. "I like it sweet but not overly." He took a sip of the coffee, and at his moan, D left the room.

Good. This was good. Caiden was finally listening to him.

On his way to the kitchen, D took the opportunity to distribute more pinhole cameras. The kitchen was huge and just as terrifying as the rest of the house. He didn't mind vintage, but the mismatch style used to decorate the mansion looked tragically outdated, and he had a feeling most of the furniture had come with the house.

Kenneth Graves was a traditional man who was not a fan of change. He indulged his wife, but from

Kenneth's profile, it was clear he liked to be in charge. Not an easy feat when he had a wife as hot-blooded and hot-tempered as Isabella.

After drinking some very fine Italian espresso, D headed for the patio, only to find Caiden and Harrison out there. *For fuck's sake. Really?* Caiden stood near one of the marble columns, and Harrison leaned into him, his fingers brushing Caiden's cheek, traveling down his smooth jaw before coming to rest under his chin. He tilted Caiden's face up to his, and Caiden smiled softly, a look not all dissimilar to one he'd given D in Vienna.

D gritted his teeth. Damn it, he couldn't be pissed at Caiden for doing exactly what D wanted him to do. Okay, not *exactly* that, but moving on. *Focus.* His earpiece came to life and Alpha's voice filled his ear.

"You have half an hour before Isabella arrives, and several rooms without camera feeds."

"Yeah, Caiden's working an asset," D replied through his teeth.

"And what are *you* doing?"

Being an asshole. "Relax. I was just getting a drink. I'm heading upstairs now to do the rest of the rooms."

"Was bringing Caiden into this a mistake?"

"A mistake for who? It was your call," D muttered as he took the steps two at a time.

"I was under the impression that night in Vienna didn't mean anything."

"It doesn't," D growled.

"Are you trying to convince me or yourself?"

Fucking Alpha. D headed down the hall toward the end of the house and remaining rooms. "Look, we discussed it. It's not a problem."

"Very well. The cameras you've installed are online, ready for you. Finish the rest and return to the safe house. Alpha out."

D hurried through the remaining rooms as quickly and discreetly as possible, refusing to think about Caiden and what he might be getting up to with Harrison. Nope. Didn't think about him at all.

After installing the tiny cameras in several more sitting rooms or whatever the hell they were, he decided to check in with Caiden. They had ten minutes before Isabella was due back. He breathed in deep through his nose and released the breath through his mouth. *Calm. Zen.*

Tapping his earpiece, he spoke quietly. "Hey, um, where are you?"

"The library. I think it's a library. It might be yet another sitting room. How many sitting rooms does one house need? There are muskets on the wall. Like the kind the Pilgrims used. Do you think they came with the house?"

"Is Harrison there with you?" *Smooth. Very smooth.*

"No. He's off doing his duty."

"Okay. I'm heading your way." D found Caiden in the library. "We have to move. Isabella's going to be home any minute."

"No, she's not." Caiden finished placing a pinhole camera inside one of the bookcases. "Harrison got a call that she was going to have a smoothie with a friend and if he could pick up her dress for tonight's dinner at the yacht club, followed by drinks and dancing." Caiden cast him a knowing smile, and D wrinkled his nose. The guy was proving to be useful. So what? "Anyway," Caiden continued as he joined D. "I managed to get a few cameras outside around the pool, guest house, and garages."

D wanted to ask how he'd managed that with Harrison drooling all over him at every turn, but he managed to hold his tongue and be the bigger man.

"Good work." See? He could be a mature adult. "I think we've covered all our bases. I got the rooms on the way to the kitchen, including the kitchen." He leaned in to Caiden as he brought up the camera feeds on his tablet. Alpha worked quickly; the feeds were ready for viewing. A few of the angles were challenging, but they also had audio. "Perfect. Let's get out of here and start the next phase."

Caiden put away his tablet. "You should go first."

D peered at him. "Why?"

"I promised Harrison I wouldn't leave until he got back."

"Are you kidding me? Why would you agree to something so stupid?"

Caiden blinked at him before fire filled his green eyes, and not the good, sexy kind of fire. *Shit.*

"I promised to wait for him because when he gets back, he's going to show me all the cool hidden features of this house. I think he's trying to impress me."

"Oh, uh, right. That's… good."

Caiden rolled his eyes. "I'll see you later." He made to move away, but D caught his arm. Caiden arched a brow at him.

"Just… be careful, okay? I know Harrison seems like a nice guy, but he still works for Graves. He's also former military, remember?"

Caiden pulled his arm out of D's hold. "Yes, I remember. Maybe *you* need to remember who I am. We're going to have a discussion about that at some point, by the way. In the meantime, maybe familiarize yourself with *my* file. I know what I'm doing." Caiden walked off, and D ran a hand through his hair, cursing under his breath.

Fuck, why did everything that came out of his mouth hurt or piss off Caiden? The guy had every right to be pissed. He was a good agent, adept at working under pressure in covert situations, had done so for years. Caiden could take care of himself. He was trained in combat, was an expert marksman, and an exceptional actor. Except when it came to D. He couldn't seem to hide from D. Not that D was about to start contemplating that nugget of information.

Leaving Caiden to do his thing, D left the house. If Caiden needed him—which was doubtful—he'd call. D got into his truck and drove off, taking the scenic route before heading back to the safe house. Once inside, he dropped his tool belt on the kitchen counter and went to the laptop on the dining room table. He signed in and pulled up the Graves mansion security feeds. He scanned through them until he found the one he wanted.

Caiden sat in the main living room area, his tablet on his lap. He wiggled his fingers at the camera, then typed away at his tablet. A message window popped up on D's laptop seconds later.

"I know you're watching. I can feel your scowl from here. Afraid of what I might get up to?"

D's fingers flew over the keyboard as he responded. *"Making sure you don't blow your cover."* It was a low blow, but he couldn't help himself. He was expecting the camera to catch fire at any moment from how hard Caiden was glaring at it. He turned his attention back to the tablet.

"How about I don't blow my cover and you don't get dead. Again."

D snapped the laptop closed and carried it with him to his room. He kicked off his boots, changed into his workout pants and an old comfy T-shirt, then headed for the home gym, taking the laptop with him. What he needed was to beat the shit out of something.

One of the townhouse bedrooms had been converted into a gym, arranged with the usual home gym equipment—treadmill, elliptical, benches, racks, weights, rower, and several other pieces. What he was interested in was the punching bag. Nothing like pounding out his frustration. He groaned. Pounding was not something he needed to be thinking about right now.

Placing the laptop on the bench next to the bag, he didn't bother looking for Caiden. Instead he quickly spun on his heels to grab a couple of hand wraps.

He rounded his shoulders and warmed up, stretching his muscles, refusing to glance over at the laptop, though maybe he should check that Isabella hadn't returned while Caiden was off exploring secret passages. D let his head fall forward with a groan.

"Fuck me. My mother was right." He really was his own worst enemy.

Sighing heavily, he checked the screen to make sure Caiden was all right. Two new camera feeds had appeared, one in a dimly lit corridor, the second in a small room that looked like some kind of storage space.

Neatly wrapped squares and rectangles of various sizes that D assumed were paintings lined one wall, while glass display cases ran across the next. The safe on the dresser against the third wall was what D *should* have been most interested in. Instead, his gaze was fixed on Caiden, who was pressed up against the wall, Harrison's body pinning him there, his thick thigh between Caiden's legs, fingers laced with Caiden's as he held Caiden's hands to the sides of his head. Caiden had his head tilted back, eyes to the ceiling as Harrison kissed his way down Caiden's neck, his hips undulating, his groin rubbing against Caiden.

The violent reaction that bubbled up through D was unexpected and scared the shit out of him. He had no right to be pissed. Not after doing everything he had to push Caiden away. Whatever happened next was on him.

Caiden had given D plenty of opportunity to stake his claim, but D had refused, and now the pleasure meant for him was being taken by another man, someone not afraid to go after what he wanted. D could easily put a stop to this. If he didn't, there was no question where this would go next. His finger hovered over the key that would bring up Caiden's phone.

"This is what you wanted," D told himself, moving his eyes back to Caiden, unprepared for Caiden's gaze aimed at the camera, an expression D couldn't read on his flushed face, like maybe he was waiting… hoping? D closed his eyes and shook his head. He slammed the laptop closed and walked to the boxing bag.

It was better this way. He repeated the words in his head as he delivered a series of fierce blows to the bag. Would Caiden get on his knees for Harrison? Or would Harrison be on his knees for Caiden? Something ignited deep inside D, rushing through him and escaping his mouth with a roar. He released every curse he knew in both English and Spanish, sweat dripping down his face as he unleashed an unrelenting assault on the leather bag, his fury coming through his fists until his knuckles were numb.

D lost track of the time while he was punching and kicking. It was only when he was gasping for breath that he stopped, throwing his arms around the bag and hugging it tight.

Was he really surprised? As if he'd be able to hold on to a guy like Caiden anyway. D dropped to the mat, one leg drawn up as he ran a finger through his sweat-soaked hair. Caiden was a good man, while D liked to pretend he was. Clearly the universe was reminding him of his place. He was a killer. No amount of good deeds would undo what he'd done, the lives he'd taken, the blood on his hands.

"Hey."

D started. He lifted his gaze, his heart stuttering at Caiden standing in the doorway. His vest was open, his shirt rumpled, and the marks on his neck had D pushing himself to his feet. He swept past Caiden only to have Caiden take hold of his wrist.

"D, wait. Nothing happened."

D flicked his fingers against one of the spots on Caiden's neck. "Yeah, really looks like that. Anyway, I don't care."

"Stop saying that," Caiden pleaded. "I wouldn't lie to you, D."

"Why wouldn't you?" D rounded on him. "We're nothing to each other."

Caiden stepped in close, his free hand going to D's cheek. "We could be."

D took hold of Caiden's wrists and gently moved him away. "No. We don't fit."

Caiden opened his mouth to reply, but D put a finger to his lips, the softness of them sending a shiver through D.

"You know I'm right."

Caiden nodded, and D released him, glad he was finally getting through to Caiden.

"I never pegged you for a coward, Montero."

D straightened. "Excuse me?"

"You heard me." Caiden poked him in the chest. "You're a fucking coward."

"Fuck you!" D shoved him, but Caiden had grabbed a fistful of his shirt, taking D with him. He raised a fist when Caiden moved in, but suddenly D had his arms full of Caiden, his mouth exploding with the taste of Caiden. *Holy fuck!* Caiden mauled D's mouth, sucking on his bottom lip before pushing his tongue against D's lips.

Opening for Caiden, D moaned around Caiden's tongue, their kiss setting D on fire, consuming every inch of him. He wrapped his arms around Caiden, jerking him up against him, their raging hard-ons rubbing against each other through the thin layers of fabric. Caiden slipped his fingers into D's hair, grabbing fistfuls of it and holding on painfully tight, sending a jolt of need through D. He hadn't felt anything this good since the last time they'd been together.

Caiden tore away from him, and D gasped, his breath coming out in pants as he stared at Caiden.

"Yeah, we don't fit at all," Caiden said, breathless, before leaving D standing alone.

What the hell just happened?

"Fuck." D ran his fingers through his hair and let his head fall back against the wall. His dick throbbed, and his chest heaved as he sucked in deep breaths, the taste of Caiden still lingering on his tongue. Dropping his arms, he stood motionless, his heart beating in his ears. *Fuck this.*

D thundered down the hall to Caiden's bedroom and threw the door open to find it empty, the only sound coming from the shower behind the closed en suite bathroom door. Not bothering to ask himself what he was doing, he stormed in, kicking the door shut behind him.

"What the hell?" Caiden had barely gotten the words out before D was walking into the shower, fully dressed, and slamming Caiden up against the tiled wall, his mouth on Caiden's. He took advantage of Caiden's gasp, and slipped his tongue inside Caiden's mouth, shivering at the low groan Caiden released before he grabbed hold of D's arms, fingers digging into his biceps.

Steam filled the bathroom as Caiden quickly divested D of his wet clothes, the material plopping to the tiled floor in a soaked heap. Their kiss was ardent and all consuming, D's hunger for Caiden ravenous. If he didn't do something, he was going to lose his mind. All he could see, feel, taste was Caiden.

Lowering himself to his knees, D took hold of Caiden's leaking cock, and swallowed it down to the root. Caiden shouted his name, his hips bucking as D sucked him hard, moaning deep in his throat at the feel of Caiden's fingers curling tightly around his hair as he held on to D. He loved how Caiden grabbed his hair, wanting to keep D near him.

Taking advantage of having Caiden shivering and naked within his reach, D slid his hands up Caiden's legs around to his ass, giving his cheeks a squeeze. He slipped one finger between those firm, round globes, and pressed the tip of one finger to Caiden's hole, his free hand going to his own cock so he could jerk himself off.

"Oh fuck. D. Oh God." Caiden tugged at D's hair, and this time D lifted his gaze, meeting Caiden's eyes, the desire in them almost making D come on the spot. He pressed his finger inside, Caiden's strangled cry music to D's ears. Caiden thrust forward, and D hummed around his cock, encouraging Caiden to fuck his mouth. "If you could see how you look with your lips wrapped around my cock. Fuck, you're gorgeous, D." Caiden pumped himself inside D's mouth while D matched Caiden's fervor, his hand moving furiously on his painfully hard cock while he finger-fucked Caiden.

"I'm so close, D," Caiden warned.

D twisted his finger, hitting just the right spot and Caiden cried out as he doubled over, spilling himself inside D's mouth with D a heartbeat away. One final touch and D was coming hard, his body trembling from the force of it.

Once Caiden had finished, D gently pulled off, then stood and kissed Caiden so he could taste himself. Caiden moaned, melting against D and letting him take Caiden's weight. They kissed until they were out of breath, and D gently moved Caiden back. He turned and Caiden grabbed his arm, his green eyes filled with panic. D shushed him softly, placing a kiss to his lips.

"Easy, baby. I'm not going anywhere."

Chapter Seven

YET.

D said he wasn't going anywhere, but the *yet* was there, hovering over Caiden's head, waiting to drop on him like an anvil in one of those old cartoons. Caiden was too blissed-out to speak, much less move. He'd enjoy this moment while he could, his heart tumbling over itself when D led him under the warm spray and started washing him.

Did D know how intimate this was? Did he care? What had prompted him to come barreling in here after Caiden? Not that Caiden was surprised. He closed his eyes, keeping his smile to himself as D's amazing hands soaped him up. Pushing D's buttons was dangerous and thrilling at the same time. Caiden had been careless, too lost in D, in his emotions, to heed the warning his brain was giving him. He'd pushed, hard, trying to get a reaction out of D, but he had to do *something*, or he was going to go crazy. He hadn't known what to expect. With D anything was possible.

D's hands on him had Caiden half-hard already. The more he tried to distance himself, the more he craved D, his touch, his taste, the feel of those wonderfully rough hands. Caiden rinsed off while D made quick work of washing himself. He turned off the water, then grabbed one of the big, fluffy towels and wrapped it around Caiden's shoulders. A quick kiss to Caiden's lips, then D grabbed a towel and dried himself off. Neither of them said a word, but it wasn't needed. The silence was calm, companionable for once.

Caiden stepped out of the shower, smiling against D's lips as he was brought into D's embrace.

"I'm just going to put some clothes on, and then we'll get some food in you."

Caiden could think of something else he'd rather have in him, and judging by D's chuckle, his expression must have said as much.

"Are you sure you don't want to walk around like that? I wouldn't mind."

D's laugh resounded through the room as he walked away. He smacked his ass on the way out for Caiden's benefit, and Caiden groaned.

"Fucker." Caiden finished drying himself off and tossed the towel into the hamper before getting dressed. They had some time before they had to change for the next phase of their mission. Dressed in lounge pants and a comfortable T-shirt, he found D already in the kitchen, the tropical sound of a Spanish pop song filling the air. It was hard to reconcile the hardened hitman with the sexy guy dancing around the kitchen. Caiden leaned against the wall, arms folded over his chest as he took in the mouthwatering vision. It occurred to Caiden how at this very moment, he was seeing Álvaro, not the intimidating contract killer, not the soldier Caiden was certain he'd been, but the man who moved as if the music was emanating from his soul.

Not only was D an exceptional dancer—his heavily muscular body moving with a fluidity Caiden hadn't expected the man capable of—but apparently, he could cook. D spun on his heels, a guilty smile tugging at his delectable lips.

"Sit," he said, pointing to one of the chairs at the kitchen counter.

Caiden obliged. He laced his fingers on the marble as D moved around the kitchen like it was the most natural thing in the world. D pulled out a rice cooker, a couple of pots, and a cast-iron skillet. "He cooks too."

D chuckled. "Are you kidding me? My parents believed in teaching their children to fend for themselves. By the time I was ten, I could cook, clean, do laundry, and change a flat tire."

Children, not child. "You have siblings?"

D's smile faded, the heartache in his eyes unmistakable. "Yeah." He turned off the music, then faced the stove, his back to Caiden. "My little sister, Luz, turned sixteen this year. She was an unexpected pregnancy." D planted his hands to the side of the stove, his head lowered.

"Oh, D. I had no idea." How could he? D's "death" had happened after he'd left Caiden, and they hadn't talked about family. Caiden stepped up beside D and placed a comforting hand on his shoulder. It was hard to see the pain in D's tear-filled gaze. Vulnerability was something he never thought to associate with D.

"I miss her so damn much," D said with a sniff. He lifted his gaze to Caiden. "I was her hero, you know?

She hung off my every word. Pain in the ass." He let out a soft laugh. "And so fucking stubborn. You have no idea."

"I think I do," Caiden teased gently, bumping D with his hip.

D chuckled. He shook his head, his smile slipping away. "I'm her big brother. I'm supposed to be there for her, look out for her. She sees a shrink because of me." He closed his eyes and let his head hang. "Because of my death."

Caiden moved his hand from D's shoulders to his back, running his hand in soothing circles. He couldn't begin to imagine how hard it must be for D, to know his family was out there believing he was gone, grieving his loss.

"You're probably wondering how it's possible." D straightened and emptied a can of black beans into one of the small pots. He didn't ask Caiden to stop touching him, so Caiden didn't.

"How what's possible?"

"That I could do what I did and have a loving family. Maybe something is wrong with me, always was. My parents didn't have the money to send me to college, so I enlisted right out of high school, joined the Army, became a Ranger. I had skills that caught the interest of certain parties, which led to me being sheep-dipped, running ops with the CIA. Next thing I knew, I was taking out dangerous men responsible for threats against our country. I became the go-to guy for contract hits." D's heart-wrenching sigh clenched at Caiden's heart.

"I was at the playground with my little sister once. She was only six at the time, and this kid's father had grabbed her by the arm when she punched his son—who, by the way, deserved it. Little shit was trying to look up her skirt. Anyway, she socked him one for being a little perv, and the kid's dad grabbed her arm, and I lost my shit. Took him out with one punch. The cops were called. It was a fucking mess.

"My mom tore into me that night. Let me have it with both barrels. And she was right. My heart was in the right place, but my view of the world around me was all out of whack. With my strength and training, I could have killed the guy. Was that the kind of example I was setting for Luz?" He swallowed hard and shook his head. "I didn't come home as much after that, afraid that my family would take one look at me and know what I was, what I was capable of. I told myself I wanted to be someone my parents could be proud of, that my little sister could look up to. The answer was out there somewhere, I just had to find it. Except I got lost along the way." He turned off the stove and motioned behind him to the counter. Reluctantly, Caiden went, resuming his seat.

"Don't get me wrong, I own my shit. I accepted those contracts, did what had to be done, and didn't lose sleep over it. By the time I realized I might never find what I was looking for, it was too late. I was bleeding to death in someone's garden, sucking in my last breath of air, knowing I'd never see Luz or my parents again."

"I'm so sorry, D."

With a shrug, D dropped some butter into the cast-iron skillet. "She's better off without me in her life. God knows I probably would have fucked it all up. Better her grieving a big brother she adored than a monster she'd hate."

"Hey, stop it. Luz loves you. You're not a monster. Those people don't matter. Luz matters. Your parents matter. And it sounds to me like they adored you. You're very lucky. Not everyone has that. Hell, I'm alive and my parents couldn't give three shits about it."

D turned to him with a frown. "Why?"

"Take your pick." He counted the reasons off on his fingers. "I'm gay, work for the government—even though they have no idea it's the CIA—instead of following in my father's footsteps and becoming a lawyer. I have opinions, many opinions, on politics that don't fall in line with theirs. I don't believe in organized religion. I don't judge a person by what's in their bank account, the car they drive, or their investment portfolio. And I love dogs, which my mother does not. She doesn't like animals, so that alone should tell you a bit about her pleasant personality." D chuckled. He started searing the seasoned steaks, and Caiden groaned. "God, that smells good. You sure you don't want to change your mind about marrying me?"

D threw his head back and laughed, the sound warm and genuine. It was good to see him smiling, and Caiden had the stupid need to see it more often. It transformed D's whole face. He really was a stunningly beautiful man.

"Need any help?" Caiden asked.

"How about you set the counter?"

"I can do that." Caiden went to work, putting out plates and cutlery while D popped the steaks in the oven to finish cooking them.

"The rice and beans are done. So's the mojo. Yucca should be ready soon. How do you like your steak?"

"Medium's good." Caiden opened the fridge to grab drinks. "Who stocked up the fridge?"

"I put in an order with David. If there's something you want to eat, just let me know and I'll get David to have it sent over."

"What do you want to drink?"

"I'll have a ginger ale."

Caiden grabbed a can of ginger ale for himself as well. "Thanks for cooking. I'd love to return the favor, but I'm not much of a cook. My mother was too busy with her tennis club for silly things like preparing her child with useful life skills."

"Who cooked for you, then?" D asked.

"Our cook."

"Ah. That's okay. I don't mind cooking. We can always order out too."

Caiden reminded himself they were in the middle of an op, and this domestic bliss he was currently experiencing with D wasn't going to last. It also brought home how lonely he was. He'd spent so much time out in the field immersed in one legend or another that he never had the time to feel lonely. His life had been fast-paced, always in motion, and now the idea of going home alone to his dinky apartment for yet another dreary winter sounded… depressing. He definitely had to change *something* in his life.

"Sit," D ordered gently before removing the steaks from the oven.

Caiden happily did, thanking D when he placed a plate heaping with rice, black beans, yucca, and a mouthwatering steak in front of him. They sat side by side, and Caiden moaned around his first bite of perfectly cooked steak.

"Good?"

"Oh my God, this is the best steak I've ever had."

D winked at him. "See? Not just a pretty face."

"I never doubted you were a man of many talents," Caiden teased, his voice going huskier than he'd intended. D almost choked on his food, and Caiden patted his back.

"Fuck," D wheezed. "Are you trying to kill me?"

"Again?"

D blinked at him, then smirked. "Smartass. Eat your food before it gets cold."

"Yes, sir!" Caiden saluted him before digging in, smiling at D's snicker. They talked as they ate. Nothing serious. Mostly small talk—sports, movies, music. Since D cooked, Caiden cleaned up. When he was done, he checked his watch.

"Looks like it's time for a little B and E."

"Let's get to it, then. Change and meet you in the dining room in ten."

Caiden nodded his agreement, then walked into his room to pull on a pair of black athletic compression pants, a long-sleeved henley that hugged his torso, and a pair of all-black hiking sneakers. He grabbed the black beanie and pulled it onto his head before snatching up his black gloves. D was already in the dining room, dressed in black workout pants and a black long-sleeved henley just like Caiden's.

"Okay," D said, glancing at him and doing a double take. He licked his bottom lip before straightening away from the table. "Wow. So, uh, that outfit is kinda… yeah, okay."

Caiden chuckled. "That made total sense," he teased.

"Shut up," D grumbled, turning back to the laptop, his eyes narrowed like he was concentrating really hard on the screen and not Caiden, who stepped up to him nice and close, their hips and arms touching. Clearing his throat, D brought up the Google Map of the Graves mansion. "Since we're so close, we'll go on foot. That way if we have to make a quick getaway, we can get lost in the trees. We've also got the small speedboat hidden and docked here." He pointed to a section of the forest near the lake.

They put in their earpieces, and Caiden checked his watch. "Eight o'clock. Isabella and Kenneth should be leaving now."

D hit a button on the laptop, and the camera feeds appeared. "There." He pointed to one of the screens outside the guest house. Kenneth opened the Ferrari's passenger side door for Isabella, then closed it after she climbed in, before getting in behind the wheel. The engine roared to life, the headlights beaming as he pulled out of the driveway and took off down A1A.

Caiden tapped his earpiece. "Alpha, targets are on the move."

"Copy that. Inform me when you're at the property, and I'll take care of the security system. Alpha out."

"Won't they know if we disable the alarms?" Caiden asked D as he took the tactical backpack D handed him.

"Alpha's not disabling it. The security system is connected to a secure network, which allows the security company to monitor it. Alpha will hack into the system using the company's own servers and trick the system into thinking it's still activated when it's not. Then they'll clone the video footage, so anyone monitoring the outside camera feeds won't see a thing. Same as when you were outside the property installing our cameras." D slipped on his backpack and pulled on his beanie before heading for the stairs. "Walk in the park. All we have to do now is avoid the security guards and the gators."

Caiden stilled. "Wait, what?"

"The gators. We're going into a patch of thick trees and bushes, and we're near a lake. Who knows what's in there?"

"Yeah, but… gators?" Caiden ran and caught up to him. "You're kidding right?"

D shook his head, his eyes lit up with amusement. "Welcome to Florida, cariño."

Did D just call him dear?

THE SUN had set, the only sound coming from the waves crashing against the shore and the occasional car driving by. They moved in the shadows, sticking close to the darkest paths as they maneuvered between houses until they reached the end of the cul-de-sac. They jumped the low wall and landed behind a row of thick bushes and trees. Listening for cars, they darted across the two-lane state road and down a path leading into the greenery ahead. The one lamppost lit A1A, but the deeper they got into the small patch of forest, the darker it would get.

"No, seriously," Caiden whispered as he stuck close to D, scanning the ground around him. "Are there going to be gators out here?"

"Maybe."

A mosquito buzzed by his ear, and he smacked it away. "Why do you have so many bugs! Ugh, I thought this was a tropical haven."

D's throaty laugh was not amusing. "Baby, Florida is a swamp."

"I can see that."

"No, really. Back in the day, it was nothing but miles and miles of water and swamp. People came in, drained the water, and built all this shit on swampland, made it pretty, but the gators were here before we were. They'll be here long after. Along with the roaches. The flying ones are disgusting."

"Oh my God, is this you trying to make me feel better? Because it's not working. At. All."

D stopped moving and crouched down. He grabbed Caiden's hand, and pulled him down beside him, his finger to his lips. They listened, faraway voices cutting through the sound of screeching bugs, buzzing mosquitoes, and God knew what else. His concentration broke momentarily when he realized D's hand was still wrapped around his.

"They're gone. Put on your night vision goggles."

"So I can see the gators. Good idea," Caiden teased, earning himself an amused head-shake. He placed the lightweight headgear on and flipped the switch. Everything around him turned green.

"Come on." D took hold of Caiden's hand again, much to Caiden's delight, and tugged him close as they made their way through the trees. The sun was gone, the night cool, especially with them being flanked by two bodies of water. They reached the small wall and both of them crouched behind it. D motioned for him to stay put, and he peeked out, ducking quickly, a finger to his lips. A radio crackled on the other side, one of the guards grumbling.

"I'm telling you, bro, Alicia's leaving me for another guy."

"Don't be an ass, Manny. Just because Alicia said she was going to have drinks with a friend and you saw her in South Beach with another guy doesn't mean she's leaving you for him."

"She let him kiss her!"

"Oh, well, I'm sure there's a perfectly good explanation—"

"I told her I wasn't ready to commit."

"After two years? Yeah, she's totally leaving you."

The guard walked off, and D grunted. "Maybe Manny needed some time to figure his shit out."

Caiden rolled his eyes. "Or maybe Manny needs to grow a pair and commit to Alicia before someone who's not afraid of going after what he wants comes along and sweeps her off her feet. She can't wait around forever."

"Maybe if she really cared about Manny," D hissed, "she wouldn't put so much pressure on him."

"And maybe Alicia is wasting her time with an emotionally stunted jerk who's incapable of seeing what's right in front of him and how good they are together!"

"Wait, are we still talking about Manny?"

With a sound of disgust, Caiden checked the coast was clear and climbed over the wall. Poor Alicia had waited two years for Manny. How much longer did he expect her to wait?

"Caiden, wait a second." D caught up to him, taking hold of his arm as they stuck to the shadows near the wall. "We are talking about Manny, right?"

"Right. Manny." Caiden pulled his hand out of D's and tapped his earpiece. "Alpha, we're at the side door near the pool house."

"Copy that. Bypassing security system now. Stand by."

A familiar voice neared, and Caiden cursed under his breath. "Manny's friend is coming back."

"Shit." D tapped his earpiece. "Alpha, we need to get in there. *Now*."

"Five seconds," Alpha replied.

Shit. Next to Caiden, D readied himself. They couldn't be discovered. If that meant knocking one of the guards out, then so be it, but Caiden would rather get in and get out without incident. They only had a few hours to search before Kenneth and Isabella returned.

"Go."

On Alpha's command, D quickly got to picking the lock.

"Ten seconds until the guard is on you," Alpha said.

"I'm working on it," D muttered, maneuvering the lock pick tools. A *click* later and they were in. "Got it." He opened the door, and Caiden followed him inside, then closed the door swiftly but silently behind him. The house was dark, but the moonlight coming in through the many windows and glass doors lit the place enough for them to see. They put away their goggles and hurried upstairs, then stopped at the top of the landing.

"How do you want to do this?" Caiden asked.

"Let's start with the secret safe." D motioned for Caiden to show him the way, and Caiden took the lead, hurried down the hall and into the library.

"The safe is in the library?"

"Yep. Behind the liquor cabinet. Alpha, you got eyes on the guards?"

"Yes. You're clear."

"And the door to the safe room isn't wired?"

"All security has been disabled."

"Good." Caiden opened the liquor cabinet doors and slowly ran his gloved fingers inside of the cabinet along the roof, feeling for any bumps. His index finger hit something, and he pushed it. Something unlatched, and the cabinet popped forward an inch. Closing the cabinet doors, he hurried to slip his fingers into the crack behind the cabinet and carefully swung it open. The light inside the room turned on.

"Quick, close the door before anyone sees the light."

D pulled the handle on the other side of the cabinet, and it clicked closed, turning off the light overhead. Rustling around in his bag, Caiden pulled out the LED camping lantern. He opened it and the bright LED lights flooded the whole room in white light. Placing it on one of the glass display cases, he turned to D.

"You're up."

D approached the safe and tapped his earpiece. "Alpha, any idea what we're looking for?"

"We're looking for a digital key. It unlocks a sort of catalog to the intel on Kenneth's clients. I'm working on the location of the intel, but without the key, we won't be able to gain access. Look for a flash drive or external hard drive."

"Any way to know what's in the safe?" Caiden asked.

"Negative," Alpha replied. "Graves hasn't opened the safe since the cameras were installed."

Caiden stepped up beside D, who was inspecting the safe, a deep frown on his face. "What's wrong?"

"This is a commercial-grade safe and a cheap one at that."

"Fuck." Caiden had been hoping he'd been wrong. He had his suspicions when he'd been in here, distracting Harrison, but he'd hoped that when they got a closer look at it that it just looked like any safe you could get from a retail chain. D removed his backpack, then opened it and took out the padded box that contained the large, round neodymium disc magnet tucked in a sock.

Standing, D stuck the magnet to the top left corner of the safe, fiddling with it and the handle until they heard a click and the safe opened.

"Something tells me what we're looking for won't be in here," D said, pulling the sock and removing the magnet from the safe. He carefully returned it to its box and packed it away in his bag. The magnet was so powerful, all the electronic gadgets had to be in Caiden's bag or the magnet would wipe everything out.

"Maybe Kenneth thinks the hidden room is enough. It's not on the floor plans of the house," Caiden reminded him.

D shook his head as he searched the safe. "No way with the list of clients and his connections to high-ranking officials does Kenneth keep something as valuable as the key to his blackmail evidence in a safe my grandmother could crack."

"What's in there?" Caiden stepped up beside him. Damn. It was nothing but the usual—passports, property documents, deeds, insurance policies, cash, jewelry. Nothing that screamed blackmail material, nothing electronic or digital. "Great. Now what?"

"We keep searching." D closed the safe.

Caiden ran his hands through his hair and groaned. "Great." An idea occurred to him. "Wait a second. If this flash drive is the key to vital intel, Kenneth wouldn't want it falling into the wrong hands."

"Right."

"And if it did, he'd have some kind of failsafe, or a way to track it down, don't you think."

D's eyes widened. He cupped Caiden's face and planted a sloppy kiss on his lips. "You're a genius." He tapped his earpiece. "Alpha, any chance Kenneth has some kind of GPS software on the flash drive?"

"Looking it up now," Alpha replied, "but it will take some time."

"Okay." D nodded. "While you do that, we're going to keep searching." He grabbed the lantern and motioned for the door.

Caiden took hold of the handle. "Alpha, are we clear?"

"You're clear."

After pulling the handle, Caiden slipped out, then held the cabinet open for D, who closed the lantern and handed it to Caiden to return it to his bag. They had moved the cabinet back into place and were searching the library when Alpha's digitized voice crackled through their earpieces.

"Kenneth and Isabella just arrived."

"What?" D hissed. "It's way too early."

"You need to get out now."

"Fuck." D grabbed Caiden's hand, and they quietly ran from the room, heading for the rear of the house toward the second set of stairs. The lights in the house turned on, and Caiden's heart leaped into his throat. The back door slammed open as well as the front, Kenneth screaming at his wife from one side while Isabella cursed her husband as she stomped up the steps from the other side.

"In here." Caiden pulled at D's arm, leading him into what looked like an alcove with a suit of armor in front of it. He pushed at one corner of the decorative scroll in the center of the alcove, and it opened. Shoving D inside, Caiden quickly followed, then closed the door just as Isabella's Italian curses echoed past. He turned and gently but firmly pushed D farther into the darkened space.

"Where the hell are we?" D whispered.

"A secret passage."

"The one you explored with Harrison?"

"Now is *not* the time," Caiden hissed. If they didn't get the hell out of here before Kenneth discovered them, they'd lose more than the mission.

Chapter Eight

THIS WAS bad.

How had they gotten stuck in a fucking wall? D *hated* small spaces. Not that he was claustrophobic or anything. He simply hated having his movements constricted, and the corridor they were in gave him an extra six inches on either side of his shoulders, at most.

"Stay close to me," D grumbled, a shiver going through him when Caiden put his hand to D's back. This really wasn't the place to start thinking about their time in the shower. "Any idea where this goes?" Light was coming in from somewhere, but he had no idea where. There was just enough for him to be able to see in front of him up to a certain point, but after that it was pitch-black.

"I don't know. We didn't get this far," Caiden said.

D ignored the way his hackles rose. He had a pretty good idea why Caiden hadn't made it through the rest of the corridor. Keeping his mouth shut, D moved as fast as he could while being silent and cautious. Judging by the cobwebs lining the stone walls, he'd say no one came in here much. It would have been helpful if this had been included in the mansion's floor plans, but then he supposed it went against the whole "secret" thing.

"Why would Harrison show you all this?" D asked. The question had been at the back of his mind since he'd seen Caiden in the safe room with Harrison. The guy was former military and a trusted member of Kenneth's staff. Why would he expose a secret escape route to someone he'd just met? Was he that desperate to get into Caiden's pants?

"Like I said, he was trying to impress me. Mostly I think because the secret passages aren't really a big deal. My guess is Harrison knows what's in the safe and feels confident I wasn't going to make off with any of it. Like you said, Harrison is former military. He has several escape plans for Isabella and Kenneth, none of which include some dusty old passages, several of which he says lead nowhere useful."

God, he hoped this wasn't one of the passages that led nowhere useful. Muffled shouts floated around them with the occasional pause. Most likely Kenneth and Isabella catching their breaths for another round. It was clear the reason they'd come back early was the topic of their epic fight. According to their profiles, screaming matches were a regular occurrence for these two. Unfortunately, they picked tonight of all nights to have one.

D tapped his earpiece, speaking quietly. "Alpha, any word on the flash drive?"

"Negative. If Graves has any kind of security software on the drive—which I'm now certain he has—it's very well hidden. The level of security makes sense, considering the connections he has and the importance of the flash drive. I'm working on it."

"Copy that."

They continued down the corridor and came across what looked like a door. "Jackpot." No handle. He inspected the doorway, light filtering through around the frame. Placing his gloved hands on the door, he gently pushed. It was one of the bedrooms. He started to open the door fully when Kenneth marched out of the bathroom.

"How many times do we have to have this same fucking conversation, Bella!"

Shit, shit, shit. D backed up so quickly, he didn't think Caiden would be right behind him. Turning, he pushed Caiden against the wall with his body, shielding him with his bigger frame as the door closed silently behind him. He leaned into Caiden, his hands to either side of Caiden's head.

"What's going on?" Caiden whispered, his hot breath against D's jaw.

"That's the master bedroom. Kenneth was in there."

"Shit. Do you think he saw you?"

They both stilled, listening for any signs of Kenneth calling in the cavalry and sending them to apprehend the intruders in his wall.

"We wouldn't be having this same conversation if you weren't so goddamn paranoid that every man who comes within a ten-mile radius of me is trying to steal me away from you!" Isabella shouted from somewhere outside the room.

"Maybe if you didn't flirt with everything that had a dick!"

D's wide eyes met Caiden's. He shook his head. "Guess that's a no."

The shouting stopped, and they froze. Shit. Maybe Kenneth *had* seen them.

"Wait." Caiden grabbed hold of D's wrists. "What's that noise?"

They listened, hearing muffled sounds followed by moaning. D's eyes widened. *No. Please no.*

Something slammed into the wall, and D jumped along with Caiden. The moans intensified, followed by another slam.

"Oh God, yes! Yes! Fuck me, baby," Isabella shouted.

Caiden's jaw dropped. "Oh my God," he gasped, eyes huge.

"Are you fucking kidding me?"

Another slam, and the moans turned into groans and shouted expletives in English and Italian. Isabella and Kenneth were having full-blown make-up sex with slamming headboard and all. D dropped his head to Caiden's shoulder. Of course this was happening to him. Who else would it happen to? Carefully but quickly, D shifted them farther down so they weren't directly behind Kenneth and Isabella's bed. Not that it helped.

The steady smacking of the headboard against the wall seemed to urge Isabella on, her screams ear-shattering.

"Wow, that's…."

D snorted. "She's faking it."

"That so?"

"Yep." He lifted his head and dropped his gaze to Caiden's lips. "Not that any women, or men, have faked it with me, but a guy can tell."

Caiden snickered. "Sure he can."

"Harrison didn't seem to think you were."

Caiden sighed. "D, just ask."

"Ask what?" Why was he still pressed against Caiden? He should move away.

"Fine. Don't." Caiden turned his head, but D took hold of his chin, forcing Caiden to look at him.

"Okay. What happened with Harrison in the safe room?" Was Caiden trying not to smile? It looked like maybe he was trying not to smile. Little shit.

"Nothing."

"Nothing?" D couldn't help sounding skeptical.

"That's what I said. He tried to kiss me, and I told him I thought I heard something. I pushed him away and said I was sorry, but if I got caught with him, I could lose my job."

"And?"

Caiden shrugged. "He understood. He said he looked forward to seeing me Friday night."

"For your date."

The headboard slammed against the wall again, and D jumped. *For fuck's sake. No. Don't think fuck. Ugh, this is a nightmare.*

"It's just drinks."

Sure it was. "You're still going, then?"

"D, he knows everything that goes on in this house. If I can get him drunk enough—"

"Are you kidding me?" D did push away this time. He ran his fingers through his hair. "The man's a Marine. He ain't saying shit no matter how drunk he is."

"I'm sure I can persuade him. He really likes me."

"Yeah, I could tell by the way he was trying to fuck you through your clothes," D growled quietly.

"So you watched us."

"We need to get out of here," D ground out through his teeth.

"Avoiding it won't make it go away," Caiden hissed.

"I'm going to disagree with you on that one. Also, this is neither the time nor the place for this."

"It's never the right time or place for you, D." Caiden let out a sigh that squeezed at D's heart. "Forget it. Let's go. Maybe there's another way out."

D took the out Caiden gave him, turned away, and walked farther down the corridor. He couldn't think about this now. If it were up to him, he wouldn't think about it ever, but Caiden wouldn't wait that long, and D didn't expect him to. His life had been easy until now. Okay, maybe not easy, but he'd known where he stood in all things. He had meaningless hookups because they didn't require any of the complications that came after. The life he led didn't leave room for happy ever after. Hell, his job *was* his life. No one could know he was alive. Caiden deserved better.

On the flip side, Caiden knew who he was and what he did for a living, and he still wanted D. But for how long? How long before Caiden had enough of the risks, the uncertainties, and went out in search of stability? Screw this. All this thinking was hurting his brain. They finally reached the end of the darkened hall.

"There's a door. Be ready." Gingerly, D pushed. The door budged half an inch. Shit. Pushing harder yielded the same whole lot of nothing. "There's something blocking it." Something exceptionally heavy that would make a fuckton of noise if he tried to move it. "Fuck!" He knocked his head against it. They had no choice. They had to go out the way they'd come in, right next to Kenneth and Isabella's bedroom.

He turned, coming face-to-face with Caiden. "It's blocked." Hadn't he said that? Genius. "Why are you standing so close?"

Caiden's lips quirked into a little smile. "You told me to stay close."

"I did?" Wait, he had? *Stay close to me.* Shit, he had. "I didn't mean that close. Anyway, our only option is the way we came. We can use the other rooms as cover, and we're going to have to be quick." He took hold of Caiden's waist to turn him around. Ooh, that was a mistake. D swallowed hard.

"D—"

"Go," D ordered gently, and with a sigh, Caiden did as he was asked, turning and heading in the direction they'd come, with D following close—but not *too* close—behind.

Reaching the alcove they'd entered through, Caiden nudged the door open and peeked out. The sex sounds had quieted, which hopefully meant the lovebirds were asleep or doing whatever they did after sex. D didn't care as long as it meant they stayed in their room. Caiden motioned for D to follow, and they slipped through the door and headed for the stairs, but then they heard a familiar voice.

"Manny, I'm sorry to say, Andy's right. You need to get your head out of your ass or you're going to lose her for good."

"Are you kidding me with this bullshit?" D pushed Caiden toward the library before Harrison reached the top of the stairs. Whoever the hell this Manny was, D was going to find him and beat the shit out of him. And now this asshole? "What the hell is Harrison doing in the house?" They took cover just inside the library near the doorway.

"How should I know?"

"He's your boyfriend, isn't he?"

Caiden shook his head at him. "Very mature."

D shrugged. Like he gave a shit. "Sounds like your boyfriend is in the main sitting room."

"He's not my boyfriend," Caiden hissed. "But you gave me an idea."

Wonderful. D couldn't wait to hear it.

Caiden removed his cell phone from the outer pocket of his bag, then pulled off one of his gloves. He tapped at the screen and held the phone to his ear.

"What the hell are you doing? Are you insane?"

Caiden put a finger to D's lips, and D glared at him. He would have said something, but Harrison's deep "Hello" had him balling his hands into fists. That and so he wouldn't strangle Caiden's pretty neck.

"Avery. What a pleasant surprise."

"Hi, Harrison." Caiden's voice was low, and although it was so Harrison wouldn't be able to tell the call was coming from nearby, it made Caiden's voice sound like he was sleepy and in bed. "I'm so sorry to bother you, but I think I might have dropped my Moleskine notebook outside your house."

What had Caiden been doing at Harrison's house? Teeth gritted, D forced himself to remain motionless, despite wanting to march out there and plant a fist in Harrison's stupidly handsome face. And that was the problem, wasn't it? How Caiden made him want to do things he'd never done before, brought out pesky feelings he had no use for.

"Why don't you come over, and we can look for it together?"

Smooth motherfucker, D would give him that. Instinctively he took hold of the strap hanging from

Caiden's backpack. Caiden noticed, his knowing smile stealing D's breath away.

"I can't, but it would be really helpful if you could check on that notebook for me. I took some notes that I need for my meeting with Ms. Draper."

"For you, gorgeous. Anything."

D made a gagging motion, and Caiden playfully shoved him.

"Aw, aren't you sweet."

Did he mean Harrison or D, because his gaze was on D.

"Going now. Walk with me. So what are you wearing?"

Way to be subtle. D rolled his eyes. Good thing Harrison couldn't see Caiden now, or he might pass out. The way the workout leggings hugged every inch of Caiden's legs and delectable ass was sinful, and the henley was all but painted on over his lean torso and sculpted muscles.

"Just pajama bottoms and an old T-shirt," Caiden purred, taking hold of D's hand and dashing out of the room. D kept an eye out for any movement or voices coming from the bedroom. They stopped at the top of the stairs, making sure the coast was clear before hurrying down, Harrison still talking away in Caiden's ear. He was far enough away now that D couldn't hear him, only Caiden's half of the conversation. "You're such a tease. Me? I never tease."

Liar. Dirty, filthy, sexy liar.

They reached the side door, and D cracked it open to check the coast was clear. *Shit.* A guard headed in their direction. D made a cutting motion, and Caiden nodded.

"Listen, Harry, I'm so sorry, but I'm going to have to go. My boss is calling me. I know. No rest for the wicked. Wouldn't you like to know? Thank you for checking. I probably dropped it in the car."

D widened his eyes. *Wrap it up.*

"Of course I'll make it up to you. Friday. Good night." Caiden hung up and returned his phone to his bag's pocket. Plastered to the wall on each side of the door, D waited, counting the seconds in his head, estimating the time it would take the guard to pass them. When enough time passed, D cracked the door open again and peeked out. The guard was several yards ahead. D slipped out and waited for Caiden to do the same before quietly closing the door, then taking off toward the trees, Caiden close to him. They jumped the small wall and hurried through the thick patch of trees they'd come through, pulling on their night vision goggles along the way.

A twig snapped to their left, and Caiden jumped. He grabbed D's arm, practically climbing him. "Is it a gator?"

D let out a bark of laughter, startling Caiden, who quickly recovered and threw his hand over D's mouth, muffling the laughter he couldn't hold back.

"Not funny," Caiden grumbled.

D's "Yes, it is so funny" was muffled by Caiden's hand—his bare hand since he hadn't put his glove back on after removing it to work his cell phone. He wrapped an arm around Caiden's slim waist and squeezed. Clearing his throat, Caiden moved away and out of his hold. Heavy, awkward silence hung between them as they reached A1A. Removing their goggles, they stood in the darkness as a car sped by, and then they darted across to the other side. Caiden pulled his glove back on before hopping over the small wall, and D followed, his eyes landing on Caiden's perfectly round ass.

"I'll make it up to you," Caiden had told Harrison. Make it up to him how?

Shaking himself out of it, D swept past Caiden, hurrying for the safe house. Once inside, D took the stairs two at a time. He pulled off his backpack and dropped it onto the floor by the kitchen, his beanie tossed carelessly on the couch when he stormed into the living room. Removing his gloves, he tapped them against his thigh.

"What's going on?" Caiden asked, stopping somewhere behind him. D could *feel* him.

Don't. Don't do it.

D spun around; his breath caught in his throat at how beautiful Caiden was. His blond hair was a mess from the beanie he'd pulled off, his cheeks slightly flushed from their mad dash, the adrenaline no doubt pumping through him the same as D.

"Don't have sex with him," D blurted.

Caiden stared at him. "What?"

"You heard me," D said, crossing the distance between them. He took hold of Caiden's chin. "Don't have sex with him."

"Why?"

"Because I don't want you to."

"Oh, okay." Caiden nodded. "Seems like a legit reason."

"I'm being serious."

"So am I. You don't want me, but you don't want anyone else to have me either? You can't have it both ways."

"I just need…." Being this close to Caiden was short-circuiting his brain.

"What?" Caiden asked softly, running a finger down D's jaw. "What do you need, D?"

You. I need you. "I um…."

"Is this what you need?" Caiden cupped D through his pants, massaging his half-hard cock.

"Fuck. Cade."

Caiden hummed, nuzzling D's temple. "Cade, now, is it?" He nipped at D's earlobe, and the noise D released was indecent. His cock strained against his pants, and when Caiden licked up D's jaw, his eyes all but rolled into the back of his head.

"This isn't—we shouldn't…."

"Okay." Caiden shrugged and walked off.

"Fuck! You drive me out of my fucking mind, you know that?"

"The feeling's mutual, I assure you." Caiden had made it as far as the dining room before D grabbed his arm, swinging him back around to face him. He cut off Caiden's protest with a crushing kiss, the heat exploding through D like a raging inferno. Caiden gasped, and D slipped his tongue inside Caiden's warm mouth, groaning at the taste of him. He tasted like everything D had ever wanted but had been too afraid to admit to. Needing air, he pulled away, his heart pounding in his ears at the decadent picture Caiden made with his blown pupils and kiss-swollen lips. Should he say something? Was Caiden expecting him to say something? As if reading his thoughts, Caiden launched himself at D, his lips swallowing D's breath.

The house was dark except for the light filtering in through the open blinds of the living room balcony doors. D walked him backward toward the living room, and they stumbled down the small set of stairs from the dining room area. Caiden laughed against D's lips, and

D loved the sound, loved that perfect mouth. They tore at each other's clothes, kicking off shoes and tugging shirts up over their heads, their mouths finding each other like magnets. The adrenaline pumped through their system, and D thought he'd scream if he didn't get inside Caiden right that second.

When they were both naked, Caiden pushed D toward the couch until the back of his knees hit it and he fell onto the cushions. Caiden stood long enough to lick his lips and drink his fill. "You are a work of art, Álvaro Montero."

The words spoken almost reverently, the way Caiden said his name, sent a tremor through D, and he was ready to come apart. "Come here," D said gruffly, holding out a hand.

"Supplies? I want you inside me." Caiden's eyes were so dark they looked black.

"Nightstand. My room."

"Don't move," Caiden ordered before rushing off. He sped into D's bedroom, and D had to calm himself or this would be over far too soon. Caiden was quick, rushing back with condoms and lube. D groaned at the mouthwatering vision Caiden made as he stilled, his eyes taking in every inch of D—and D could have sworn he felt it as if it had been Caiden's hands. It would seem his gorgeous man needed a little incentive to come over. He spread his legs and palmed his cock, using his precome to ease the friction.

The whimper Caiden let out was sexy as fuck. Caiden stalked over to him, tossed the supplies on the couch, and knelt between D's legs, batting his hand away.

"This is mine," Caiden growled before taking hold of D's cock at the base and swallowing the rest.

"Fuck!" D bucked his hips, and Caiden moaned around him, his free hand sliding up D's thigh, then down to his balls, cupping him and toying with him. D's moan was loud, and he slipped his fingers into all that thick blond hair, petting Caiden, stroking his hair as Caiden tortured him with his mouth, alternating between sucking, licking, and nipping at D's skin.

D threw his head back against the couch cushions, his eyes closed as pleasure swept through him like a tidal wave. Caiden's hot mouth on him, stroking him, sucking him like he was dessert, was driving him crazy. He opened his eyes and groaned when their gazes met.

"Fuck, you look so good on your knees sucking my dick." Watching Caiden's lips around his rock-hard shaft had to be the most erotic thing he'd ever seen. His muscles tightened, and he stopped Caiden. "If you keep that up, I'm going to come."

Caiden popped off to snatch a condom and lube packet from the couch. He handed D the lube and tore at the condom packet with his teeth. D's rapt attention was focused on Caiden, and he dug his fingers into the couch when Caiden flicked a tongue out over D's slit, lapping up the drops of precome.

"You're gonna kill me," D said with a groan. The smile he received was wicked. Caiden sucked the head into his mouth, and D cursed under his breath, ignoring Caiden's chuckle when he pulled back. He placed the condom to the tip of D's cock and rolled it down painstakingly slow. Taking the lube packet from D, he opened it and slathered it over D before standing to straddle D's lap.

The feel of Caiden's hot naked body against his, of his soft skin and firm muscles, felt so damned right. Caiden took hold of D's hand and lubed up two of his fingers. Just when D didn't think he could get any harder, or want Caiden any more than he already did, Caiden proved him wrong.

"Get me ready for that gorgeous cock," Caiden murmured before running a tongue along D's bottom lip.

D ran a hand up Caiden's thigh, the fine hairs feeling so damned good beneath his hands. He tapped Caiden's flank, and Caiden leaned forward. Spreading his asscheeks, D pressed a finger to Caiden's hole. Caiden sucked in a sharp breath, and D captured his lips and shoved his tongue inside Caiden, taking his mind off the burn he was surely feeling. He then sucked on Caiden's thumb, one hand kneading his left asscheek while he carefully fucked Caiden with first one finger, then two.

Caiden writhed on top of him, seeking more of D.

"D," Caiden pleaded against his lips. "Now. Do it now."

Lining himself up with Caiden's hole, D pressed the tip inside, sweat beading his brow as he paced himself, going slow so as not to hurt Caiden. He'd already hurt Caiden in many ways; this wouldn't be another one. Caiden, however, was very impatient, and he sat down, impaling himself on D's cock, both of them crying out at the sudden thrust.

"Oh. Fuck." Caiden dropped his head to D's shoulder, and D ran a soothing hand down his back.

"You okay, baby?"

"Yeah, just… give me a second. You're not exactly a small guy."

"Hey, you're the one who couldn't wait," D teased.

"You complaining?" Caiden rolled his hips, and D saw stars.

"Holy fuck!"

"Yeah, that's what I thought."

"Such a fucking smartass," D grumbled, his toes curling when Caiden started moving. "God, you feel good." Caiden undulated his hips, moving slow at first, his fingers digging into D's shoulders. Every muscle in D's body was pulled tight, his pulse in the clouds as Caiden picked up his pace, alternating between rolling his hips and bouncing on D, who took the opportunity to run his hands all over Caiden.

Placing his hands on D's thighs, Caiden leaned back, his beautiful cock slapping his stomach as he fucked himself on D. D'd never seen anything more stunning. He palmed Caiden's dick, using his precome to jerk him off, his movement matching Caiden's pace. A light sheen of sweat made Caiden's fair skin glow. D needed his hands on him.

"Come here," D ordered, his voice rough with need.

Caiden quickly sat forward, wrapped his arms around D's neck, and brought their lips together. D couldn't get enough of Caiden's taste, of his hot mouth and wicked tongue. Tearing his mouth away from Caiden's, he moved his lips to Caiden's neck, sucking on his tender flesh. He took hold of Caiden's asscheeks, spreading him wide so he could pound into him. Caiden cried out his name, his fingers in D's hair holding on tight. The sound of D's balls and groin slapping Caiden's ass filled the room along with their panting, moans, and groans.

"Harder, D," Caiden begged, bouncing on D and meeting each of D's deep, hard thrusts. "Oh God, yeah. That's it, baby. Fuck me. Fuck me hard."

D grabbed a fistful of Caiden's hair. "You like my big cock inside your tight hole, don't you?" Caiden groaned, and D nipped at his chin. “Say it,” he demanded gruffly. “Say how much you love being stuffed full of my cock.” D snapped his hips up hard, and Caiden cried out.

“Oh fuck! Yes. I love having your big cock filling me. Please, D.”

“Damn, you’re beautiful.” D pulled Caiden against him, his arms wrapped around Caiden in an iron grip. He kissed the hell out of Caiden, swallowing his ragged breaths and loud moans. D’s muscles ached as he drove himself into Caiden over and over until he couldn’t tell where he ended and Caiden began. His orgasm stormed through him like a hurricane, and a roar tore from his throat as he filled the condom, Caiden’s scream following shortly after, his come trapped between their stomachs as his body convulsed before he collapsed on D.

“Holy. Fuck.”

D let his head fall back, a small aftershock going through him from how hard he’d come. “Yeah, that was… wow.”

Caiden smiled. “As good as the last time, or better?”

“I don’t know. We went at it for hours last time.” It had been one of the best nights of his life. A feeling of rightness he’d never felt before had made the sex out of this world.

“I’m game if you are.”

D blinked at him. “Really?”

“Is that a trick question?” Caiden rotated his hips, and D inhaled sharply. He hissed as he carefully pulled out. With a sinful smile, Caiden teased one of D’s nipples. “Remember how long I spent tasting every inch of you? The way you begged me to stop the torture?”

"You played with my ass for hours." It had been glorious.

"And you loved every minute of it."

D had. He so had. "When I didn't feel like I was going to die from edging. It could have totally happened." He nodded for emphasis. "True fact."

Caiden barked out a laugh. He shook his head at D. "What am I going to do with you?"

D waggled his eyebrows. "I have a few ideas."

"Mm-hm." Caiden brushed his lips over D's before climbing off him. "How about you share some of them with me in the shower?"

D removed the condom and jumped to his feet. "Lead the way."

Chapter Nine

CAIDEN APPROVED of D's ideas. The man had many, *many* good ideas. After breaking records for the quickest shower ever, D had dried him off and dragged him into Caiden's bedroom to push him onto the bed, where Caiden now lay sprawled with D kissing his way down his torso.

"Mm, you smell so good. I think I need to invest in some essential oils shower gel," Caiden said, running his fingers through D's hair. The style suited him. Short on the sides, long on top. "Why don't you come up here so I can kiss you?"

"Because it's my turn to torture you." D flicked one of Caiden's nipples with his tongue to demonstrate his point.

Caiden sucked in a breath, moaning as D toyed with the sensitive bud. First one, then the other, one elbow propping him up, his left hand roaming down Caiden's torso, slipping between them so he could fondle his balls, rolling them in his hand. D did torture oh so well.

God, he loved the feel of D's callused hands on his skin, the strength of his fingers, his powerful body. D took his time, lavishing attention on every inch of his body, using his mouth, his tongue, his fingers.

"Knees up and spread your legs."

Caiden did as D prompted, pulling his knees up and spreading his legs wide, a groan escaping him as D slid down his body, getting on his stomach between Caiden's legs, moving them over his shoulders, and holding on. His gaze met Caiden's, and a sinful smile spread onto his face. His tongue darted out and he licked at the precome on the rosy tip of Caiden's cock before he sucked it into his mouth.

"Oh God, D." Caiden let his head fall back, his eyes closed until D popped off him.

"Look at me, Cade."

Caiden opened his eyes, and D nodded his approval.

"You're going to watch me, and you're not going to touch yourself."

"You're evil," Caiden said with a pout.

"That's right. I am. Try not to interrupt me again."

Caiden had a very articulate and zingy response, but it turned into a strangled gurgle when D swallowed him down to the root. The man had no gag reflex, and sweet molasses, did he know how to work that wicked tongue. He swirled it around the tip before tonguing Caiden's slit, all the while denying Caiden any form of relief. He sucked, licked, and laved, a finger toying with his rim but nothing more, simply ghosting his entrance, teasing. *Fuck.* Caiden was going to lose his mind.

D pulled off him, and Caiden growled his displeasure, receiving a chuckle in response. Then D speared his hole with his tongue.

"Holy shit!" Caiden arched his back up off the bed. What followed was a rambling mess of grunts, groans, and unintelligible half sentences as D made a meal out of him. Caiden tried to touch himself, only to get his hand batted away. "Please, D."

D lifted his head, his grin evil. "How's that payback feel?"

"Like fucking heaven and hell at the same time."

"I don't know about the rest, but fucking comes after I'm done with you. I just started." D lowered his head, his tongue tasting and massaging. Caiden writhed, his body feeling like it was going to catch fire from the heat spreading through him. Every nerve ending seemed attuned to D, sparking with need. He desperately wanted more. More of D's tongue, his cock, his heart. Caiden wanted it all.

D alternated between fucking Caiden with his tongue and his finger, until Caiden thought he was going to expire. Sweat dripped down the side of his face, his skin flushed with heat, and his panting breath mixed with the sounds of the ocean. Moonlight trickled in through the blinds, and Caiden couldn't think of anywhere else he would rather be than right here.

"D," Caiden begged. "I need you inside me." If he left D to it, he'd feast on Caiden for hours, but Caiden couldn't wait that long. He wanted D inside him, filling him. Who knew how long they had together, and he wanted his memories of D to be of his limbs tangled with Caiden's, their bodies fused together. As if sensing his thoughts, D pulled away. He climbed off the bed, stopped by the nightstand, and was ready to open the drawer when Caiden took a chance. He put a hand to D's.

"We don't have to."

The fire in D's eyes was unmistakable, but it was mixed with something else, something Caiden couldn't read. "Are you sure?"

Caiden nodded. "I'm negative." Relief washed over him when D climbed into bed and straddled him.

"Me too, I swear. I might take stupid risks on the job sometimes, but not in this. Never this. I've got the test results."

Caiden brushed his fingers down D's cheek, his smile warm. "I trust you."

With a nod, D leaned over, opened the drawer, and pulled out the lube only. He poured a generous amount onto his hand, then stroked himself a few times before he leaned over Caiden and kissed him. His mouth was hot, and Caiden couldn't taste him enough. He twirled his tongue around D's, his fingers in D's hair, tugging, stroking, combing.

D pressed the tip of his cock to Caiden's entrance and gingerly pushed in. "Fuck. I love how tight you are."

Caiden wrapped his legs around D, his hands on D's face as he kissed him again, letting himself get lost in D's kiss instead of the initial pain and discomfort. He could spend hours kissing D and nothing else and be content. His heart swelled with every kiss. When D was buried inside Caiden, he pulled back onto his knees, his arms around Caiden's thighs. Slowly he started to move, rocking his hips in tiny movements, and Caiden gasped at the ripple of pleasure it sent through him.

"Takes a really fucking stupid man to walk away from you," D said, breathless.

"Not stupid," Caiden replied, palming his cock. "Complicated, maybe. Infuriating, for sure."

D snapped his hips, and Caiden cried out. A laugh tumbled out of Caiden, and he shook his head at D.

"Fucker."

"I'll show you just the kind of fucker I am," D teased, snapping his hips again. His movements picked up, his groin smacking against Caiden's ass as he thrust in and out, speeding up, then slowing down and rotating his hips.

"D, please." Caiden jerked himself off. He reached for D, needing to feel D's mouth on his. To his relief, D obliged, leaning in to bring their mouths together, swallowing Caiden's cry when D thrust his hips hard.

"Yes!" Caiden threw his head back and screamed, feeling lighter than he'd had in forever. "That's it. Come on, tiger!"

D laughed. "Tiger, huh?"

"Grr," Caiden growled, and D's throaty laugh was music to his ears. His smile reached the corners of his dark eyes, forming little wrinkles. If it were up to him, he'd never let D go, but it wasn't up to him. Caiden quickly pushed those thoughts aside. For now, he'd enjoy the magic that was the both of them together like this.

"Okay." D pulled almost all the way out, then plunged back in, and Caiden's toes curled. He dug his fingers into D's flesh, pulling him down against him. They ravaged each other's mouths as D snapped his hips over and over, thrusting deep and hard inside Caiden, the bed moving beneath them with every thrust.

"Oh God, yes. Oh, baby, I love how you fuck me. I love you buried deep inside me, love how you fill me." Caiden didn't know where the words came from.

He'd never been vocal during sex. Nothing outside the usual grunts and groans, anyway, but with D every experience was new, out of control, as D unleashed some wild part of him he'd never known was buried deep inside him.

"You're so damn beautiful. I can't tell you that enough, Cade. You're the most beautiful, sexiest man I've ever known. Everything about you is so fucking stunning." D punctuated the compliment with a snap of his hips, and Caiden groaned loud. Good God, this man was going to kill him.

Their panting breaths and soft curses filled the room as they moved together, D's fingers lacing with Caiden's, bringing his hands above his head. He changed his angle, hitting Caiden's prostate and sending a jolt through Caiden.

"Oh fuck!"

"Yeah, that's right, baby. Your body was made for me."

Caiden wanted to say they were made for each other, but he didn't. He bit down on his bottom lip to keep the words inside, to stop himself from blurting something out that neither of them was ready to hear. Instead, he urged D on, gasping when D took hold of Caiden's cock, pumping him fast and hard. Caiden met every one of D's deep thrusts, his muscles tightening as the pleasure swept through his body along with his orgasm.

"Come for me, cariño."

At D's roughly spoken endearment, Caiden cried out, his fingernails digging into D's biceps as he came, ribbons of come hitting his stomach. D's movements were wild, and then he roared his release, cursing in both English and his native tongue as he filled Caiden with heat. He thrust inside Caiden several more times before collapsing on him.

Caiden wrapped his arms around D's broad back, enjoying D's weight on him. For now, they were safe, secure, hidden away from the outside world. The ocean waves crashed against the shore, and peace Caiden had never felt before washed over him. He closed his eyes as he ran his fingers through D's hair, and D let out a happy sigh, settling against Caiden, no intention of moving in sight. Caiden smiled, his breathing evening out. He didn't care that they were sticky or sweaty. The breeze coming through the doors cooled his hot skin, and he was content.

I'm falling for him.

Caiden had been on dangerous missions in foreign territories, had come close to death many a time, but this right here, right now, was truly terrifying because he was losing his heart to a man he wanted more than anything, a man who would walk away from him the moment the mission was over.

"I guess I should move," D grumbled.

Caiden chuckled. "Or not."

"Very tempting, Cardosa. Very tempting." D nuzzled Caiden's temple, placing a feathery kiss there. He slid lower, his fingers slipping between Caiden's ass-cheeks. "My spunk is inside you."

"Has anyone ever told you how wonderfully romantic you are?"

"Shut up," D grumbled. "It's hot as fuck. Also… it's a first for me."

"What is?"

D hesitated. "Leaving a part of myself inside someone."

Whatever Caiden had expected him to say, it hadn't been that. He stroked D's hair, smiling softly when D placed his chin on Caiden's stomach, his eyes meeting Caiden's. "It's a first for me too." He'd never had sex without a condom. In his line of work, relationships would only bring complications. Maybe because he'd never met anyone worth complicating his life for. He'd been satisfied with his casual hookups. Now….

D pushed himself to his hands and knees and dropped a quick kiss on Caiden's lips before climbing off the bed. "Come on. Quick shower."

Caiden didn't question it. He let D lead him into the bathroom and beneath the showerhead, the warm water heavenly on his skin. They took turns bathing each other. This was the second time D had bathed him, and Caiden told himself he couldn't get used to it. They washed and rinsed, then dried each other off before heading into the bedroom. Caiden expected D to head back to his own room, but he didn't. He climbed in underneath the blanket and held Caiden's side up for him.

"Hurry up, I'm cold."

Caiden hurried, climbing into bed and holding back a smile when D grabbed him around his waist and brought him in close, nuzzling his temple before rolling onto his back.

"That's better," he murmured, eyes closed.

Caiden stared up at the ceiling. This man was going to kill him dead, so dead. He was already on his way to making off with Caiden's heart, thieving it. The only way to avoid heartbreak was to enjoy D while he could, to accept this second chance for what it was—temporary. Nothing permanent would come from this, but that didn't mean it couldn't be good. D wasn't the forever kind of man, and Caiden couldn't change that. He'd known it back in Vienna.

"Go to sleep," D said softly.

"So bossy," Caiden teased quietly, rolling over to face him, one arm flung around D's waist. Looking into D's eyes, Caiden hid his feelings for D behind thoughts of Vienna. "I can't wait to get my hands on that son of a bitch who called the cops on me and ruined my life."

D stiffened beneath him. "What?"

"In Vienna. That night, after we had sex, I had a blind date—a meet with an asset—at the Vienna State Opera, but the police showed up at my hotel room. I didn't want to blow my cover. I opened the door, intent on getting them off my back. They told me someone had reported suspicious activity and asked me to go down to the station. I complied."

"What happened?"

Caiden sighed. He traced the lines of D's abdomen, thinking of the night that had changed his life forever. "They questioned me at the station, and I did what I've been trained to do. I assessed the situation and fabricated a story that would appeal most with whoever I was dealing with. From the moment we walked into the station and saw the way they interacted with their coworkers, men and women, I had my story. I apologized, said I was there for business, and how I *had* been sneaking around because I was meeting a 'friend,' and how it would be bad if I got caught, because I was married. They ate it up, teased me about it, and let me go."

"I thought you said your cover was blown?"

"I was on my way out when the same officers approached me and arrested me for being a terrorist."

D covered Caiden's hand in his and squeezed but didn't respond, so Caiden continued.

"They said they had evidence. I denied everything of course, and let them put me in a cell, biding my time. I needed to get out of there and get word to my CO. A few minutes later, these men showed up, stating they were going to transport me for questioning."

"They were going to interrogate you." D's words were so quiet, Caiden wouldn't have heard him had he not been so close. He nodded.

"My guess was they hadn't contacted our government. They wanted a go at me first. On the way to the transportation van, I made my move, took them down, swiped one of their rifles, and stole the transportation van. While I was on the run, my name was cleared, but my cover was blown. The Austrian government confirmed I wasn't a terrorist, but an American spy, but someone was still after me. I got the hell out of there as fast as I could, changed cars, took the back roads, and then crossed into Slovakia on foot. I found a safe place to stay, contacted my CO, and waited. I was holed up for three weeks while whoever the hell wanted me dead hunted me."

"Jesus." D rolled onto his side to face Caiden and brought an arm around him. "I'm so sorry."

Caiden smiled at him, touched by the sorrow in D's eyes. He cupped D's face and stroked his thumb across D's cheek. "It's not your fault."

D swallowed hard and closed his eyes. He brought their mouths together, his lips soft and his kiss tender. They kissed for what seemed like hours, until sleep came for Caiden, and he surrendered.

THE NEXT morning, Caiden woke to an empty bed. Stretching, he sat up, feeling the sheets beside him. They were cold. D had gotten up some time ago. Movement caught his eye, and he smiled. D stood outside on the balcony, arms leaning on the rail as he stared off at who knew what. Seagulls called to the sea and the ocean responded. Dawn was approaching, golds and yellows bleeding into the purples and blues. For a split second, Caiden could fool himself into believing he was on a tropical vacation with his sexy new man.

After getting up, he walked around the end of the bed and out onto the balcony, stepping up behind D and wrapping his arms around his waist, chuckling when D jumped.

"Easy there, tiger. Just me." He let his chin rest on D's shoulder, his morning stiffness rubbing against the seam of D's boxer-briefs over his crease. Talk about an incredible ass. Would D let him fuck him? That was a question for another time. For now, he'd enjoy D's firm muscles beneath his hands. He slid one hand down to cup D, humming at the half-hard cock he found there.

"We need to get dressed. Alpha will be calling soon," D murmured, moving out of Caiden's embrace.

"What's wrong?" Caiden asked, following him inside. Something was going on. He might not have known D long, but in the short amount of time he'd known him, he'd become adept at reading the grumpy man.

"Nothing. I didn't sleep well. I usually don't when I'm on a mission, especially with the safe house being so close to the target."

"Oh, right." That made sense. Caiden followed D to the bed and took hold of his wrist, turning him to face Caiden. He slipped his arms around D's neck and brushed his lips over D's. "How about we take a shower, and you let me relax you?"

D removed Caiden's arms from around him, and Caiden frowned. It had to be more than a bad night's sleep.

"I already showered. Why don't you take yours and I make us some breakfast?" D kissed him, a quick brush of the lips, before he was out of the room.

Caiden wasn't stupid. Something was off. Why wouldn't D confide in him? Had he not earned D's trust by now?

You know what, I'm going to let him be. Maybe D needed a little time to recenter himself. A lot had happened in a few short days. Caiden was moving fast, far too fast. He needed to slow his roll. How could the guy not be freaking out? D had probably never expected to see him again, and then Caiden showed up out of the blue, they're thrust into a mission together, and not long after start having sex. Caiden shook his head at himself. Jesus, give the guy room to breathe.

Caiden left to shower and get dressed.

The kitchen smelled amazing, and Caiden resisted the urge to attach himself to D's back like an octopus, especially with D standing at the stove in nothing but a fitted black T-shirt, and boxer-briefs—which Caiden realized were pink and teal and covered in pineapples.

"Nice undies."

D smirked at him over his shoulder. "Thanks."

"What are you making? It smells amazing."

"Bacon, cheese, and mushroom omelet. Do you like mushrooms? I haven't made yours yet."

"I love mushrooms. Thank you."

"No problem." D turned back to the stove and started on the second omelet. He motioned to the counter and the two coffee machines. "There's regular coffee and Cuban espresso. I wasn't sure which one you liked, so I made both. Personally, I don't know how anyone can drink that watered-down stuff." He shrugged. "But, hey, to each his own."

Caiden chuckled as he rounded the counter and removed a coffee mug from the cabinet. "Why don't you tell me how you really feel?"

"What?" D asked, eyes wide.

"About the coffee," Caiden said, pointing to the pot.

"Oh, and yeah, I don't drink that shit."

"What about decaf?"

D squinted at him. "Why are you trying to ruin my morning?"

Caiden threw his head back and laughed. He popped a kiss on D's lips. "You're adorable." Turning, he removed the milk from the fridge. "I suppose you have an opinion on creamer?"

"Oh, I have opinions all right," D groused. "That shit tastes like chemicals, and the flavored ones?" he scoffed. "French vanilla, my ass. Why would anyone ruin perfectly good coffee with a flavor, anyway?"

"Oh, you're one of those." Caiden poured himself a large mug of coffee and added some milk to it and a tablespoon of brown sugar since it seemed to be the only sugar in the house.

"One of what?" D frowned, his eyes following the movement of Caiden's mug as he lifted it to his lips.

"A coffee snob." Caiden took a sip. "Mm, latte."

"I'm not a coffee snob. I just don't like shit coffee. And that's not a latte." D took the cup from him and emptied it into the sink.

"Hey, my latte!"

"Like I said, that's not a latte." He turned off the stove, moved the frying pan with the second omelet off the burner, then washed out Caiden's mug. "I'll show you what a real latte tastes like. Sit."

"So bossy," Caiden teased, taking a seat at the counter.

D grunted and filled Caiden's mug with milk nearly to the top, leaving about an inch and a half of space below the rim. "This is the quick way because there isn't always time to steam milk. Add your desired sugar amount to your mug. Brown sugar works best. Then fill your cup of milk almost to the top but leave enough room for the espresso and froth."

"Okay. Got it."

D eyed him but continued. "Pop into the microwave and heat just under two minutes, depending on how hot you like it. I heat mine for a minute and forty-nine seconds."

"Why not an even one fifty?"

"Did I say one fifty?"

"No, but I mean, it's a second. Does it really matter?"

D put the mug in the microwave and set the cooking time to a minute and forty-nine seconds. He turned and arched a thick brow at him. "It matters."

"Whatever you say." Caiden held back a smile when D flipped him off. Unable to help it, Caiden laughed. When the microwave dinged, D removed the mug.

"Now you froth the milk. If you have a fancy espresso machine, it'll have a milk steamer and frother so you can do both at the same time. You can't travel with an espresso machine most of the time, but you can travel with a frother."

It took everything Caiden had not to bark out another laugh. "You travel with a milk frother?"

"Do you want this latte or not?"

Caiden nodded. "Yes, please. I would very much like your delicious, creamy sustenance."

"Don't ever say that again," D deadpanned. He pulled a battery-powered frothing wand from one of the drawers, held the mug over the sink, and frothed away. When he was done, he washed up the frother—because D always seemed to wash up as he went along—and then poured in the espresso. He picked up a teaspoon, stirred, then moved some of the foam aside.

"What are you doing?"

"Checking the color. It'll indicate how strong it is. The darker it is, the stronger the latte." He slid the cup in front of Caiden. "Taste. Tell me it's not a hundred times better than what you'd been about to drink."

Caiden picked up the piping hot mug, and took a sip, ready to tease D and tell him it was just okay, but he all but melted into his chair. "Oh my God, this is *so* good." The latte was fucking phenomenal, a thousand times better than what he'd been about to drink, but the beaming smile on D's face was the best part of all. "Okay, you were right."

"Of course I was." He turned back to the stove and moved their omelets onto plates, complete with garnish. Toast soon followed, with D making himself an espresso latte before taking a seat beside Caiden. D lifted his coffee mug. "¡Buen provecho!"

"Mahlzeit!"

D's smile faltered at the Austrian expression, but he quickly recovered.

What was that about?

"Dig in," D said, not giving Caiden a chance to think any more on it. The food was as good as he'd come to expect from D, and they ate together in companionable silence. At the end of the meal, Caiden washed up, though thanks to D's tidiness, there was only their plates, forks, and mugs to wash. After that, they each went to their rooms to get dressed before their meeting with Alpha in half an hour. They were both due back at the house that morning as part of their cover.

Caiden dressed in another one of the tailored three-piece suits he'd been supplied with. This one was a charcoal gray windowpane check with a polka dot tie. He loved the bold styles they'd picked out for him, styles he would have never chosen for himself. All spruced up, he headed out into the dining room where D stood by the dining room table in his porn outfit. Caiden's pants got a little tighter as he took in the sight of that tight ass in those snug jeans, and the all-but-painted-on white T-shirt. His brain helpfully reminded him of the reason for the outfit, and he frowned.

If Isabella flirted with D, would he flirt back? Not that he had any grounds to complain. Harrison would no doubt flirt with Caiden, not to mention invade his personal space. The guy couldn't seem to keep his hands to himself around Caiden. They both had a job to do, and a little flirting was part of the game. D looked over his shoulder at him, then turned, his gaze raking over Caiden.

"What do you think?" he asked, totally fishing for a compliment. He loved the way D subtly shivered, his eyes dark and filled with heat.

"You know you look good."

Caiden stepped up close to him to murmur in his ear, "Yeah, but I love hearing you say it." He licked a trail up D's ear, his heart doing a little jig when D sucked in a sharp breath, his entire body shuddering. With a wicked grin, he leaned in to whisper, "Maybe tonight you can do a little work on me." He smiled at D's low groan. "I have all kinds of naughty things in store for you, Mr. Rivas. Maybe I'll even let you keep your tool belt on."

D's soft Spanish curses had Caiden wishing it was already evening.

Chapter Ten

D WAS so fucked.

Thankfully he didn't have time to think about just exactly how fucked he was, because at that moment, the screen on the laptop came to life, and Alpha's voice filled the room.

"As I mentioned yesterday, if Graves has some kind of tracking software on the flash drive, it's not activated. It's possible it may only be activated in emergency situations."

"So how do we find it?" D asked, frustrated. "Searching the house for something that could potentially be the size of a thumbnail will take far longer than we have."

"Maintain your cover," Alpha instructed. "Continue the search of the house during your scheduled work hours. Renovations start next week, which means you'll have to be extra careful to maintain your cover. In the meantime, set up surveillance on Kenneth.

Maybe he'll lead us to it. I'm going to keep monitoring his computers, and I have eyes inside his office. I'll let you know if I come up with anything."

"Got it," Caiden replied.

"Caiden, Harrison seems to have taken a liking to you. I would suggest you use that to your advantage tomorrow night. See if you can get some information out of him that could help us locate the flash drive."

D straightened, his fingers curling into fists. That's right. Tomorrow was Friday.

"Um, right." Caiden cleared his throat.

"Is there a problem?" Alpha asked.

"No," D said, aware of Caiden staring at him. "There's no problem. He'll be there."

"Very well. Alpha out."

Caiden frowned at D. "What the hell was that about?"

"That was about us doing our jobs. We have a mission, remember?" He turned to go, but Caiden caught his arm.

"D, what's going on? Talk to me."

"Nothing. I'm trying to focus on the job, which is what you should be doing."

"Including going on a date with Harrison?"

Now it was a date. What happened to just drinks? "Yes. Like Alpha said, he likes you. You might be able to get good intel from him."

"By what means?" Caiden searched D's gaze, and D rounded his shoulders. He removed Caiden's hand from his arm.

"By any means necessary. That shouldn't be a problem. It's not like you're emotionally compromised or anything."

"Not emotionally—what's happening right now?"

This was going to hurt like hell. "You mean us? It was sex, Caiden. That's it. A little fun while we're stuck in this house together."

The hurt in Caiden's eyes almost had D backpedaling, but he kept his mouth shut. This was how it had to be. He'd done enough to ruin Caiden's life.

"Right. Yeah. Sorry. Fun." Caiden smiled wide, but it didn't reach his eyes. "You should go on ahead. I'll follow in a few minutes."

D took the out, heading off like someone lit his ass on fire. He hurried down the stairs and into the garage, where his truck was parked. Climbing behind the wheel, he shut the door and stilled.

"I can't wait to get my hands on that son of a bitch who called the cops on me and ruined my life."

Caiden had already gotten his hands on that man. His hands, his mouth, his come. D let his head fall against the steering wheel.

"Fuck! Fuck, fuck, fuck!" He sat up and rubbed his hands over his face. He'd set out to do the right thing, and instead he'd ruined Caiden's life, destroyed his career. Last night, D had been happy and foolishly hopeful. He'd started getting all kinds of crazy ideas in his head about the two of them, about maybe asking Caiden to stay. And now? D scoffed. "Now nothing." It was over. Even if D came clean, Caiden would never understand, never forgive him for the betrayal. His cell phone went off, and he picked up. "Yeah?"

"What's going on, D?" Alpha asked, their tone sounding almost… concerned.

"I fucked up."

"How?"

It was strange trusting someone he'd never met. Confiding in them. "I ruined his life."

"Can you elaborate?"

"Caiden. I ruined his life. *I* was the one who called the cops on him in Vienna. I don't know who accused him of being a terrorist, because I didn't say shit about that, but I set the whole thing up. If I hadn't called the cops, maybe he'd have stayed off their radar, maybe—"

"Maybe he'd be dead," Alpha offered, and D flinched.

D let out a sigh he felt down to his bones. "It doesn't matter. Either way, he'll hate me again. Worse this time."

"And you don't want that."

"No. I thought maybe after the mission…."

"You care about him."

D turned on the truck and hit the button on the garage door opener. "Doesn't matter. When this mission is over, I'll tell him the truth. He deserves to know."

"It would be a shame to lose him."

"Yeah," D agreed as he pulled out of the driveway and onto the street. "It would. I'm going to put my earpiece in now. I'll keep you posted."

"Stay safe."

"I will." He hung up, then pocketed his phone and put his earpiece in. The drive to the Graves mansion took minutes, but to D it felt like hours. He had to get his head in the game or he'd be risking a lot more than the mission. Whatever illusion of a happy ever after he'd allowed himself to fall into had gone up in smoke almost as quickly as it had appeared.

After parking by the guest house, he climbed out. Several cars were in the drive, including Isabella's car and Kenneth's. Furniture purchase issues had been ordered, and construction was starting. Furniture would begin arriving next week. Hicks's construction crew was on-site, and D greeted some of the guys as he made his way through the house. D was scheduled to be on-site until 11:00 a.m. He'd check in with Caiden later so they could rendezvous at the safe house, change, and head off to Graves Financial for some surveillance.

Inside the house, D checked in with Hicks for appearances' sake. The guy was clearly not fond of D, and the amount of judgment in his gaze when he looked D over spoke volumes. D couldn't give a shit. He wasn't here for Hicks. If Hicks owed Alpha, he wasn't that innocent. The guy was in his mid to late fifties, tall, with leathery skin from years of exposure to the Florida sun.

"Did no one tell you not to wear clothes that cut off your circulation?" Hicks grumbled, motioning to D's shirt.

"Did no one tell you not to piss off the guy who could take you out before you take your next breath?"

Hicks glared at him, mumbled something under his breath, and sent D on his way. D headed down the hall as Isabella came out of her bedroom.

"Oh!" She put a hand to her chest. "You scared me."

"I'm so sorry, ma'am." D made to go around her, but she closed the distance between them and put a hand to his arm, her eyes taking in every inch of him.

"That's no problem, Mr.…?"

"Rivas, ma'am. Lorenzo Rivas."

"Lorenzo," Isabella purred. "How very nice to meet you." She held a hand out to him, and he took it and brought it to his lips for a kiss.

"It's so very nice to meet you too," he replied, letting his voice go throaty and low. She hummed, the hand on her chest slipping lower, drawing his eyes to her cleavage and the way the maxi dress hugged her ample breasts. He released her hand, and she placed it on his bicep.

"Look at these arms. Goodness. It must be all that—" She lifted her gaze to his, her red lips curling at the corners. "—hammering."

D leaned in, his voice husky. "I'm good with my tools, and I *always* hit the right spot."

A shiver went through her, and she trailed a nail down his arm. She opened her mouth to say something, but then someone called his name.

"Mr. Rivas, can I see you a moment?"

Schooling his expression, D smiled warmly at Isabella. "Duty calls. Excuse me." He could feel her eyes on his ass as he walked away, his smile dropping into a scowl at Caiden, who stood with a tablet in his hand, his disdain clear as day. D plastered on a smile. "What the hell are you doing?"

"My job," Caiden said, his eyes hard. "Just like you should be doing yours."

"I *am* doing mine," D hissed.

"Is that what that was?" Caiden blinked at him.

"Yes. Now if you'll excuse me—"

Caiden glanced around, then grabbed D by the arm and hauled him into the closest room. He slammed D up against the wall.

"What the fuck, Caiden?"

"What happened to *Cade*?" Caiden snapped. "What the hell is going on with you? Why are you acting like an asshole?"

D shoved Caiden away from him. "This ain't acting, sweetheart."

"Stop," Caiden pleaded, his tone soft, and it was like a punch to the gut. He cupped D's cheek and brushed his lips over D's. "This isn't you." He pressed his lips to D's, and heat roared through him, threatening to consume him. Unable to stop himself, he jerked Caiden against him, and mauled Caiden's mouth, their hard bodies pressed together.

"Caiden?"

Fuck! Goddamn cockblocker Harrison. No, wait. This was good. D managed to push Caiden away from him before Harrison entered the room.

"Oh, there you are." Harrison looked from Caiden to D and back. "Everything okay?"

Harrison wasn't an idiot. Caiden's lips were swollen, his face flushed, suit rumpled. D turned away so Harrison couldn't see how out of breath he was.

"Yes," Caiden said, smiling brightly. "I needed to clear up a few equations with Mr. Rivas." He turned to D. "Thank you. I'll let you know if I need anything else."

"Sure," D grumbled. He cast Harrison a sideways glance; the man's sharp eyes were narrowed on him. If they'd fucked up, Harrison wasn't about to say. Probably because a heartbeat later, he was too busy fawning over Caiden, who'd wrapped an arm around Harrison's.

"Could I trouble you for some water? I have a bit of a cough. Must have had something in my throat."

Yeah, D's tongue.

Caiden fanned himself, and Harrison patted his hand where it lay on his arm. "Of course, gorgeous. Anything for you. And you know I mean *anything*."

"You're such a flirt," Caiden teased, playing up the giggly-schoolboy-with-a-crush routine. D hated it. He also wanted to punch Harrison in the face. Or the balls. Either would be highly satisfying.

With Caiden led away by Harrison, D made himself useful by searching the room he was in. After pulling on his gloves, he kept an ear out and checked the furniture for any hidden compartments or secret hidey-holes that might contain a flash drive. He moved quickly, inspecting every inch of the room before moving on to the next room. Arguing coming from next door stilled him. Isabella and Kenneth were at it again. D slipped out of the room and inched closer to the doorway. Why wasn't Kenneth at the office?

"I said I was sorry," Isabella huffed.

Had Kenneth seen Isabella with D?

"Baby, you know what that bracelet means to me," Kenneth said, his tone softer. "It was my grandmother's. The house is full of strangers. If I hadn't seen it, who knows what would have happened to it?"

"I know. I'm sorry. It won't happen again. You know I never leave it anywhere. I was momentarily distracted."

"By that construction worker with the shirt two sizes too small. Yeah, I noticed."

"No. That was after I returned from the pool. Besides, you really think I'm going to leave this," she purred, followed by a moan coming from Kenneth, "for a construction worker?"

"Damn it, Isabella. I'm running late as it is. Be more careful, okay?"

"Yes, baby."

D hurried into the room and waited for Kenneth to leave before he slipped out, making sure to run into Isabella again. She'd been distracted by him. He could use that.

"Hey," he said, smiling wide. At her startled expression, he frowned, looking concerned. "Are you okay? I thought I heard shouting."

"Oh, Lorenzo. Yes." She waved a hand in dismissal. "My husband was upset with me. It was my fault, really." She touched one of the bracelets on her wrist fondly, her smile warm. "He gave me this bracelet on our wedding day. It was his grandmother's."

"It's beautiful," D said, admiring the wide gold band.

"I cherish it. It reminds me of that perfect day. It's obscenely expensive, and I never take it off except when I shower or go in the pool. With everything going on, I wasn't thinking, so when I went to the pool, I forgot to put it back on and left it outside. He was very upset, understandably so. I was careless." Her eyes widened. "Not that anyone would steal it, but you know."

"I understand. It means a lot to you both, and he's right. Your house is full of people you don't know." D felt bad for her. She clearly had no idea who her husband was. Though Becky was right. The woman was a notorious flirt.

"Anyway, crisis averted." She hooked her arm around his. "I don't know what it is about you, Lorenzo, but I find it so easy to talk to you. Why don't you join me in the kitchen for some sweet tea?"

"Oh, um, what about your husband? I'd hate for him to get the wrong idea."

"Don't you worry about him. He left for work and won't return until tonight. It's his late night at the office since he gets off early on Fridays for our date night."

Date night. Fun-fucking-tastic. Though it did present a perfect opportunity. While Caiden was out doing whatever with Harrison, and Isabella was out with her husband, D would do another search of the house. What he would *not* do was think about Caiden.

That worked for as long as it took them to reach the kitchen, where Harrison had Caiden crowded against the counter, a hand gripping Caiden's hip, the other tipping Caiden's face up.

"Well, hello, boys."

Harrison and Caiden jumped with a start, and D suppressed a growl. Guilt flooded Harrison's face, and he took a step away from Caiden, his face flushed with embarrassment.

"I'm so sorry, Isabella."

Isabella laughed and waved a hand in dismissal. "Come on, Harrison. You know I don't care." She winked at Caiden. "Don't worry, Mr. Ashwood. This will stay between us. You have your fun."

"Um, thank you, Mrs. Graves. I should, um, get back to work." Caiden excused himself and hurried out of the kitchen. He didn't so much as glance at D.

"Oh my God, Harrison." Isabella slapped the huge man's arm playfully. "He's gorgeous! Tell me you've had that man in your bed."

What the fuck? Had she forgotten he was right here? Not that she had any reason to care.

Harrison chuckled and shook his head. "Not yet. But we have a date tomorrow night, so I'm confident he'll be coming home with me then."

It wasn't a date. It was just drinks.

Isabella fanned herself and groaned. "That one's going to be a handful. He has that look about him. All prim and proper on the outside, wild on the inside. Mm, talk about hot."

Fuck my life.

Harrison seemed to think it over, and D gritted his teeth to keep from shouting at Harrison to keep Caiden out of his filthy thoughts.

"You're right," Harrison said, releasing a groan and adjusting himself. "Fuck, I can't wait. He's going to look so good naked in my bed."

"Are you kidding? With those legs and that ass?"

Was this happening? Was this *really* happening right now?

"And that mouth?" Harrison pitched in.

An image of Caiden on his knees with his mouth wrapped around Harrison's cock popped into D's mind oh so helpfully, and he cleared his throat. Harrison moved his gaze to D.

"Oh, sorry, man. Didn't know you were there. Didn't mean to make you uncomfortable." Harrison's gaze hardened, and D frowned.

"Why would I be uncomfortable?" He wasn't uncomfortable. He was ready to dropkick Harrison.

"All this gay talk in front of the straight guy."

There go those fucking stereotypes again.

"What makes you think I'm straight?" D asked.

Harrison looked him over, and Isabella's brows drew together. Wonderful, how was this about *him* now?

"I'm pansexual," D said.

Isabella turned to Harrison. "What does that mean?"

"The short definition? He's attracted to people regardless of their gender or sex."

"Oh, okay." She sauntered over to D and wrapped her arms around his neck. "Oh, well, aren't you just full of surprises, Mr. Rivas? So, let's say, hypothetically, if you were invited into a threesome with Harrison and Mr. Ashwood, you'd be open to that scenario?"

No. Fuck no. All the fucking nos. Kill me now. Dead. Done.

Harrison's interest was suddenly piqued, and he raked his gaze over D again, this time appearing to see him in a new light. He licked his lips and cocked his head to one side. "Hmm, me, you, and a sexy blond in the middle. What do you say?"

"And I get to watch," Isabella purred.

Oh, no fucking way. No one was laying his hands or eyes on a naked Caiden but him. Thankfully before his brain got carried away, or an answer was expected, a swarm of workers came into the kitchen, distracting Harrison and Isabella, who quickly switched to host and hostess mode. D slipped out of the room and hurried back upstairs. If this mess with Caiden didn't kill him, this mission would. Wonderful, now Harrison wanted a threesome. That was easy enough to avoid. He'd just say he wasn't into that kind of thing, which was a lie, but he sure as hell wasn't into it when it involved Caiden.

Speaking of the blond devil, Caiden looked up when D approached the living room Caiden was standing outside of, as if the man could sense he was near. His brows drew together in concern, and D subtly shook his head. It was fine. He was fine. His world was Kumbaya-singing levels of fucking fine. Nothing to see here, folks.

D only had to avoid Harrison, Isabella, and Caiden for a few hours until it was time to get the hell out of here and shut himself in a small space with Caiden for hours of surveillance. Perfect.

In that time, he'd managed to search a total of three rooms, leaving no hideously patterned piece of furniture unturned. He'd also managed to avoid thinking of Caiden a grand total of zero times. Checking his watch, he tapped his earpiece. "Caiden, time to go. Meet you at the safe house."

"Copy that."

D scanned his surroundings, then slipped out of the house unseen. He climbed into his truck and drove the long way to the safe house. At the end of their cul-de-sac sat a gleaming white AC Repair van. Parking the truck inside the garage, D climbed out, locked up, and hurried inside where he changed into his regular jeans, a faded Johnny Cash T-shirt, his scuffed black biker boots, and his leather jacket.

Checking no one was around, he made his way to the van and climbed behind the wheel to wait. Less than fifteen minutes later, the passenger door opened and Caiden climbed in, dressed in black jeans, a black T-shirt, and black motorcycle jacket. Like the guy wasn't a distraction enough in his tailored suits. How could he possibly get hotter? D was so boned.

"You ride?" D asked, pointing to Caiden's jacket.

Caiden smiled, clearly bemused by the odd question. "Yeah. Kind of have to in a lot of European cities. Having a car is too much of a hindrance."

D nodded. He started the van as Caiden buckled up. They headed south on A1A and drove a whole seven minutes to Kenneth Graves Financial, then made a left on Lake Avenue and pulled into the large beach parking lot behind Kenneth's building. With Lake Worth Beach Park mere feet away, there was plenty of public parking and enough trees to provide cover. D parked the van beneath a couple of palm trees facing Kenneth's building.

"Let's do this." He climbed into the back of the van, ducking his head before getting to the surveillance console, where he took a seat, Caiden joining him. Powering up the equipment, he glanced over at Caiden, who was uncharacteristically quiet. The guy always seemed to have something to say, and D chastised himself for missing the sound of Caiden's voice, as if he hadn't heard from the guy in years. Man, he was such a sap.

Once the computers were online, D logged in, the screens bringing up the surveillance feeds Alpha had told him about. They had eyes inside Graves Financial, the entrance located on the A1A side, and Kenneth's office, where the man currently sat with what looked like a client. The building was typical Florida architecture—a Spanish-style villa with cream walls, arched entryways, and a clay-tiled roof. Kenneth's office was at the end of the two-floor building, taking up a good chunk of the top floor. His neighbors were a pharmacy, a medical group—because this was Retirement Central, aka Florida—a Realtor, salon, and small bank.

The silence was excruciating. D cleared his throat. "So, uh, there's a possibility Harrison is going to bring up a threesome with you, him, and me."

Caiden choked on air. "*What*? What the hell happened in the kitchen after I left?"

"Things. Awful things. Anyway, just tell him you don't like me."

"Shouldn't be too hard," Caiden grumbled.

D opened his mouth to respond, then thought better of it. They were going to be stuck in this damned van for God knew how long. It was best he not make it harder than it needed to be. Sitting so close to Caiden and not being able to touch him or kiss him was driving D crazy. He forced himself to turn his attention back to the monitors. Even if Caiden hadn't told him what happened in Vienna—though D was certain it would have come out eventually—it wasn't as if he'd had any definite plans about their future. He'd had fantasies. Ideas that were easy to get lost in while they were at the townhouse on the beach, away from everything and everyone.

After the mission, real life would encroach on their fantasy. Caiden would go back to Virginia, to his life, his career. He'd make new friends, go out to bars and clubs, pick up guys, meet someone he could introduce to his friends and coworkers at the Company picnic without worrying someone might recognize him. His new guy wouldn't have to constantly look over his shoulder, worrying his past might come calling. Whoever Caiden met wouldn't have a list of enemies a mile long.

"You're thinking awfully hard over there," Caiden murmured.

"Check Kenneth's schedule," D said, clearing his throat. "I think he has a lunch meeting with this guy."

Heavy sigh. Caiden typed away at the keyboard in front of him, bringing up Kenneth's itinerary for the day. "They're scheduled to have lunch at the pier." Caiden checked his watch. "In ten minutes."

"Great. You hungry?"

Caiden shrugged. "I can always eat."

"Don't I know it. I don't know where you put all that food." The guy loved to eat, and D loved a guy with a healthy appetite. Not that he loved Caiden, he just—

He really needed his brain to stop. Like, right now.

"I probably work it off," Caiden said, without realizing what that sounded like, or what it'd sound like to both their dirty brains. D quickly grabbed a black baseball cap and handed it to Caiden.

"Let's go. It's a five-minute walk. The place is big enough for us to blend in." He grabbed a cap for him and pulled it low before getting out of the van.

Caiden hopped down, and D locked up after him. What he didn't think about as he walked side by side with Caiden, down the palm-tree-lined trail that led to the restaurant, was how good it would feel. The day was beautiful, the sun shining in the sapphire-blue sky, the ocean sparkling beyond the sandy white beach. It was calm and peaceful.

They hung back beneath one of the roofed events areas and waited. D leaned against the concrete pillar, with Caiden next to him like they were a couple of bros hanging out and chatting. Kenneth's Lexus pulled into the parking lot behind them, and they waited for the two men to pass by. It was lunchtime, and the place served some stellar food, so they had the advantage of a nice crowd.

"Let's move," D murmured, stepping onto the pier where the restaurant was located. Kenneth and his client chose to eat outside, so D asked for a table inside, making sure it was one where they could see outside to Kenneth's table. They thanked the hostess, put in their drink orders, and picked up the menus.

"Suddenly I'm starving," Caiden said as he looked over the menu.

D chuckled. A young waitress with a messy bun on her head and friendly smile came over with their drinks. "Hi, I'm Crissy. I'll be your server today. Do you know what you'd like to order, or do you need more time?"

Caiden smiled brightly at her, and D could have sworn she swooned a little, but then who wouldn't with those big green eyes and gorgeous smile aimed at them?

"Hi, Crissy. I'll have the seared tuna tostada, please."

"That's my favorite too," Crissy whispered conspiratorially.

"Well, now I know I'm gonna love it." Caiden frowned, pointing at a nasty bruise on Crissy's wrist. "That looks painful. You okay?"

Crissy's smile faltered before her chipper smile was back in place. "Oh, yeah, it's nothing. I sometimes ride my bike to work and I lost control riding over some sand in the pathway, but thank you for asking. That's so sweet." She turned to D. "And what can I get for you?"

"I'll have the same," D said with a smile. "Thank you, Crissy."

"You got it." With another bright smile thrown in Caiden's direction, she walked off.

D took a sip of his water as Caiden spoke quietly. "You think we're going to find this thing? The guy's probably all kinds of crazy careful."

"We'll find it," D assured him. Before they did, D would have to come clean. Caiden was expecting to find evidence of the guy who called the cops on him on that drive, but Alpha was certain the man who betrayed Caiden was the same man who had D killed, and since he hadn't put a hit out on himself, it meant Caiden still wouldn't know who called the cops. Either way, it spelled the end for whatever was between them.

Caiden stared off into the distance. "It's so beautiful out there."

The small smile of contentment on Caiden's face had D averting his gaze. He hated knowing the pain he was going to bring Caiden. The moment of reckoning was swiftly approaching—D could feel it in his gut. The heaviness of it loomed, rolling over him like a thunderstorm, the dark clouds hovering over him, darkening with every passing minute before it let loose. He was going to lose Caiden, and for the first time in his life, he wasn't sure his heart would recover.

Chapter Eleven

WHAT THE hell was he doing?

Caiden's mind kept going to the memory of his kiss with D when Harrison had almost caught them. He had been so lost in D, he almost blew his cover. *Again.* Not that he'd been the one to blow his cover the first time, but at the mansion, that had been on him. The way Isabella hung all over D, touching him, tempting him? Caiden had seen red. He allowed his emotions get the better of him and reacted like some jealous asshole.

If D hadn't moved fast and pushed Caiden away, Harrison would have walked in on them mauling each other, and although they might have been able to cover it up, it would have caused problems. The last thing they needed on this damned mission was more problems. Maybe that's why D was pulling away. At least that's what Caiden kept telling himself. He couldn't deal with D being everything Caiden wanted, making Caiden believe they were moving toward something, and then having the rug pulled out from under him again and again.

For now, he'd concentrate on their objective, keep an emotional distance from D until they completed their mission. Then they'd talk, and Caiden could open up about how he wanted them to have a future together. He no longer questioned whether D felt something for him. It was clear as day in D's eyes, in his touch, his kiss. They were good together, and once this was over, he'd show D just how right they were for each other.

The food came, and Caiden chuckled at the way D's face lit up at the mound of goodness placed in front of him. He did a little wiggle in his chair, and Caiden snickered, Crissy's giggle joining in.

"What?" D said, looking from Crissy to Caiden.

"Nothing." The man had no idea how stinking cute he was. "Eat up." Caiden winked at Crissy. "Thanks."

"My pleasure. You boys enjoy. Let me know if you need anything."

"Maybe a bib for this guy," Caiden said, motioning to D, who crunched down on a giant section of tostada. D flipped him off, and with another giggle, Crissy left to attend to her other customers.

"Oh my God." D moaned around his mouthful of food, the sound going straight to Caiden's dick. "This is so good."

"Yeah? I couldn't tell."

D flipped him off again, and Caiden laughed before digging in to his food. He groaned and nodded. "Okay, yeah. You're right."

"When will you learn? I'm always right."

Caiden shook his head, amused. They kept an eye on Kenneth as they enjoyed their food. The view was stunning, the food fantastic, and the company....

Caiden glanced over at D and picked up his napkin to wipe the corner of his mouth. "So messy."

D rolled his eyes but continued eating, like them being here together was the most natural thing in the world. He stole a piece of Caiden's avocado, and Caiden poked his side, making him laugh.

"Hey! Stop thieving my food, you food thief. You have your own."

"Oh man. This aguacate with sriracha is fucking amazing." D made his sex face, and Caiden coughed into his hand.

"You do like your avocado."

"I *love* avocado."

Caiden speared one of his avocado slices and placed it on D's plate. "There you go."

D dropped his gaze to the slice before lifting his eyes to Caiden and letting out a dreamy sigh. "Aw. Are we having a *Lady and the Tramp* moment?"

Caiden burst into laughter, and D joined him, both of them laughing until they had tears in their eyes. "Wait, which one of us is the tramp?" Caiden asked with a wink.

"Clearly I'm the tramp," D said. "You're obviously the sweet lady."

"Fuck off." Caiden shook his head and laughed again. God, he was so damned fond of the man. D waggled his eyebrows, and Caiden snickered. "You're impossible."

"Yeah, but I'm also adorable. You said so yourself."

Caiden took a bite of his tuna. "You're something all right."

They bugged each other as they ate, talked about food, and afterward split a dessert. No way was Caiden leaving without dessert. Naturally, he chose the tropical lemon bar.

"Like lemon, do we?" D teased.

"I'm the same with lemon desserts that you are with avocado. Can't get enough of it."

D took one more bite before pushing the rest in front of Caiden.

"You haven't had half yet," Caiden said even as he pulled the dessert closer to him.

"Like you wouldn't stab me with your fork right now if I tried to take it back."

Caiden hunched over the remaining dessert, his arm on the table keeping D away. "Not gonna lie. I might draw blood."

The man was so beautiful, and when he laughed there was no way not to get drawn in. D teased him some more, and when Crissy brought them their check, they fought over it and of course D won, though he'd played dirty by grabbing Caiden's thigh under the table and making him jump, giving D the opportunity to snatch up the receipt wallet.

Once they'd paid, leaving Crissy a generous tip, they slipped out of the restaurant and waited outside for Kenneth to leave.

"He's on the move. Let's go." They walked slowly and stopped to admire the view from the pier when Kenneth paused to chat. Once he started walking again, so did they, keeping enough distance and people between them. As soon as Kenneth had driven off in his Lexus, Caiden and D headed down the path, but then a woman's soft cry caught Caiden's attention, and he paused, D stopping beside him. In the shadows of the roofed space they'd stood under earlier as they waited for Kenneth to arrive, their waitress, Crissy, looked like she was trying to shrink into the concrete pillar, her hands up in front of her as she trembled with fear.

"Please, Ignacio. I'm sorry."

"Are you fucking stupid?" Ignacio growled, smacking her on the side of the head. "I told you I needed the car to hang with the boys tonight."

"But I couldn't change my shift, and Ginny said if I called in sick one more time that she'd have to let me go."

Ignacio grabbed her by the hair, giving her a shake. "Because you're a fucking moron, that's why."

Oh fuck no. Caiden stormed over, kicked at the back of the man's knee, forcing him to release Crissy, who gasped, eyes huge as Caiden grabbed Ignacio's arm, twisted it behind him, and grabbed a fistful of his hair, jerking his head.

"You fucking lay a hand on her again, and I'm going to hunt you down and put a bullet in you, do you hear me?"

"Fuck you," Ignacio spat out. "She's my girlfriend, and I'll do whatever the fuck I want with her."

"Wrong answer." Caiden slammed the guy into the pillar, a satisfying crack filling the air before Ignacio dropped to the ground.

"My nose!" Ignacio cried, blood dripping down over his mouth. "I'm gonna kill you, motherfucker." A shadow passed over them, and D crouched down beside the man.

"You're still not listening, are you?"

"Who the fuck are you?"

"No one important," D said. "What does matter is that you not hurt your girlfriend again, because we'll know." He took two of Ignacio's fingers and snapped them back. Preempting the scream, Caiden slapped

Ignacio's hand over his mouth, not wanting to get the man's blood on him. "Now," D said, a smile splitting his handsome face. "Let's try this again. Are you going to put your hands on her in any way that might hurt her?"

Ignacio smartly shook his head fervently.

"Good. See. You're learning. Now, stop being a piece of shit and show a little respect." D snagged a hold of the guy's jacket, and together they hauled him to his feet. Caiden turned to Crissy, who shook like a scared kitten.

"Crissy, anyone who makes you feel scared or puts their hands on you in a way that makes you feel uncomfortable or hurt, is someone you shouldn't be with. You deserve better. Now why don't you go home, or better yet, go to a friend's house. If you feel threatened at any point, call the police. Okay?"

She nodded, turning to go, but then stopped and threw her arms around him and hugged him. "Thank you," she said with a sniff. After pulling away, she ran off, got into a beat-up Toyota, and burned rubber.

D released Ignacio and motioned behind him. "There's the bus stop. I suggest you go to the hospital and get that nose looked at. Don't forget what I said."

Ignacio scrambled away, his hand cradled against his chest as he made like the wind.

"I really hope she doesn't go back to that asshole," Caiden said with a sigh.

"The only one who can do right by Crissy now, is Crissy," D said, and Caiden nodded in agreement.

"Thanks for backing me up." Caiden suppressed a smile at the warmth that spread through him. D hadn't questioned him. He'd been right behind Caiden, jumping in to help.

"Of course," D said, frowning, as though he couldn't imagine how Caiden would think anything otherwise.

The walk to the van was nice, same as the walk to the restaurant had been. D opened the door for Caiden, and he climbed in and took a seat at the console. D sat beside him, and they returned to watching Kenneth. Despite sitting in a van for hours on end, Caiden had a good time. He and D fell into an easy banter, keeping things light between them. D picked them up dinner, and they ate in the van. Kenneth didn't leave the office except to go to the men's room. The guy was a definite workaholic.

It was just before five thirty when movement outside the building caught Caiden's eye. A woman with a toddler was headed for the bank. The little girl skipping along, holding her mother's hand, was dressed like Wonder Woman. She couldn't have been more than four or five years old.

"Aw, that's adorable," D said, pointing to the screen. "She's even got a little lasso of truth."

Caiden held back a smile. "Wonder Woman fan, are we?"

"And if I am?" D shrugged. "She's a total badass."

"Hey, I agree." A van pulled into one of the parking spaces across from the small bank the mother and little girl had just gone into. The side door slid open, and four men in masks with firearms hopped out. "Oh shit. Someone's about to rob the bank." He made to get up when D grabbed his wrist.

"What do you think you're doing?"

"We need to do something. That mother and her little girl are in there. Innocent people could get hurt."

"That's for the police to handle."

"D, we can help those people."

D closed his eyes before letting out a curse. "Fine. But we get in, take care of it, and get out. The last thing we need is the cops looking for us." D tapped his earpiece. "Alpha?"

"I heard. I'll take care of the bank's security feed, make sure the cameras don't get your faces. The bank only had one security guard on-site, and he's been knocked out."

"Copy that." D unlocked one of the drawers beneath the console, removed two Glocks, and handed one to Caiden. "Let's go."

Baseball caps and gloves on, they hopped out of the van, tucked the Glocks into the waistband of their jeans, covered them with their shirts, and ran across the parking lot. They hurried around the building, the whole place eerily quiet. As they neared the bank, they could hear the shouts, the orders to get the money in the bag.

"Follow my lead," D said as he motioned for Caiden to walk with him. "Bro, what did I say? Didn't I tell you not to go all in? Did you listen? No, you never listen."

"Never played poker, my ass," Caiden groused as they walked into the bank, and the four armed men spun to face them, guns aimed at them. "Holy shit!" Caiden put his hands up in front of him as the men shouted at them.

"Hands in the air," the shortest of the four barked.

"Okay, yeah, take it easy," D said, hands raised. "We don't want any trouble." He stood with his shoulders hunched and head lowered, making himself appear smaller, nonthreatening.

"You, over there. Your friend over on this side," Shorty spat out, and they quickly did as ordered, Caiden stepping in close to the trembling mother while D stepped in beside a man and his young son. Beside Caiden, tears streamed down the mother's cheeks as she cradled her terrified little girl to her, the child's screams intensifying with every shout. One of the masked men stormed across to them, looming over the mother, a gun to her temple.

"Make her shut up!"

"Hey, man," Caiden said cautiously, drawing the guy's attention away from the mother and her child. "She's just a scared little kid." As he'd expected, the man moved his gun away from the mother to Caiden.

"You thinking of being a hero, motherfucker?"

Caiden shook his head, his hands up. "No, I don't want anyone to get hurt. Please."

"Yeah?" The guy slammed the butt of his rifle into Caiden's face, and Caiden doubled over at the sharp pain on his brow. D shifted, and Caiden discreetly put a hand out to stop him from making a move. They had to play this carefully. Caiden counted eight adults, three children. Something hot trickled down the side of his face, and he touched his brow, hissing at the sting.

"Anyone else have an opinion?" the guy growled.

Caiden straightened. He inched closer to the woman while the four men were busy. Turning, he smiled reassuringly at her.

"It's going to be okay," he promised. "When I give you the signal, you run out of here as fast as you can." The bank was small enough, and the distance to the door was only a few feet. Her eyes were huge, but she nodded quickly. Caiden put a hand to the little girl's back. "Don't worry, sweetheart. Close your eyes.

Everything's going to be okay." Caiden turned and met D's gaze across the small lobby. He nodded, and D returned the gesture, whispering something to the dad, who pulled his son in closer with a nod.

Two of the men were near the counter, the other two had their guns aimed at their hostages. The number of armed men was nothing. Caiden had taken out far scarier men more heavily armed, but the civilians crowded into the small space changed the narrative. D shifted from one foot to the other, drawing the two men's attention, allowing Caiden to tap his earpiece.

"Alpha, I need you to set off the fire alarms."

"On it."

Caiden nodded at D and readied himself. The fire alarms screeched, and the four men's heads shot up to the ceiling at the flashing red lights. Caiden and D charged, D going for the men by the counter and Caiden taking care of these two. He grabbed one guy's rifle and momentarily stunned the other with an elbow to the face as he shouted.

"Everybody, run!"

The hostages didn't hesitate. They took off as Caiden delivered a hard jab to Shorty's solar plexus before maneuvering the rifle strap over the other man's head and twisting it. The guy let out a gurgling sound before he passed out. Caiden released the strap, and the guy crumpled to the floor next to his friend. The two guys by the counter were also out and on the floor. They patted the guys down and removed backup weapons. D held out a trash bin, and Caiden tossed the weapons inside.

Police sirens filled the air in the distance. The bank manager came out from behind the teller's window. He took Caiden's hand.

"Oh my God, thank you. Thank you so much." He took D's hand and shook it as well. "Thank you."

D handed the manager the trash can of weapons. "Keep this locked up until the police arrive. When you tell them what happened, you never saw our faces."

"But you guys are heroes, you—"

"You never saw our faces," D insisted.

Caiden turned to the confused manager. "We're undercover. No one can know we were here or the case we're working on will be a bust. It's important."

The manager nodded. "Okay. Yes, of course. Thank you again."

Caiden and D walked swiftly out of the bank, heads lowered, caps pulled down over their faces. They were halfway to the van when the police arrived. After climbing inside, they dropped down into the seats behind the console.

"Well, that was fun," Caiden said, smile wide as D opened one of the locked compartments on the console and pulled out a first aid kit.

"Turn this way," D ordered, placing the kit on the counter in front of them.

Caiden swiveled his chair around to face D, holding back a smile as D removed antiseptic wipes and a bandage from the red box. On the screen to Caiden's right, police rushed the bank and cuffed the unconscious men. They were hauled away while some of the witnesses who'd taken cover in their cars or around the property came out. The police began their questioning, some of them inside talking to the bank manager, while another one went into the bank manager's office. Caiden's earpiece crackled to life, and Alpha's voice spoke up.

"Security footage has been taken care of, the cameras angled away from your faces. The police are viewing the footage now and the witnesses seem to be having trouble recalling what either of you looked like."

Caiden smiled. "Thanks. Copy that." He beamed at D.

"What?" D muttered, tearing open one of the antiseptic wipe packets. "You look like a crazy person. Why are you smiling at me like that?"

"We make a pretty good team, Montero."

D snorted. "You're such a dork. Lean forward."

"Maybe." Caiden leaned in. "Feels good, though, doesn't it?"

"Easy there, hotshot. Don't go swapping your jeans for tights and a cape just yet." D placed the wipe to Caiden's brow, and he hissed at the sting. D chuckled. "Poor baby."

"Funny." Caiden punched him playfully in the shoulder. "Ass."

Cut cleaned, D placed the tiny white bandage on Caiden's brow, his hand cupping Caiden's face. "There." He stroked Caiden's brow with his thumb, his face so close to Caiden's, he could feel D's warm breath on him. "Nice job out there."

"Thanks, you too." Caiden placed his hand over D's and smiled.

Clearing his throat, D pulled away, and Caiden pushed down the sigh trying to escape. They spent the next couple of hours doing what they'd been doing before the excitement of the bank heist. A little old lady with a cane struggled to push her shopping cart with groceries across the lot from their van, and Caiden lolled his head in D's direction. He waggled his eyebrows, and D groaned.

"Really?"

"Kenneth's been doing paperwork for the last two hours. Come on."

"Yeah, because two big dudes in a dark parking lot coming toward her isn't going to freak her out in the slightest."

Caiden considered this. "You're right. You should go on your own."

"What?" D stared at him like he'd sprouted antlers or something. "The fuck are you on?"

"Come on, D. Help the poor old lady. She's probably someone's grandma."

With an exasperated sigh that told Caiden exactly how exhausting he was, D climbed out of the van. Caiden watched on the screen as D approached the white-haired woman hunched over her cane, her other frail hand on the shopping cart's handle. D stopped in front of her, opened his mouth, and received a whack on the leg from the woman's cane.

"Ooh!" Caiden sucked in a breath and cringed as she whacked him wherever she could get him. D tried to jump out of the way, but the tiny old woman seemed to be some kind of secret ninja, because she moved quicker than D, swinging her glittery cane at him. Caiden was laughing so hard he could barely breathe. At one point she swiped her cane at him, and he tried to jump it, but she moved it away, and he tripped, falling on his ass. Caiden fell out of his chair. "Oh," he wheezed, "my," gasped for breath, "God." No air. "Can't. Breathe."

When he managed to push himself to his feet, D said something, and the old lady put a hand to her chest, her scowl converting into a beaming smile. She nodded, and he scrambled to his feet before walking the cart to her car. He helped her load the groceries, and she reached into her purse. He shook his head, said something, but then she removed what looked like a handful of something. His pasted-on grin had Caiden laughing again. D pocketed whatever she gave him since she seemed to be waiting for him to do so. As soon as he had, she climbed into her little Kia and drove out of the lot.

D spun around, his murderous glare on the van.

"Oh shit." Caiden jerked open the van door, jumped out, then took off across the empty lot like he was being chased by the devil himself, which considering who was chasing him, wasn't a far-off assessment.

"I'm going to kick your ass!" D sped after him, and despite the danger he was in, Caiden couldn't help but laugh, calling out behind him.

"How was I supposed to know she had combat training?"

"You're a dead man, Cardosa!"

Caiden skidded into a sharp turn, dodging and faking as D tried to get his hands on him. He probably shouldn't poke the homicidal hitman, but he couldn't help it. "Did she pay you in candy? Tell me she gave you grandma candy."

D removed something from his pocket and lobbed it at Caiden, who caught it as he ran. It was one of the old-school strawberry candies. He let out a bark of laughter, momentarily faltering, and was tackled into the grass, D on top of him.

"You fucker!"

Caiden's cackle was loud as D straddled him. "Oh my God, she paid you in grandma candy. Best surveillance job ever."

D shook his head at him, but Caiden could see he was fighting hard not to smile. "You're a bastard, you know that?"

"Yeah, but I'm a bastard who got you some free candy to suck on."

D grabbed his crotch. "I got something you can suck on right here."

"Is that supposed to be a threat?" Caiden said, running his hands up D's thighs. "Because I fail to see how my sucking you off is a bad thing."

D's eyes filled with heat, and he cursed under his breath. He stood and held a hand out for Caiden, who took it, allowing D to pull him to his feet. He dusted himself off and followed D to the van.

"Can I have a candy?"

"No fucking way. I bled for those candies. You can bite me."

"Wow, she drew blood? Are you okay? Do you need a medevac? Should I have Alpha send in emergency medical reinforcement?"

D flipped him off and climbed into the van, Caiden laughing behind him as he sat.

"Come on. Don't be selfish. Give me a grandma candy."

"Fuck you," D growled.

"Again, not a threat." Caiden poked him in his side as D reached into his pocket and pulled out a handful of the sweets. He chucked them at Caiden like he was throwing ninja stars.

"You want candy? Here's your candy."

"Ow! Those wrappers are pointy!" Caiden laughed as he swatted at the tiny projectiles.

"Ass." D swung back to the console, and Caiden picked up the candy and placed them on the console between them.

"Unlike *some* people, I believe in sharing."

D grunted, and for the next hour they watched Kenneth until the man climbed behind the wheel of his Lexus.

"Well, today was a bust," D muttered, climbing into the driver's seat.

"I'd say it was productive on a different level. We didn't catch Kenneth doing anything shady, but we had some good food," Caiden said, fastening his seat belt. "We stopped a bank heist, and you helped that little old lady." He fished a candy out of his pocket and unwrapped it, but D grabbed it and tossed it into his mouth.

"Hey, that was mine."

"Actually, it's mine. I was letting you hold it for me."

Why did everything D say sound so suggestive? Or was it Caiden?

They followed Kenneth, keeping two cars between them at all times. When Kenneth turned into the drive outside his home, D drove past, made a U-turn ahead, then doubled back. They left the van at the end of the cul-de-sac for Alpha to have picked up, then left for the safe house.

"I'm gonna shower," D said before disappearing into his room, his door closing behind him.

After a quick shower and change into comfy pajama pants and a T-shirt, Caiden walked out into the dining room. D sat at the table, laptop open.

"What's on the agenda for tomorrow?" Caiden asked, stopping by D's chair. He itched to run his fingers through D's hair, but he refrained.

"We're back on the clock at the mansion, and then in the evening while you're on your date with Harrison—"

"Not a date," Caiden said. "Just drinks."

"Anyway, with Harrison off the property, and Isabella and Kenneth out of the house on their date night, I have the perfect opportunity to search the house."

Made sense. "I can let you know when Harrison is on his way back."

D nodded but didn't respond.

He didn't believe Caiden. Didn't D trust him? Caiden had no intention of sleeping with Harrison or even letting the man get too close. He could handle Harrison. D on the other hand? Caiden was still trying to figure that one out.

Chapter Twelve

THE UNIVERSE was far from done screwing with D, as evidenced by the new form of torture presented to him. Caiden emerged from beneath the water's surface like some mythical god, rivulets of water rolling down sun-kissed skin as he pushed his hair away from his eyes. His sculpted muscles glistened in the bright sun as he climbed the stairs at the end of the pool, revealing more of his sinful body, the soaked blue beach shorts—*short* beach shorts—clung to his skin, outlining his mouthwatering ass and leaving nothing to the imagination in the front.

D cursed under his breath and adjusted his loose shorts. At least they'd been loose when he'd come out here. Now he had his knees drawn up to hide the very stiff erection in his swim trunks.

"You sure you don't want to go for a swim?" Caiden asked, drying off his face with the towel draped over the back of his lounge chair.

D shook his head. "Nope. I'm good." Thank God for his sunglasses. At least he could hide behind those.

"Okay." Caiden gulped down some water before heading back to the pool.

Every day it was the same torture. Caiden out here, almost naked, swimming laps in the pool. The search of the Graves mansion last Friday night had gone off without a hitch but without success, and D managed to keep himself busy long enough not to think about Caiden on his nondate with Harrison. True to his word, Caiden notified D when Harrison left him, and by the time D got home, Caiden was already there. D should have been glad, and a part of him had been giddy—*take that, Harrison, you douche*—but the other part of him, the one that dreaded hurting Caiden, because he *would* hurt Caiden, had been disappointed.

D hadn't asked what happened, but considering the short amount of time Caiden had spent with Harrison, he doubted it was much. Not that certain things couldn't happen in such a short time, but not with Caiden, who'd returned frustrated after managing to get very little out of the man. Apparently the guy was too busy trying to get into Caiden's pants to discuss anything else, especially not his employers. With a well-timed phone call from Ms. Draper, Caiden said he'd bid Harrison farewell with a promise to make it up to him some other time before leaving, charming the man to the point Harrison hadn't even been upset.

The days that followed were miserable for D, which made no sense, seeing as how he and Caiden were getting along great. They carried on as if nothing was wrong, and maybe that was the problem. They teased, laughed, ate together, and did their job, alternating between following Kenneth around and searching the house. In the evening, they watched TV in the living room, and even enjoyed the pool. Well, Caiden enjoyed the pool. D saw it as a lesson in self-restraint. By the time D climbed into bed each night, he had a severe case of blue balls. His hand worked fine, but with Caiden sleeping in the next room and images of Caiden writhing underneath him fresh in his mind, D's nights were long and sleepless.

The longer it took to find the damned drive, the more frustrated D became. For one, he was horny as fuck and preferred to take his frustration out on Caiden's ass rather than the punching bag, but he couldn't. Second, it was getting harder for Caiden to put off Harrison's advances. Something had to give, or the guy was going to get suspicious. Either Caiden was interested or he wasn't. For now, Harrison seemed to enjoy the thrill of chasing Caiden, but that would only last so long. Meanwhile, Isabella took every opportunity to flirt with D. She'd made some not-so-subtle hints that he was more than welcome to pay her a visit at the house while her husband was attending to business.

"I'm going to take a shower and get ready for work," Caiden said, stopping beside D to towel dry his hair. A drop of water rolled down his torso, and D followed it with his eyes as it traveled over his abs to his belly button. "D?"

D shot his head up, eyes wide. "What?"

"I said, do you want to go first."

"Go first? Huh? What?"

Caiden chuckled and flung the towel over his shoulder. "Maybe you shouldn't sit in the sun so long. I said, do you want to head out first. To the house."

"Oh, uh, no. You go first. Hicks doesn't look so pissed when you show up first."

"Okay. See you at the house." Caiden walked off, and D's eyes were glued to Caiden's ass like it held the world's greatest secrets. "It's here whenever you want it," Caiden said, smacking his ass.

Shit, Caiden had a clear view of D through his reflection on the sliding glass door. With a groan, D sat back against his lounge chair, ignoring Caiden's husky laugh as he disappeared inside.

D waited until Caiden was out of sight before he hurried into his own room, closed the door, and leaned against it. "Fuck." He lifted his eyes to the heavens. "Cut me a break, man. I'm trying to do the right thing here."

A quick cold shower later, and D got dressed before heading out. When he arrived at the mansion, the only words to describe the scene around him were organized chaos. Trucks delivered furniture, fittings, and decor. Upstairs, Caiden was tapping away at his tablet as he checked inventory while Harrison hovered around him, pretending to help. Mostly he ogled Caiden's ass whenever Caiden bent over or crouched down to check the contents of a box. D pulled out the small Moleskine notebook from his tool belt and stood close enough to hear Harrison as he took an invoice Caiden handed him.

"After work, come over to mine," Harrison said, his hand sliding from between Caiden's shoulders to his lower back. "I promise to take things slow and have a conversation with you before I try to taste those gorgeous lips of yours."

Caiden put a finger to his own lips. "Hm. I'm not sure I'm convinced, Mr. Caveley."

"Then give me the chance to convince you. I'll make you a nice dinner, we'll have some wine, you tell me how you got into doing what you do, and I'll tell you how I ended up going from soldier to house manager for Graves."

That bastard was going to cook for Caiden. D was the one who cooked for Caiden! Okay, he needed to get ahold of himself. D jotted down measurements on the dining room table, pretending for all the world that he wasn't listening in. Caiden's answer was obvious. It was what D would have done.

"Okay, but only if you promise to behave yourself. I'm not that kind of boy," Caiden teased.

Harrison groaned. He put a hand to his heart. "Promise."

"Okay, but I have to go home and change first, so how about six o'clock?"

"Perfect. I'm going to go pick up a few things. Call if you need me."

"Thank you, Harry."

Fuck you, Harry.

As soon as Harrison was downstairs, D strolled over to Caiden, his eyes on his notebook. "So, another date, huh?"

"You heard him. He's going to talk."

"Before or after he tries to 'taste those gorgeous lips of yours,'" D hissed.

Caiden opened his mouth to reply, but Isabella appeared and hooked her arm around D's. She raked her gaze over at Caiden and *tsk*ed.

"Such a shame you're not interested in having a little… get-together."

Threesome. What she meant was threesome with an audience.

"Sorry, it's not really my thing," Caiden said. His eyes flicked to D before moving back to Isabella. "I don't like to share."

"I can understand that. If you had been interested, tonight would have been perfect." She gazed up at D as she ran a nail down his arm. "What with my husband having a business dinner. They run so very long. I suppose I'll simply have to entertain myself while I'm home all alone."

As D patted her hand, he noticed her wrist was bare. "Mrs. Graves—"

"Isabella," she insisted.

"Isabella, your bracelet?" he asked, feigning concern.

"Oh, you're so very sweet for noticing. It's okay. I didn't forget it this time. Kenneth is taking it to get it cleaned. With how rarely I take it off, it needs to be professionally cleaned regularly. I swear, he's more careful with it than I am. Don't get me wrong, I adore it and I take very good care of it, but it's not the same. It's an heirloom, after all."

"Isabella," Ms. Draper called from the living room. "I'm so sorry to interrupt, but I need to discuss these swatches with you."

"Excuse me," Isabella purred, running her hand from D's arm to over his shoulder before leaning into him. "If you find yourself in need of some company tonight, I'll be happy to offer my services." With a lick of her lips, she sauntered off.

"Well, that just happened," Caiden murmured, eyebrow arched.

D scanned the room, making sure no one was paying attention to them before motioning for Caiden to follow.

"We need to talk." He led Caiden down the hall and into the billiard room, away from all the construction, noise, and more importantly, Isabella. D closed the door behind them and turned to face Caiden.

"I think I know where the flash drive is."

Caiden's eyes widened. "You do? Where?"

"The bracelet." He couldn't believe he hadn't thought of it sooner.

"What?"

"Last week I overheard her and Kenneth arguing, and after he left, I asked her if she was okay. She showed me the gold bracelet on her arm, told me Kenneth had given it to her on their wedding day, how it meant a lot to him because it belonged to his grandmother. He was pissed because she'd taken it off while she was in the pool and forgot it there. He found it and lost his shit. That bracelet never leaves her wrist."

Caiden's soft gasp was cute. "Except when it goes out for cleaning."

D nodded. "Exactly. How much do you want to bet Kenneth's taking it to access the catalog?"

"Shit."

Caiden tapped his earpiece. "Alpha, can you get me the name of the jeweler where Kenneth supposedly takes Isabella's bracelet to get cleaned?"

"Sending the details to your phone now."

"Thanks." Caiden's phone beeped, and he tapped the screen before putting it to his ear. "Hi, this is Harrison Caveley, Mrs. Graves's house manager. I wanted to double-check that the bracelet her husband dropped off will be ready in time for tomorrow night's gala event. I know it's very last-minute, and I apologize profusely. Of course I'll wait."

D paced in front of Caiden. *Please let me be right.*

"He didn't? Oh, wait. Silly me. I checked my notes, and I see here she decided to go with the diamonds. There was a sudden change from the gold sequined dress to the rose gold, which meant a completely different set of jewels. My apologies. Have a nice day." Caiden hung up and waggled his eyebrows.

"Let me guess. No one delivered any bracelet."

"Bingo."

"Which means Kenneth is accessing the drive." D tapped his earpiece. "Alpha?"

"Searching for a signal now. I'll notify you as soon as I have confirmation. If the flash drive is indeed inside the bracelet, he'll be returning it to Isabella the moment he's finished with it. If that's the case, you must retrieve the bracelet."

"Copy that."

"So what's the plan?" Caiden asked.

"Alpha's right. Kenneth's not going to lose sight of that thing, and the minute he's done, it's going back on Isabella's wrist." D grabbed Caiden's tablet from him and accessed Kenneth's schedule. "Isabella's telling the truth. Kenneth has a business dinner planned for tonight across town, and he's blocked out time until 2:00 a.m." This was it. A way for them to finally get their hands on the truth. It was also the end of him and Caiden. He handed the tablet back to Caiden. "I'll get it off her."

Caiden eyed him. "What do you mean, you'll get it off her?"

"You heard her. She'll be alone tonight. I'll show up, say I left some tools behind, get close to her, distract her so I can take it without her knowing."

"Distract her how?"

D arched an eyebrow at Caiden, and his heart lurched in his chest as the color drained from Caiden's face.

"You're going to sleep with her?"

When D didn't reply, Caiden's eyes filled with fury.

"I didn't realize whoring yourself out was part of the mission," Caiden snapped.

Wow. Okay. "Is that what you called it when you did it for the Company?"

"That was different, and you know it."

"How was it different? You used whatever means necessary to obtain your objective, including seducing men. How is that different to what I'm doing?"

"I wasn't sleeping with anyone I cared about at the time!"

D flinched, and Caiden took a step back.

"I shouldn't have said that. Any of it."

"Cade...."

"No. It's fine, D. This is my issue, not yours. You've been clear about where we stand from the beginning. I'm the one who muddied the waters by bringing my stupid emotions into this. You wanted to keep things professional, and I kept pushing. I know better." Caiden shook his head with a humorless laugh. "I was so fucking stupid. Naive, really. I'm sorry." Caiden made to walk around him, but D stopped him.

"Caiden, wait."

"Just... let me go, D. It's what you want."

It wasn't what he wanted, far from it, but what he wanted wasn't possible. Not now that they were so close. Caiden would have his answers soon.

"We have a chance to find out the truth."

"Were the roles reversed, I would have found another way," Caiden said, eyes searching D's.

"It's worth the cost."

Caiden put his hand to D's cheek. "Not to me, it isn't."

"You're saying you would give up knowing the truth… for me?" D cursed himself for leaning into the touch, but he couldn't not seek Caiden's warmth, his soft skin, and tenderness.

"I would have given up a lot more, but that's me. You do what you have to do. I need to go. We both have dates tonight."

"Shit. Right. Your date with Harrison. Have fun." D cringed the moment the words were out of his mouth. The coldness in Caiden's bright green eyes had the bile rising in his throat. It was starting, and D couldn't do a thing to stop it.

"That's it?"

D shifted, uncomfortable. "What do you mean?"

"Never mind," Caiden said with a sigh. "Are you going to be wearing your earpiece?"

"What for?"

"In case you need backup."

"Oh, um, no. I'll have it with me in case of emergency, but I won't be wearing it while I… obtain the device."

"Fine. I'll have mine on me in case you need me, though I guess neither of us should wait up, huh?"

Was Caiden baiting him? D didn't appreciate it if he was, but if Caiden was pissed, he had every right to be. Especially with the way D kept spinning them in circles, being hot one minute and cold the next, and now this. Was he really going to go through with this? The hurt was rolling off Caiden in waves, and he stopped by the door, his eyes pleading as he paused long enough for D to change his mind.

"Be safe," D said.

Caiden's jaw muscles worked. "You too." He left the room without looking back, not that D expected him to. D waited a few breaths before checking the coast was clear, then headed out. He was on his way to the living room when his earpiece came to life. For a second, he hoped it was Caiden, but quickly shook that thought away.

"I found the flash drive. It's on the move and surrounded by heavy security. The key was accessed; then it went offline. It looks like Graves is already on his way back to the mansion."

"He's going to return the bracelet to Isabella's wrist. There are too many people around for me to make a move on it. I'll get it tonight." Alpha made no response, and for a second, D thought they'd been disconnected. "Alpha?"

"Are you sure that's what you want?"

"No, but I don't have a choice."

"There's always a choice. It's just not always the easy one."

"Copy that. D out." Since when did Alpha give him relationship advice? Whatever. Time to get this done. He went to work, making sure to stick close to Isabella for when Kenneth arrived. He didn't have to wait long. Less than an hour later, Kenneth walked up to Isabella, kissed her cheek, and slipped the bracelet around her wrist. He murmured something at her that made her smile, and then he was off again.

Time to put his plan into motion. After a quick scan of the area and refusing to give any thought to Caiden's absence, D sidled up beside Isabella. He leaned in to murmur in her ear.

"Your husband still going to be busy tonight?"

She hummed, her hand discreetly going to his thigh and squeezing. "He is. I'm going to be all alone."

D brushed his fingers down her bare arm. "Maybe you won't be." He walked off, heading back to work, feeling her heated gaze on him. For the rest of his shift, he felt her eyes on him, but the gaze he wanted to feel was absent. Caiden was nowhere to be found—not that D had gone out of his way to find Caiden, but it was obvious Caiden was no longer in the house. Had he decided to meet Harrison early, now that D had determined the fate of their relationship? Was he taking comfort in Harrison's arms? In his kiss, his body?

This was what D had wanted. He could hardly be upset for getting it. His shift ended, and he headed for the stairs, with one last look at Isabella, whose red lips pulled into a seductive smile. She turned and sauntered off, her A-line dress clinging to her swaying hips and rounded ass. *Deep breath.* He could do this. She was a beautiful woman and interested. That was all he needed.

On the drive to the safe house, he hoped to avoid any awkward moments with Caiden, but when he arrived, the house was empty.

"Damn spook," D grumbled. It looked like Caiden was the one doing the avoiding. Taking a nice long shower, he stood under the warm spray and closed his eyes. His stomach was full of lead, his heart was pissed, and his head chastised him. He was saving them both a worse heartache. Caiden thought he knew D, but he didn't. He knew what D had done before he'd been killed, but he didn't really know. When the excitement and newness wore off, Caiden would realize what he'd given up to be with a killer, with a man who'd ruined his career, his life.

After turning off the water, he got out of the shower and dried himself, then pulled on a pair of boxer-briefs and made himself something to eat. The house was silent, and as he stood in the kitchen, surrounded by nothing but the sounds of him cooking for himself, he'd never felt so alone. Which was ridiculous, really. He'd been alone from the day he was born.

Making friends had never been easy for D. His oh-so-pleasant personality had been a part of him since he was a kid. While other children laughed and squealed in delight while they played, looking to socialize, D had kept to himself, preferring it that way. He'd been a daredevil. Jumping off furniture and playground equipment. From the moment he could walk, he wanted to go faster, be better than everyone else, do what they couldn't. It was what drove him to enlist, not just the lack of college tuition as he'd told Caiden. Something inside him needed to be moving, acting, in the thick of it, to feel his blood pumping in his veins, terrified he'd feel nothing at all otherwise.

Being with Caiden, that drive was there, but it seemed to still around him. D was like a kite, always fighting against the wind to go higher, perform death-defying feats, but instead of wildly thrashing against the sky until he plummeted to earth, Caiden held his strings, gave him the distance he needed to be himself yet kept him close enough not to lose himself.

Leaning his arms against the counter, he hung his head. He'd survived a bullet to the chest; he'd survive losing Caiden. Hopefully it wouldn't take a miracle like it had the first time he'd needed saving.

His dinner hit his stomach like a lead balloon, but he ignored the heaviness surrounding him. He dressed in a pair of snug jeans, a tight black T-shirt, his biker boots, and leather jacket. Running a comb through his wet hair, he slicked it back, then headed out. He drove far too fast for his own good and made it to the mansion in less than two minutes. After parking at the end of the drive, he got out and closed the door to his truck harder than he'd meant to, but he hadn't been thinking, his focus on the guest house. Caiden's car was parked next to it.

D's fingers flexed, balling into fists. His heart screamed at him to march in there, drag Harrison off Caiden, and punch him in the face, then take Caiden home and show him who he belonged to. Instead he walked to the side door of the house and rang the bell. A shaky breath later, Isabella opened the door, dressed in a silk-and-lace slip with matching robe, and nothing else.

"Hi," D said, hoping he didn't sound as awkward as he felt. Fuck, like he hadn't done this before.

Isabella looked him over, her tongue poking out to run over her bottom lip. "Hello." Her voice was husky and dripping with sex.

"I'm so sorry to bother you at this time. I left some tools behind, and I was hoping you'd let me…." He looked her over and grinned lecherously. "Inside."

"Please, do come in." She stepped back, giving him room to enter before closing the door behind him.

"Thank you." He glanced upstairs, pretending he didn't already know the answer to his next question since he'd checked the surveillance cameras. "Is your husband home?"

"No. He left for that business dinner an hour ago and won't be back until late. Very late." She took hold of his hand and led him upstairs, smiling at him over her shoulder. At the top of the stairs, she spun around and threw her arms around his neck, and seeing as how he was two steps below her, she could easily reach him. She moved in to kiss him, and he turned his head, pretending he'd heard something.

"Someone could see us here," he said roughly, putting his hands on her waist to get her moving.

"There's no one here," she purred, her eyes on his lips.

"What about your house manager?" He had to ask, didn't he? How dumb and how much of a glutton for punishment could a guy be?

"Don't worry about Harrison. He's got his hands full of a certain sexy blond tonight. The man's not leaving his house for anything short of an invasion."

"Still…." D slid his hand around her back to cup her ass. "How about we take this somewhere a little more private?" He leaned in to whisper in her ear, "Wouldn't want the guards to mistake your screams of pleasure for something else."

She gasped and trembled in his arms before taking hold of his hand and leading him into her bedroom. After closing the door behind them, she pulled him over to her bed. She slipped out of her robe, letting it drop to the floor before her hands were on him again, sliding up his chest to his shoulders.

"Are you okay?" she asked, nipping at his jaw. "You seem a little… distracted."

"Just nervous, if you can believe it. I can't believe I'm here." *Tell me about it.* "A guy like me with a woman like you."

She pressed her body to his, straddling his thigh. "What do you mean?"

"Wealthy, beautiful. Hot for me."

"It's one night, handsome." She booped the tip of his nose. "It's not like I expect you to marry me."

Marry.

D had never seen himself getting married. Getting tied down to the same man, being all domestic, getting a dog? None of that shit had ever interested him. He never believed he'd enjoy cooking for someone, waking up to the same man in his bed every morning. Never imagined someone who could be his best friend and husband.

Who was he kidding? Marriage was never in the cards for him. He was *dead.* His name would never be able to go on a marriage certificate. Unless….

"You look a little uncomfortable. Why don't I help you with your jacket?" She took a step back and pushed his jacket off his shoulders, the lightweight leather dropping to the floor around his boots. She tugged his shirt out of the waistband of his jeans, her lips pulling into a lustful smile as she slid the shirt up and off him where it joined his jacket.

"Let me guess. You played sports in college. Football?" She raked her nails over his pecs and down his abs.

"Baseball."

"Mm, I bet you looked so damned sexy in that tight uniform. Those pants hugging you in all the right places." She cupped him through his jeans, and he jumped. What the fuck was wrong with him? If he didn't get his head out of his ass, she was going to suspect something was up. He should have been mauling her by now, have her naked underneath him in bed. "Why don't you let me take the lead."

Before he could say a word, she was turning him and pushing him. The back of his legs hit the mattress, and he fell onto it, with Isabella not wasting any time in straddling his lap. She caught his face in her hands and covered his mouth in a kiss. In that moment, all D could think about was Caiden—his laugh, his smile, his hands on D, his kiss that was warm and filled with so much need and emotion.

Oh God, he'd made a terrible mistake.

Chapter Thirteen

IT WAS happening. He was up there with *her*.

Caiden had been in the living room while Harrison had gone off to get them another bottle of wine, when headlights caught his attention. He'd sneaked a quick peek, his breath hitching at the sight of D climbing out of his truck. When Harrison returned, Caiden was back on the couch, trying to keep his heart from falling to pieces. *Keep it together.* D had made his choice. Nothing Caiden could do about it now.

"What's wrong?" Harrison asked, his gray eyes filled with concern. He placed a hand to Caiden's knee. "You've gone quiet all of a sudden."

"What? Oh, sorry." Shit, he needed to pay attention. "I have so much going on with this whole renovation thing, and…." He sighed before beaming up at Harrison. "I'm sorry I've been such a flake. I've had a lot on my mind."

Harrison nodded. He cupped the back of Caiden's neck and leaned in, but before his lips could touch Caiden's, he paused. "Avery, God knows I want you. Hell, I want you more than I've wanted anyone in a long time, but if you're not interested, you can tell me. I'm a big boy. If this wasn't meant to be, it wasn't meant to be."

Meant to be.

Caiden jumped from the couch. "I'm sorry, Harry, but you're right. I won't lose him."

"What? Lose who?"

Caiden ran from the house, aware of Harrison close behind, calling out and asking him what the hell was going on. *Please don't let me be too late.* If D decided to continue his mission after Caiden told him what he needed to say, at least Caiden would know he'd done as much as he could.

"Caiden, stop!"

Caiden took the steps inside the mansion two at a time, making a run for Isabella's bedroom, his pulse through the roof at what he might find when he got in there. The lack of moaning was a good sign, and he stormed into the bedroom, his fists at his sides as he walked in to find D sitting on the edge of the mattress, his hands wrapped around Isabella's wrists as she sat straddling his lap.

"I need a word with Mr. Rivas," Caiden ground out through his teeth. "*Now*."

"Harrison, what the hell's going on?" Isabella demanded, looking from Harrison to Caiden and back. "What's he doing here?"

"I'm so sorry, Isabella. He was determined to get in here. I have no idea what's going on."

"And you couldn't stop him?" Isabella asked incredulously.

D gently moved Isabella off him. "Excuse me for a second."

"Are you kidding me?" Isabella huffed, plopping onto the bed, her arms folded over her ample chest as she glowered at Caiden.

He really didn't give three shits. No way was she laying one more manicured nail on his man.

"I'll be right back," D told her. "Why don't you make yourself comfortable."

"Like hell you are," Caiden whispered hoarsely at D when D reached him. He grabbed D's wrist, dragging him toward the door, but D stopped him, pushing him into the walk-in closet.

"What the hell is going on, Caiden? What are you doing here?"

Caiden cupped D's face. "Don't do it. Please."

D's expression softened. "Cade, baby, what are you doing here?"

"Don't do it. I don't care about the evidence. I don't care who betrayed me. I don't want to lose you."

"What are you talking about?" D's smile was sad, and it hurt Caiden's heart.

"If you do this, I can't—" Caiden brought their mouths together, and he put everything he had behind the kiss, everything bubbling up inside him, hoping D understood the depth of emotion in his heart for this complicated, infuriating man. He pulled back, smiling at D's wide eyes. "I love you."

"What?" D wrapped his hands around Caiden's wrists, Caiden's hands still cupping D's face.

"I love you. You might not be ready to hear it, but I do, D. I never believed in the whole 'love at first sight, soul mates' thing, but from the moment I met you, I couldn't get you out of my head. Wherever I was, whatever I was doing, you were there in the back of my mind. I was so pissed at you for leaving, for not sticking around to see where things led us, because I knew you felt it too." D swallowed hard, his eyes glassy, and Caiden frowned. "What's wrong?"

"Cade, I… I was the one who called the cops on you in Vienna."

Caiden's heart stuttered to a halt. Or so it felt like. No. That couldn't be right. "What?" He shook his head with a laugh. "That's not funny, D. If this is your way of—" D pressed his lips in a thin line, his brows drawn together, and Caiden took a step away from him. "Tell me you're fucking with me." When D didn't say anything, his dark eyes filled with heartache and pain, Caiden turned away. He thrust his fingers through his hair. D had been the one to betray him? But… the mission. What? How…? He spun around, bringing his raised fist with him, but D ducked, his hands coming up in front of him.

"Baby, please. I have a good reason. Hear me out."

"A good reason?" Caiden was so livid he could barely see straight. "For ruining my career. My *life*?"

"I don't know who accused you of being a terrorist, but that wasn't me, I swear. I told them there was a suspicious-looking man in the hotel and that maybe he had a gun. I had no idea what happened after."

What? This couldn't be happening. Caiden paced the large closet. "They said I was a terrorist, that they had proof." He rounded on D. "I could have been killed, and if my CO hadn't gotten me out of the country, I probably would have! They were going to transport me for questioning, D. I don't have to tell you what that means in our line of work. How could you?"

D tried to inch closer. “Listen to me. Cariño, please.”

“Don’t you fucking dare! You betrayed me, and then you lied to me about it! All this time, you could have told me, but you didn’t. You waited for me to fall in love with you, you heartless son of a bitch!” Caiden’s heart shattered. Had this whole mission been a lie? A setup? Why bring Caiden in on this mission to find evidence that would incriminate D? It made no sense.

“Yes, I called the police, but I didn’t tell them you were a terrorist! I knew you’d get yourself out of it. Any good spook would have been able to talk his way out of that situation.”

Then it hit Caiden. “You knew I was CIA.”

D swallowed hard.

“How did you know? If *you* weren’t the one who accused me, then why did you know what I was? Tell me!” Caiden spat out.

“I—”

An explosion rocked the house, the walls around them bursting, smoke and chunks of stone sending Caiden hurtling into something solid and hard, stealing the breath from his body. He slammed into what he assumed was one of the closet walls, or maybe a shelving unit. Hitting the floor, he wheezed and coughed as smoke tried to choke him. His body screamed in agony, and he forced his head up, a thick fog of smoke, ash, and falling debris obstructing his view.

D pushed himself to his feet and leaned heavily against the doorframe as shouts and the roar of helicopter blades splintered the silence. The bedroom flooded with armed men in masks, and D glanced at Caiden over his shoulder, the look in his eyes sending a rush of panic through Caiden.

"No," Caiden wheezed. "Don't." He tried to push himself to his feet, a sharp pain in his side forcing him back down. "D!"

"I love you too, Cade. I'm sorry."

Before Caiden could reach him, D slipped out of the closet and closed the door, the lock clicking into place with a finality that shook Caiden to his core. No. *No.* That son of a bitch was *not* sacrificing himself like some fucking white knight when he'd just confessed to loving Caiden. If they survived this, Caiden was going to fucking kill him! Caiden pushed through the pain and stood, checking his side at the blood staining his shirt. He'd been grazed with something sharp, but it wasn't deep. Hurrying to the door, he heard Isabella screaming and the sound of fighting.

"No, please! Don't kill him! He's my house manager."

Harrison. Shit. The man was a former Marine. Of course he wasn't going to stand idly by and do nothing while hostiles tried to kidnap Isabella. Caiden didn't doubt that's exactly what this was. Someone with heavy firepower and a whole army of men had discovered the flash drive and its location. How, he didn't know, but D was out there fighting, and as skilled as he was, he needed backup, and Caiden was locked in a fucking closet.

"Tranq them!" a gruff voice shouted, and Caiden grabbed the doorknob. *Fuck!*

D, you fucking asshole!

Caiden turned the closet inside out, searching for something, anything he could use to get the damned door open. Outside the noise and shouts continued, followed by the sound of a helicopter flying away.

"No, no, no." Caiden grabbed one of Isabella's stilettos and broke the heel off. Snatching one of the thick platform boots, he used the items like a chisel and hammer to remove the pins from the door hinges. Pins off, he jerked at the door, letting it fall to one side as he rushed out into the bedroom, or what was left of it. Police and emergency service would be here any minute. He tore from the room and ran down the stairs, then sped out of the house. Guards were scattered about the lawn, some knocked out and others just coming to, wondering what the hell had happened.

"Stop right there!" A guard with a familiar name sewn onto his uniform ran in front of Caiden, gun aimed at Caiden's chest.

"I don't have time for your shit now, Manny," Caiden said, grabbing the gun and swiftly disarming him. He released the magazine, tossed it across the lawn, then expelled the bullet in the chamber before tossing the gun. "Find your balls, tell Alicia you love her, and fucking commit. Good luck." He patted Manny's shoulder, the guy standing dumbstruck as Caiden took off for Harrison's living room.

Flipping open his messenger bag, he grabbed the earpiece he'd stupidly left behind in his haste to get to D, like some '80s movie hero out to stop his girl from marrying the wrong guy. D would love that analogy. He put his earpiece in and tapped it to connect. "Alpha, this is Caiden." Grabbing his bag, he ran outside and climbed behind the wheel of the Audi, then burned rubber, nearly hitting incoming traffic as he swerved out onto A1A.

"Where the hell have you been?" the garbled voice demanded. "I've been trying to get ahold of you two, and no one answered me!"

"We were ambushed."

"I gathered as much when I lost the feed inside Isabella's room after your heartfelt declaration," Alpha growled. "I tried to warn you, but you were both offline." Of course Alpha knew. Alpha knew everything. They had eyes and ears all over the Graves mansion.

Caiden skidded to a halt in front of the safe house's garage and hurried inside, leaving the door open for Zed and his guys. If anyone who wasn't them tried to get into the house, Alpha would let him know. "Yeah, things got messy. You can yell at us later. I need to find D. Do we know who took him?" He rushed up the stairs and made straight for his bedroom.

"Mercenaries, but I don't know who they're working for. Yet. Zed and his team are en route to the safe house. ETA twenty minutes."

"Do you know where they took D?" He grabbed the black tactical uniform that had been delivered for him along with the rest of the equipment from the supply closet. David seemed to have anticipated all kinds of shit going wrong, because Caiden had been supplied with three times the amount of stuff he'd originally picked out. Caiden would have to send the guy a gift basket.

"I'm tracking him now through his GPS."

Caiden strapped himself into one of the tactical vests. "Whoever took him is smart. If they strip him, we'll lose the signal. They've probably already taken his phone."

"They won't find the GPS."

Caiden paused. Why wouldn't they— "D has a GPS implant?"

"Yes. As do Si and Zed."

Was that for their security or Alpha's own?

"I know what you're thinking. The trackers are for emergencies such as this. I would never leave them behind. Never."

"Okay. Smart thinking on the implant." Caiden had to give them that. Without a tracker, the chances of finding D would have gone down exponentially.

"I'm glad you approve."

"Which direction are they headed?" Caiden clipped and secured accessories to his vest before grabbing the armored case from the closet. He dropped it onto the bed and placed his thumb to the biometric lock screen.

"You're not going without backup. Wait for Zed and the others. I'm working on a plan of action as we speak."

"We're wasting time," Caiden growled, the lock on the case opening. He threw back the lid, revealing a host of weapons tucked securely into their padding. Caiden removed a Glock, checked the magazine, and secured it into the holster in his thigh rig before clipping the strap of the SIG MCX Virtus Patrol with tactical riflescope to his vest.

"Caiden."

"What?" Caiden snapped, snatching up extra loaded magazines, which he stuffed into the pockets on his belt.

"D trusts me. You can too."

Caiden swallowed hard. He closed the lid on the case and secured the lock. "Okay." If D trusted Alpha, Caiden would put his faith in them as well.

"Hello?" a male voice called out from the kitchen. "Anyone home?"

"They've arrived," Alpha informed him.

"I'm here! Be right there!" Caiden quickly returned the case to the closet and headed out into the kitchen, which now seemed small with the six large men in tactical gear taking up most of the space.

"Hey, I'm Caiden."

A man who looked to be in his early forties, with dirty-blond hair and piercing blue eyes, stepped forward. He wasn't the biggest and tallest of the six men, but certainly the one with the most presence. His smile was warm as he took Caiden's hand for a shake. "Hey, I'm Zed." He pointed the guys out one by one. "This is my band of misfits—Theta, Iota, 42, Mess, and R-Man."

"Orion's sword," Caiden said. "Mess is short for Messier, and R-Man is Running Man."

Zed smiled in bemusement. "That's right." He tilted his head in question, and Caiden shrugged.

"My college boyfriend was an astronomy major."

"Ah." Zed nodded. "Alpha's briefed us on what's happened. Let's go get your man."

His man. Caiden liked the sound of that more and more. They had a lot to discuss, but first he'd have to get D back. They'd work it out somehow. The idea of not having D was worse than anything D could tell him. Not that there could be anything worse than the possibility of him blowing Caiden's cover, but was Caiden going to let their past ruin the chance of a future? D had said he had a good reason, and other than this one major time, D hadn't lied to him.

The laptop on the dining room table came to life—at least the sound did, the only image being the blue sound wave that undulated when Alpha spoke.

"Everyone's here. Good. D, Isabella Graves, and Harrison Caveley are being transported to the Aerojet-Dade Rocket Facility in the southwest region of Homestead, five miles from Everglades National Park.

It was built in the sixties during the Space Race and abandoned in the eighties when NASA decided to have someone else build their rocket. The place is crumbling, but satellite imagery shows recent activity around the site. It would seem our mercenary friends have been operating out of the abandoned hangar and old building. I'm sending schematics of the site to your phones. It's hard to say how many hostiles are on-site, but they are armed and dangerous. Still no intel on who is behind this. Whoever they are, they're good. My guess is someone from the intelligence community. I'll be in your ear the whole time. They've got the lead, so get moving."

"I don't suppose we have a chopper handy?" Caiden asked.

Zed shook his head. "Sorry, man. Can't have black ops helicopters flying over US soil. Someone's bound to notice, and we can't have that kind of heat coming down on us." He put his hand to Caiden's shoulder. "D's one tough son of a bitch. He'll buy us some time."

Caiden nodded. Zed was right. He had to have faith in D. Whoever was after the flash drive would keep D alive until they got what they wanted. After that....

Following the guys out of the house, Caiden stopped abruptly. "What the fuck is that?" He stared in horror at the shiny black vehicle parked in the driveway.

"It's our ride," Zed said, patting the hood lovingly.

"The fuck it is. That's a soccer mom minivan."

"It seats seven, gets great gas mileage, and is inconspicuous. What, you thought we'd be driving around Florida in an armored tactical vehicle?" Zed snorted and climbed in behind the wheel.

Theta pointed at one of the black windows. "It's got tinted windows."

"Tinted windows." Caiden arched a brow at him. "Are they ballistic?"

Blink. Blink. "It's a minivan, bro."

"Great," Caiden grumbled as Mess rubbed his hand in circles over the door. It was a little disturbing.

"We call her Mrs. Brady."

Nope. *That* was disturbing, and clearly his expression said so, because the guys all laughed.

Mess grabbed the passenger side door handle. "I get shotgun!" *Whack.* "Ow, man! What the fuck you hitting me for?" He glared at Theta, who shook his head at him.

"Where are your manners? Our guest gets shotgun."

"Fine." Mess opened the passenger side door and bowed at Caiden. "After you."

Caiden rolled his eyes before climbing in. The rest of the guys shoved one another with no one wanting to be stuck in the back seat.

"Guys," Zed warned, narrowing his eyes at them through the rearview mirror. "How about we not piss off the hitman by showing up late, huh?"

"I'll take the back," Iota said cheerfully, his huge ass climbing in and making the van tip to one side.

"Suck-up," R-Man declared as he climbed over 42, who was the smallest member and managed to crawl in while the others tried to push one another out of the way.

"Get your ass out of my face," 42 protested.

Caiden turned in his seat to face Zed and threw his hands up. "A fucking minivan?"

"Mrs. Brady," Mess corrected before resuming his wrestling match with Theta.

"Guys, sit your asses down *now*," Zed barked, and the van fell into immediate silence as everyone parked their butts in seats and the door closed. They sat facing forward, seat belts on, and gloved hands on their laps. Zed turned his attention back to Caiden, whose jaw was on the floor. A smile quirked his lips. "Seat belt."

Caiden quickly fastened his seat belt as Zed pulled out of the driveway. They merged onto I-95 South not long after, and Caiden still had no idea what to make of this whole surreal experience. He cast a sideways glance at Zed in his full tactical uniform, gloved hands on the steering wheel and Oakley sunglasses on his face as he drove an elite tactical team armed to the gills.

In a minivan. A minivan dubbed after an old sitcom TV mom.

"You really drive around the state in this?" Caiden asked.

Zed smiled. "Like I said. Less conspicuous. It's big enough to fit the team and our gear comfortably. We're on the road for hours on end sometimes, so comfort is important. It's deceptively quick and has some great safety features."

Caiden nodded. "Right. Safety features." He sat back and faced forward. "Tell me, is everyone Alpha hires slightly unhinged?"

The guys burst into laughter, and beside Caiden, Zed chuckled. He shrugged. "I guess you have to be a little bit nutty to do what we do. Don't you think?"

Caiden frowned. "I don't work for Alpha."

Zed hummed.

"What's that supposed to mean?"

"Nothing."

The guy looked a little too smug for his own good. Was there something he knew that Caiden didn't?

"Z, please put on some music, bro," Mess pleaded. "If I have to listen to Theta breathing in my ear for the next two hours, I'm going to lose my fucking mind."

"Fuck you," Theta snapped. "I don't breathe loud."

"No country music," 42 protested.

"Hey, what's wrong with country music?" Iota grumbled.

"No one wants to listen to your backwater, sheep-fucking, sister-marrying shit music," Mess ground out, getting another whack to the side of the head from Theta.

"Don't insult the man's music just because you don't like it."

"I swear on my madrecita, Thay, if you whack me upside the head one more time, I'm gonna dump your ass in the Everglades and let the gators eat you."

Caiden snickered. At least the guys were keeping him from drowning in his fear. What were they doing to D? Were they hurting him? Torturing him for information? A hand on his arm had him looking up, and Zed offered him a reassuring squeeze.

"He's gonna make it through this."

"Zed's right," R-Man said, his deep baritone resonating through the van. "D's one of the strongest, most stubborn guys we know."

"That fucker's got nine lives," Mess added. "Always lands on his feet."

"Yep," Theta agreed. "Nothing can break that dude."

"Thanks, guys. I appreciate it." And he did. It was nice to have backup.

No wonder D liked these guys. They were soldiers, or at least had been in another life, though Caiden wasn't about to pry. It wasn't his place. Had what happened to D happened to the rest of the guys? Had they been sacrificed to keep someone's dirty secret? They were a tight-knit bunch, bickering and teasing one another. A brotherhood. What would it be like to have that? The few times Caiden had worked with teams, he'd enjoyed it, but the majority of the time, he worked on his own, and trust was hard to come by. He never knew when an asset would get turned or someone who said they were a friend was actually preparing to double-cross him. Friendship didn't exist in the spy game, simply connections you hoped wouldn't turn on you. He'd been lucky to have Savannah and Gibson.

As the guys argued over music, Caiden let the sound wash over him, soothe him. He was safe here. Like Alpha, D trusted these men, so Caiden would too. He closed his eyes, D's smiling face appearing in his mind. That night, D had called the police on Caiden. What reason could he have had? At the time they'd known little to nothing about each other. Something had happened when Caiden went to the bathroom after they had sex that night. D had known who Caiden was, at least who he worked for. Various scenarios ran through his head, but none of them made any sense. The only way to find out was for D to tell him.

Either way, Caiden was going to get D back. They still had a chance at a future.

"I love you too, Cade."

Caiden smiled, his heart swelling. D loved him. Everything else would sort itself out. They'd get that damned bracelet, find out the truth, and Caiden would leave the past behind him for good, with D the part of it he'd be bringing with him into the future.

Hang on, baby. I'm coming for you.

Chapter Fourteen

D JOLTED awake, his vision blurred before slowly coming into focus. He tried to rub his eyes, only to find the movement denied—his wrists and ankles were zip-tied to the metal chair he sat on. Dropping his head, he frowned down at himself. Damn. They'd stripped him of everything except his boxer-briefs. He kinda wished he hadn't gone with the candy hearts. Good thing this was Florida, or he'd be freezing his nuts off. There was a chill in the air, as it was. With this being November, the temperature could drop to the low fifties, maybe a little more.

Where the hell was he? By the derelict state of the place around him, he was somewhere abandoned, and that most likely meant far out in the middle of nowhere. Graffiti covered the concrete walls. Debris, dirt, glass, and garbage littered the floor. Moonlight shone through missing pieces of roof, and the portable work lights positioned in the corners of the room allowed him to get an idea of his surroundings. He needed to get himself out of this chair, find Isabella and Harrison—if Harrison was still alive. Just because they took him alive didn't mean he'd stay that way. It would have been real helpful if they'd left D with something. Whoever he was dealing with wasn't leaving anything to chance.

All D had to do was bide his time until Alpha sent in Zed and his band of merry men. Caiden would be with them because he was a stubborn little shit, but Zed would look after him, keep him safe. Not that Caiden wasn't a capable agent, but D would rather not take any chances. Now that he'd managed to get his head out of his ass and had stopped pretending he wasn't in love with the pain-in-the-ass. Man, Caiden was going to be *so* pissed at him for locking him up in that closet. His reasons were many, and as much as he'd love to say his decision had been a purely tactical one, it hadn't. He'd simply wanted to keep Caiden safe.

How had Alpha not known a third party was involved? Alpha knew everything, listened to chatter on all the right channels, was tapped into the intelligence community—albeit not fully, so it was possible they were dealing with someone who knew how to operate undetected, or maybe they were dealing with a rogue organization. Something wasn't right. The armed men who'd taken them were mercenaries, D knew that much. The million-dollar question was who were they working for? Did they know Isabella had the flash drive on her? D ruled out that possibility. If they knew, they would have killed D and Harrison and just taken Isabella. Somehow they'd known the flash drive was connected to one of the three of them. It was the only explanation for why they'd gone after Isabella and not

Kenneth. Unless they already had Kenneth. Fuck, too many variables in this scenario.

D twisted his wrist, gritting his teeth against the pain of the sharp plastic digging into his skin. A shrill scream met his ear, and his heart leaped into his throat. Isabella. *Fuck.* D was in the middle of jerking at his wrists when a shadow moved in his peripheral vision. He slowly sat back, waiting for the large figure to show himself. It didn't take long. D narrowed his eyes at the white-haired man. Who the fuck was this guy? He was over six and a half feet tall, a wall of muscle, bigger and wider than D, with a short military-style haircut.

"Look who's awake. The killer with a heart."

D squinted at him. "Do I know you?" He was good at remembering faces and recognizing voices, but he'd never seen or heard this man before. The guy was in his early fifties maybe, strong, with several scars running along each temple. His square jaw was covered in stubble, and the way he stood in the tactical uniform screamed former military, or current, for all D knew.

"You don't know me, but I know you," the man said, his voice deep and gravelly, like maybe he had dirt stuck in his throat. D didn't know him and yet felt an odd sense of familiarity. His gut never steered him wrong. Even when his head or heart fought him, he trusted his gut. He knew this man from somewhere.

"Care to share with the rest of the class?" D asked, not taking his eyes off the guy, who slowly paced in front of D, studying him. Another earsplitting scream filled the air, and D struggled against the restraints. "Whatever you think she knows, you're wrong."

"She insists she doesn't know where the flash drive is."

"That's because she doesn't know," D growled. "She has no idea who her husband is or what he does, but I'm guessing you do."

"I've been hunting for that flash drive for years, and *finally* I've found it."

"Must be some pretty fucked-up shit on there for this kind of play. Let me guess. Someone found out all your dirty little secrets, gave Kenneth the evidence, lubed you up and shoved their hand so far up your ass, they're moving your mouth like the good little puppet you are. You got tired of getting fucked, and here we are."

"You know all about getting fucked, don't you, Montero?"

D chuckled. "Nice one. Never heard that before. You seem to know plenty about me, yet I don't know a thing about you, Mr.…?"

"You don't need to know who I am."

"Oh, I beg to differ. I want to know the name of the man I'm going to put a bullet in."

"So cocky. For now, you can call me Sir."

D snorted. "Yeah, no. I don't think so. How about we kick it old-school and I call you Dickface. How's that?"

Dickface stepped in front of D and grinned down at him. "Old-school. I like the sound of that. Let's see what old-school gets us." He cracked his knuckles, and D snorted.

"I'll save you the trouble and tell you right now. The only thing that's going to get you is one pissed-off dude in his undies. Granted, I get pissed fairly easily, especially when someone tries to blow me up, but you know, that's me."

"A smartass. I really hate smartasses."

The punch that landed across D's jaw had his head snapping to the side. Well, that hurt. D tongued the inside of his mouth, tasting blood on the fresh cut. He laughed as he lifted his gaze.

"Oh, then you are going to *hate* me, because let me tell you, even my mama used to say, 'Cariño, one of these days your smart mouth is going to get you into trouble.' She was right. But then mothers usually are, aren't they? Or at least they like to think they always are. It's your job to nod, smile, and then climb out of your bedroom window to meet the cute guy from biology who promised to blow you if you got him an A on his test. Spoiler alert, he got a B, but I still got my blowjob. I'm naturally charming that way."

This time the blow came to his stomach, knocking the wind out of him, the pain making him double over as he gasped for breath. The blows came hard and fast, and D tried to curl up on himself as much as he could. He tugged against the restraints, the sweat from his body allowing for a little wiggle room, but not enough to free himself. His body screamed with pain, his flesh tender, and his skin mottled with bruises and cuts.

Dickface stepped back, his knuckles bloodied and bruised. "Tough guy, huh? Fine. Time to change the game." He turned toward the doorway. "Bring them in!"

Fuck.

Four armed men appeared, one dragging Isabella zip-tied to a chair like D, and the remaining three dragging a bloodied and growling Harrison tied to a chair in nothing but black boxer-briefs. They dropped the chairs near D before walking off.

"Lorenzo? What's going on?" Isabella asked with a sniff, her eyes red and face flushed. Her bottom lip was split, and a bruise was forming on her cheek where she'd been struck.

Dickface chuckled. He ran a hand over Isabella's head.

"Don't touch her," Harrison spat out.

"You poor, poor naive woman. His name isn't Lorenzo, and he's not who you think he is."

Harrison glared at D. "I knew there was something strange about you. My gut kept telling me to be on my guard around you, but I was—"

"Too busy trying to get into his boyfriend's pants?" Dickface offered.

"Boyfriend?" Harrison stared at D. "Avery's your boyfriend?"

The bark of laughter Dickface let out startled Isabella. "Avery? You mean Caiden Cardosa? The CIA agent you've had in your house?"

D closed his eyes and let his head hang. Fucking wonderful. This shit show just got better and better.

"That's right." Dickface grabbed a fistful of D's hair and forced his head up.

D's eyes flew open, and he gritted his teeth, eyes narrowed up at the bastard. How did he know who Caiden was?

"CIA?" Isabella gasped, looking to D. "You're CIA?"

Another round of laughter from their unpleasant friend. "Oh no, sweetheart. At least not anymore. He was a contract killer. A cold-blooded hitman for the Company. I don't know what he is now, other than fucked. What I can tell you is that he and his boyfriend have been looking for the same thing I am, and I think he knows where it is."

"You have to tell him," Harrison demanded.

"Shut the fuck up, *Harry*. You don't know what's at stake here."

"Your lives," Dickface said with a shrug. "That's what's at stake." He opened his mouth to continue when one of his men hurried into the room. "What? I'm a little busy."

"Sorry, boss, but we're, uh, still having trouble locating the target."

"Are you fucking kidding me? How hard can it be?" Dickface marched to his guy, pausing only long enough to growl over his shoulder, "Why don't I give you all a moment to talk it over. Your lives for the flash drive." He strolled off and disappeared into one of the other rooms.

"What the hell is going on?" Harrison hissed as he tried to free himself from the zip ties.

"What flash drive is he talking about?" Isabella asked. "I don't know about any flash drive. And what would the CIA want with it?"

Officially the CIA didn't know it existed, though if they did, they'd be all over it. "That depends. Do you want the truth, or do you want to keep your marriage?"

"What?" Isabella looked from him to Harrison and back.

"For fuck's sake, say it," Harrison growled.

"Kenneth has a flash drive that's a key to a catalog system filled with evidence against everyone, from criminals to the government, people in positions of power. People like our dickhead friend who kidnapped us."

"But… why would Kenneth have this?"

D hesitated. Poor Isabella looked so lost. She truly believed her husband was an innocent man. "Because he's not the man you think you married. They call him the Steward, and—"

"Steward?" Isabella gasped, her eyes huge. "My uncle Benny called him that one day by accident. I thought he'd gotten Kenneth's name mixed up with someone else."

"Your husband is a butler of sorts. He offers services to these people—his clients—gets them what they need, including storing their dirty laundry."

"And why do you and that liar Cardosa want it?" Harrison asked, his eyes filled with hurt. D almost felt bad for him. Almost.

"Because there's evidence on the main drive that will tell Caiden who betrayed him while he was on a covert mission abroad, ruining his career and almost getting him killed. It will also tell me who *did* kill me."

Harrison frowned. "Who killed you?"

D sighed. "Yes. Someone sent a hitman after me. Fucking hilarious, I know. But whoever went after Caiden also went after me, only they succeeded. Sort of. Point is, this asshole here is willing to kill for this information. If that intel gets into his hands, a lot more innocent people are going to die."

"I can't believe he lied to me." Tears filled Isabella's eyes before she jerked against her restraints, cursing up a storm in Italian. Pissed didn't begin to cover it. If he were Kenneth, he'd be guarding his loins.

"We need to get out of here," D said, quickly scanning the room for something, *anything*, he could use.

"Are you crazy? We need to give him what he wants," Isabella cried.

Harrison released a heavy sigh. "We can't do that, Isabella."

"What are you talking about?"

"If Lorenzo, or whatever his name is, is telling the truth, and God help me, I believe he is, we can't let that man get his hands on that information."

"That's easy for you to say," Isabella spat out. "You're a Marine! You're trained for this shit. I'm not!"

"Listen to me," D told Isabella, hoping his tone would soothe her. "Kenneth, for all the bad shit he's doing or done, only holds on to that information. It's why his clients trust him. He accesses the flash drive to add or delete at his clients' request. He never looks at any of it and never uses it. This guy, if he gets his hand on all that blackmail material, you bet your ass he's gonna use it, and the world as we know it will burn around us."

"So we let him kill us?"

"No. The only thing keeping us alive is that flash drive. Once he gets his hands on it, we're dead. Caiden's on his way with some of our guys. We need to buy ourselves some time."

"We need a distraction," Harrison said, looking around. "I think I got something, but it's going to involve you hitting the floor just right."

D craned his neck, spotted what Harrison's gaze had fallen on, and grinned. "Okay. Let's do this."

"Do what?" Isabella asked.

"Don't worry. We'll get you out of this alive. I promise." The less she knew, the better. This whole thing could go sideways, but D had to try everything in his power to get them out of this.

Dickface returned and stood near D, his grin smug. "So what's the verdict?"

"The verdict," D said, pursing his lips, "is that you're an asshole, and steroids will fuck you up, man. Don't do that shit. I know you're getting on in years, but think of your poor dick. I mean, as it is, getting it up is gonna get harder, no pun intended." As expected, their friend did not appreciate the response. He swiped his gun from its holster and marched over to Isabella. With a sneer, he pressed the gun to her head.

"How about I start with her?"

"No, please!" Isabella cried.

"You kill her, you kill him, and you get nothing," D said calmly. "I'm the one who knows where the flash drive is. You seem to have a thing for old-fashioned. How about we settle this old-school. You and me."

"Are you kidding me?" Dickface let out a bark of laughter. "You think I'm going to let you go? Do I look stupid to you?"

D squinted at him. "Is that a rhetorical question or…?"

"This is a waste of time. I'll kill all three of you. You're not the only one who knows where the flash drive is."

D laughed at that. "Right. And remind me why you didn't grab Kenneth in the first place?"

The man's murderous glare said it all. God, D fucking loved Alpha. He had no idea how Alpha had done it, but he'd guess Alpha had seen the bastard heading for Kenneth and warned him. Kenneth, being the smart man that he was, probably used one of his many emergency evacuation plans and went underground. It didn't explain why he left Isabella and the bracelet behind. Even if he was confident no one would find the bracelet, it was quite the risk he was taking.

"That's right," D said. Well, now was as good a time as any. "Because you don't know where the fuck he is."

Dickface marched over to D and backhanded him, making D laugh. He whooped loud.

"Man, I do love it when I'm right!"

"Shut the fuck up." The guy put his gun to the middle of D's forehead. "Tell me where it is, or I'll blow your brains out."

"But you told me to shut up. Now you want me to talk? Did you forget already? Are you having memory trouble? It's nothing to be ashamed of. That sort of thing happens at your advanced age."

With a roar, the guy moved the gun and marched away before swinging back around, nostrils flaring as he kicked at the side of D's chair. D toppled over, hitting the floor hard, the blow shaking him from head to toe. Teeth gritted, he twisted his wrist while Dickface was pacing, thinking. Thank God he was up-to-date on his shots. D gingerly maneuvered the long, slim shard of glass closer until he could palm it.

"Tango Five," Dickface called out, and one of the mercenaries came running.

"Yes, sir?"

"Where are we on locating Graves?"

The younger man shook his head. "We're trying, sir, but he's gone underground. The men he sent to get his wife have been intercepted and are being questioned, but they're not talking."

"Keep trying," Dickface spat out.

The guy ran off, and D lifted his gaze to Harrison, then motioned to their captor. He needed a little more time. Dickface had turned and headed for D, when Harrison spoke up.

"I know where the flash drive is."

That… wasn't what D had in mind. What the hell was that idiot doing?

Dickface turned to Harrison, his gaze wary.

"Look, I don't want anyone to die. That goes against everything I stand for. Kenneth gave me the drive for safe keeping. Just promise me you'll let us go once you have it."

"Where is it?" Dickface demanded.

"Promise me," Harrison growled.

The guy put his hand to his chest, his sneer oh-so convincing. "You have my word. I'll release you once I have the drive."

Always read between the lines. He'd kill them, then release them.

"It's in my phone. The SD card."

Dickface threw a hand out and grabbed Harrison by the neck as he leaned in. "If you're lying to me, I will take pleasure in breaking you. Do you hear me?"

"I just want this over with."

The guy marched off, and D moved as fast as he could, his fingers and hands stinging as the glass cut into his flesh.

"Hurry up," Harrison hissed. "The moment he finds out I was bullshitting him, he's gonna be pissed."

"Master of the fucking obvious," D growled. When he'd cut the plastic enough, he jerked his hand, and it snapped. He sliced through the second tie, then moved to his feet.

"You're a dead man, Caveley!"

Shit. D darted over to Harrison, put the glass in his hand, and made it back to his chair on the floor as their pissed-off friend charged into the room. He didn't even look at D, just went straight for Harrison, gun in hand. The moment he stepped in front of Harrison, D launched himself at the larger man and threw an arm around his neck in an attempt to choke him.

"Montero, you fuck!"

D wrestled the gun out of Dickface's hand, and it went skidding across the floor. A fierce elbow to the ribs had D scrambling away. The guy might be older than D, but he was just as strong, with more years of experience behind his belt, and God only knew what kind of training. He also had the benefit of wearing protection, from his combat boots to his tactical vest. He came at D with fierce punches made to inflict some serious pain, left hooks, right hooks, close-quarter-combat moves that had D fighting to protect himself while attempting to get his own hits in. The fact the asshole hadn't called for reinforcements yet said enough about the guy's confidence in his skills. He had every intention of taking D down.

Sweat slicked D's skin as he sidestepped his assailant, grabbed at his vest, and flipped him over his shoulder with a fierce growl. The guy hit the floor, but kicked at D's leg on the way down, forcing him onto one knee. D rolled when Dickface lunged at him, his body screaming from the jagged pieces of debris digging into his flesh. Jumping away, D ducked under one of his opponent's hooks, and came up fast, fist catching the guy in his side. Fucking vest. D threw his arms around the guy and lifted him off his feet with a yell, then ran with him and slammed him into the wall. He swiped the guy's knife from his thigh rig, ready to plunge it into Dickface's side beneath his vest, but the guy caught his wrist. He slashed at D's back with something, and D cried out.

Fighting through the pain, D caught the guy's wrist, and they wrestled for the knife. D gritted his teeth, his muscles straining and pulling as he tried to get the upper hand. He brought a knee up, but the guy continued to block him when a slam of the guy's head to his own had D seeing stars, momentarily stunning him and giving the asshole the opportunity to swipe his legs out from under him.

D hit the floor hard, and his ankle was grabbed and his body dragged across the floor. D cried out as glass and metal scratched and cut the shit out of his naked body. Kicking, he caught the guy in the face, giving him the chance to get to his feet. D came in fast and hard, putting all his force behind his punches, managing to land a blow to the man's leg, giving him a dead leg. He was lunging at the guy when Harrison screamed his name, but his warning was too late. Several men tackled D, grabbing his arms, legs, around his torso, and his hair, forcing him to his knees.

D let out a frustrated roar as he fought against their hold, managing to push himself to his feet despite their unified attempt to keep him on his knees. *Fuck them.* The only man D got on his knees for wasn't here, so they could kiss his ass. Dickface pushed himself to his feet with a groan. He wiped the blood from his mouth and stepped in front of D.

"You think you're so fucking smart, don't you?"

D spat a mouthful of saliva mixed with blood in the guy's face. "Definitely better-looking," D said with a grin, earning him a punch to the face.

"When I'm done with you, I'm going to find your boyfriend and make you watch while I take him apart piece by piece."

"Fuck you," D spat. No way was this asshole going to get his hands on Caiden. Not while D had breath left in his body. His lungs and skin burned; his breath came out ragged. His chair was set right, and he was shoved down into it. He struggled against his captors, managing to kick one in the face.

"For fuck's sake, restrain him already," Dickface snapped.

A punch to the balls had D doubling over with a curse. He gritted his teeth, his glare on the asshole who'd punched him in the nads. "When I get my hands on you, I'm going to rip yours off."

The guy snorted and finished restraining his legs.

For fuck's sake. Where the hell was Caiden?

Hands and legs once again zip-tied to the chair, D sat back with a sigh. The men left the room, and D was once again faced with Dickface.

D grinned up at the guy and shrugged. "Can't blame a guy for trying."

"You're a resilient motherfucker, I'll give you that." Dickface cracked his knuckles as he approached D. "Let's see if we can't soften you up a bit."

Fuck. This was going to hurt.

Chapter Fifteen

"YOU'VE HEARD of the song that never ends? This is the road that never ends," Mess grumbled.

The dirt road they were on was shrouded in darkness, with nothing for miles except overgrown bushes, trees, and dead grass. Signs warning against trespassing were littered about the place, most of them tagged with graffiti.

"I can't see shit," Theta said. "At least they won't see us coming."

"The only lights in this place are gonna be the ones they've installed, so yeah," R-Man agreed.

Zed had turned the headlights off so as not to give them away. "They probably have armed men guarding the perimeter. Our objective is to get D and the hostages out alive. Stealth mode, guys." He parked the van away from the buildings. Concealing the vehicle wasn't a problem, considering how overgrown and abandoned everything was. They moved through the trees, rifles at the ready as they made their way to the first building. Who knew what the hell was going on in there.

Portable floodlights were scattered around the buildings, the low hum of a generator filling the air. As they moved closer to the main building, Zed put his fist up, motioning them to stop. He put up two fingers, then pointed left before motioning three and pointing right. The team split up, Caiden staying with Zed as they continued to move forward, using the trees and bushes to conceal them. They'd agreed that it was unlikely whoever was in charge had D and the others in the hangar. It was too big a space, too open, too easy to infiltrate, which left the main building that had once been filled with offices and labs, with its many rooms and corridors as the most likely choice.

The entrance to the main building had no door, and Caiden followed Zed in. The facility was covered in graffiti tags, the hallway inside the doorway narrow and lined with more doors and boarded-up windows. They crouched whenever they reached a closed door, as each one had a small window, the glass gone ages ago. When Zed moved, so did Caiden.

Caiden listened for movement, for talking. Sound bounced off the walls, and they stilled. It came from somewhere ahead to their left. Zed tapped his earpiece, speaking quietly. "Possible location on our hostages. I need a SITREP."

Mess was the first to speak up. "Three hostiles are Tango Down."

"Four hostiles are Tango Down," Theta said.

Iota, 42, and R-Man followed up giving them a total of fifteen targets incapacitated.

"Affirmative," Zed replied. "We're Oscar Mike." He motioned for Caiden to follow, and they turned down another corridor, the voices growing louder. Several of the rooms ahead were lit up, and they crab-walked beneath a wall with a large open window, then slipped into the next room. Several doors down, familiar voices filtered out of a room that looked to have three entrances, two guards in front of the larger doorway.

Zed let his rifle hang and signaled that he'd take the guard on the right, Caiden would take the left. They slipped back out into the shadows of the corridor, moving silently. Zed tossed a pebble in the opposite direction, and when the guards turned, Zed and Caiden made their move. Caiden covered the guard's mouth with one hand, while he choked the man with the other until he was out. Dragging him to one side, Caiden took his rifle in hand and followed Zed, who waited by the doorway.

They moved through the outer room, which connected to several smaller ones and dark corridors, toward the room where the voices were coming from. Zed stood on one side of the window, while Caiden stood beside the other one. He was going to peek in, but then he heard a familiar voice, one that turned his blood to ice.

"You should have killed him, Montero."

It couldn't be. No. He was wrong. Hearing things.

Caiden edged closer to the window and sneaked a peek. The man's back was to him, but Caiden would know the set of his shoulders and that haircut anywhere. His heart slammed in his chest at the realization of who'd betrayed him. Countless questions flooded his brain, but the one he kept coming back to was, why? Caiden had looked up to him, respected him, come to see him as a friend. The man had played a part in saving

Caiden's life. In getting him out of Vienna. How could Gibson betray him?

Across from the bastard, D sat in a chair, bloodied and stripped down to his underwear. Harrison was in the same state, blood trickling down the side of his head. Isabella was quietly sobbing from where she sat, the bracelet still on her wrist.

D's head snapped up, his eyes going huge as he stared at Gibson. "What? Wait. You. It was *you*." D shook his head. "No."

"You accepted the contract. You *never* go back on a contract."

"You lied," D spat. "You said he was a terrorist. A traitor to our country, but he wasn't any of those things. He was one of our own."

Caiden slapped a hand over his mouth to stifle a gasp. Oh God, it got worse. Zed's brows drew together, and he motioned in the man's direction. Caiden nodded. Yes, he knew who that was. The last time he'd seen him was in Vienna. His Chief of Station, Ryan Gibson. His friend, a friend who'd accused him of being a terrorist and put a contract out on Caiden. His heart pounded against his chest as if trying to escape.

"Did you decide not to kill him before or after you fucked him?" Gibson said with a snort of disgust.

"What?"

"You think I don't keep tabs on my people? Why do you think I told you to go to that particular café to await instructions? I knew you wouldn't be able to resist. He was just your type—pretty face, fuckable lips."

"Fuck you, you son of a bitch! When I get my hands on you, I'm going to rip your fucking throat out!"

Gibson ignored D's raging. "It was the perfect setup. You fuck Caiden Cardosa, receive your target, and take him out. Instead you fuck it all up by calling the cops?"

The fight seemed to go out of D at that moment. "It was the only way to protect him. To make sure you didn't send someone else in. He'd be safe."

That was it. The reason D had called the cops. To protect him. To keep Gibson from sending someone else in to finish the job, but Gibson had sent someone else anyway, even after Caiden's name had been cleared. Gibson had ruined Caiden's career and tried to kill him.

"Which is why I took matters into my own hands, except those incompetent assholes let him get away before my new guy could get to him. I mean, I handed him over to them on a silver platter. Told them he was a terrorist, provided evidence, and they bring in a bunch of amateurs."

"Then his people got him out, and you were done," D said, his grin feral.

"But so was he."

"Say it," D spat out. "Say it!"

"Whatever do you mean?"

"You fucking had me killed!"

Caiden blinked the tears from his eyes. He shook his head as Gibson confirmed D's words.

"Of course I did! What the fuck good is a hitman with a conscience? You betrayed me, so I had you taken out, except you seem to have a problem with fucking dying, Montero!"

The rest of the team slid into the outer room with them, and Caiden slowly aimed his rifle at Gibson's head, but then his earpiece came to life.

"I need him alive," Alpha ordered, and Caiden pulled back his rifle, cursing under his breath. "I know you want to take him out, but it's vital we take him alive. Retrieve the bracelet and detain Gibson."

Caiden was tempted to ignore Alpha, but when he lifted his gaze to Zed, the man shook his head, his eyes pleading with Caiden not to do anything stupid. Caiden nodded.

Fine. Have it your way.

Zed motioned that he and the team would go through the window while Caiden went for the door and Gibson. They were going to provide a distraction and cover him. Caiden nodded. He could work with that.

Readying himself, he pulled the tactical knife from his thigh rig. All he had to do was cut one of D's restraints loose, leave the rest to D. He peeked around the corner, silently urging D to look his way. Sensing eyes on him, D glanced over. His man gave nothing away, and when Gibson turned, Caiden motioned for him to close his eyes. D nodded, sending a silent signal to Harrison, who murmured to Isabella. Caiden nodded to Zed.

Zed pulled a flash bang from his vest and tossed it into the room. The ringing was loud, and Gibson instinctively ducked, covering his ears as the room exploded with light and smoke. The team moved in, catching Gibson's attention while Caiden moved in fast through the open door. He managed to cut D's right wrist and dropped the knife onto his lap before spinning, knowing Gibson was coming for him.

Gibson tackled Caiden, both of them hitting the ground hard as gunfire erupted in the corridor, but true to his word, Zed and the team took care of Gibson's mercenaries while Caiden busied himself with Gibson. From the corner of his eyes, Caiden noted D was cutting himself free. Gibson hauled Caiden to his feet by the vest, holding him in place to throw a punch. Did he think Caiden was going to just take the hit?

Caiden blocked the blow and used his free hand to swipe his backup knife, twirl it in his hand, and use it to lash out in swift bursts, slicing through the fabric of Gibson's uniform in several places: arm, leg, shoulder, thigh.

"You son of a bitch," Gibson growled, pushing himself away from Caiden and putting some distance between them.

"Better that than a traitor! How could you?"

"You made it easy," Gibson snarled. Behind him, D was out of his chair and cutting Isabella free. He was unsteady, beat to shit, but the determination in the set of his jaw, the way he pushed through, had Caiden's heart swelling. His man was fierce, and together they made one hell of a team.

Caiden launched himself at Gibson, faking right and going left only to get blocked and punched in the ribs. He reeled away but moved in fast, coming in hard and dirty, ducking under Gibson's right hook to deliver a right hook of his own, followed by a left. The hits did very little with Gibson wearing a vest, but they were a distraction. Each time Caiden got in close for a punch, he used his other hand to expertly slice through the straps of Gibson's vest until one good jerk had the thing coming right off.

"What is with you two and not dying when you're fucking supposed to," Gibson growled, charging Caiden and grabbing him around the waist, hauling him off his feet, and slamming him onto the floor, the air whooshing out of Caiden's lungs and sending his knife soaring across the concrete. He gasped, sucking in a lungful of air. Gibson brought a heavy booted foot down, but Caiden rolled out of the way before Gibson could crush his skull. He tried to scramble to his feet, but the kick to the chest had him falling. Thankfully his vest absorbed most of the blow, but it still hurt like a motherfucker. A fierce roar resounded around them, and Caiden rolled onto his back just as D landed a jump and punch across Gibson's face.

Gibson stumbled but recovered quickly. He spat out saliva mixed with blood and charged D, who did his best to protect himself in between trying to land a hit. Caiden pushed to his feet, lunging for Gibson when D slammed into him, knocking them both off their feet.

"Christ. What the fuck is this guy made of?" D ground out, allowing Caiden to help him to his feet.

"You schoolboys think you can take *me* on? I've faced off against bigger, harder men than you. I survived torture in the harshest conditions in the deepest, darkest hellholes no man should ever know exists."

D made a talking motion with his hands. "Blah, blah, blah, my dick is bigger, I'm harder, yeah, yeah. Tell me, when they tortured you, was it some asshole trying to talk you to death, because I gotta say I'm feeling a little tortured right now."

Caiden snickered.

"I've had enough of your shit," Gibson spat out, rolling his shoulders, the sound of gunfire echoing through the empty rooms around them. Across the room, Mess was getting Isabella out, and Caiden smiled to himself when he noticed Mess slipping the bracelet off her wrist without her realizing. Harrison had a rifle in his hand and was showing Gibson's mercs what he was made of.

"Hey, eyes off the naked Marine," D groused.

Caiden chuckled. "I only have eyes for you, baby, you know that."

"You better," D grumbled.

"By the way, Alpha wants him alive."

"Fuck."

"Yeah."

They each took a fighting stance, fists up as Gibson let out a war cry and attacked. The man was skilled and trained in various fighting styles, most of which he employed while D and Caiden made their assault, the idea to cause as much damage as possible without killing the guy. They needed to knock him the fuck out without getting knocked out themselves. The guy's fists were like boulders, the force behind his hits lethal.

Caiden came in from the front, while D took the rear. Any weapon they tried to use, Gibson managed to disarm them, forcing them to use only their fists. *Fuck that.* Caiden did his best to block and avoid Gibson's fists as he edged the guy back. Catching on to what Caiden was doing, D shifted to Gibson's side. When they were close enough, Caiden ducked out from underneath one of Gibson's hooks while D took Caiden's place. Using D's chair for leverage, Caiden swung his legs around Gibson, hoping to bring the guy down with the momentum and his weight, but Gibson spun into it, using Caiden's move against him, and throwing Caiden into the wall. He hit it hard and landed on his front.

"I've had enough of this bullshit." Caiden jumped to his feet and came up swinging, landing an uppercut under Gibson's chin, followed by a fierce right hook to the head with all his strength behind it, sending Gibson reeling. Snatching his tactical knife off the floor from where he'd dropped it earlier, he spun low when Gibson charged him, D on his back trying to slow him down. Rolling out of the way, Caiden lunged forward, and plunged the knife into Gibson's thigh.

Releasing a roar, Gibson stumbled but kept going, slamming D against the wall. Trapped between Gibson and the wall, D gasped for air, but refused to let go.

"It's over," D growled at Gibson.

"If I'm going down, I'm taking you with me." Gibson reached into his pocket and pulled out a grenade. Caiden was on him, grabbing his thumb and jerking it. Gibson's howl filled the room as Caiden broke his fingers, the grenade landing at their feet. Caiden kicked it away.

"No fucking way," Caiden snarled. "You're going to pay for all the misery you've caused, you fuck." Maybe he couldn't kill Gibson, but he could sure as hell inflict pain and make him bleed. He pulled a fist to punch Gibson in the solar plexus when Gibson flipped D over his shoulder, sending him flying into Caiden. They hit the floor, and Gibson ran for one of the exits.

"Shit, we can't let him get away," D wheezed as Caiden helped him up. They hurried after Gibson, and Caiden handed D his backup Glock. He tapped his earpiece.

"Anyone have eyes on Gibson?"

Theta's voice came through the line. "He's heading for the silo."

"Copy that." Caiden turned to D. "You—"

"I swear to God, if you tell me to stay here I'm going to—"

Caiden arched an eyebrow at him, and D sighed.

"Going to be miffed at you." He dashed off to one of the mercs out cold on the floor and lifted the guy's leg.

"What the hell are you doing?"

"Go. I'll catch up."

Caiden nodded and darted off into the corridor, rifle in hand as he ran for the silo. The strategically placed floodlights offered some lighting, but there were still too many dark areas and shadows for Caiden's liking. Movement up ahead caught his eyes, and he spotted Gibson running for the hangar. Shit, if Gibson had a getaway vehicle parked in there and got to it first, they were screwed. Caiden wasn't going to let that happen. If Alpha wanted this asshole alive, there was a damned good reason for it.

"Gibson, stop!" Caiden shouted, firing warning rounds that Gibson ignored, disappearing into the shadows of the hangar. Caiden steadied his breathing and calmed his pulse, relying on his training, using stealth to hunt his prey. He wasn't letting Gibson get away, not after what he'd done, the number of people he'd hurt. The hangar was pitch-black in certain places, other parts lit up by the floodlights around the property. Caiden could feel the bastard moving around in the darkness, but there were no signs of any vehicle. Why the hell would Gibson run in here?

"It was you, wasn't it?" Caiden said. "You're the one I was looking for in Vienna. The one my asset was going to turn over evidence against that night."

"You were like a dog with a bone," Gibson growled from within the shadows. "I tried to lead you astray, but you kept coming back to the same fucking bone over and over. I gave you a chance, Caiden."

"*I* was doing my job. How did they get you to turn? Money?"

"Isn't it always about the money?"

"A little bit on the side here, a little bonus to look away there," Caiden said, inching closer in the direction Gibson's voice came from.

"It was easy. They gave me shit-tons of money and perks. I helped them move the chess pieces around, got rid of the competition, helped the elections along. They have a plan, a vision for what they want for their country, same as Uncle Sam."

Yeah, Caiden had opinions on that too. "Let me guess. Once the pieces were in motion, you got in a little over your head, and someone with a bigger chess board decided to make you their pawn."

"As charming as all these analogies are, I really need to get going."

A floodlight flipped on, the blinding light spearing Caiden's vision.

"Shit." He threw an arm up to shield his vision, spots dancing in front of his eyes when a dark object launched itself at him, and he pushed away from the wall but couldn't see a damned thing. Something hard hit the back of his legs, and he fell forward onto his hands and knees. Snatching up the closest thing to him, he swung the piece of metal pipe up, the clang it made against the steel pipe in Gibson's hands resonating around them. Caiden blinked several times, his eyesight clearing as he put all his strength into pushing the metal pipe against Gibson's.

"Cade!"

At D's shout, Gibson swiped his Glock from his holster and fired.

"No!"

D was thrown off his feet, the bullet hitting him in the chest. Caiden kicked at Gibson, his boot slamming into the man's balls. After scrambling to his feet, Caiden tackled him to the ground, swinging the pipe against the side of his head. Gibson stilled, and Caiden checked his pulse. Son of a bitch was still alive, just out for the count. Throwing the pipe to one side, Caiden ran for D, who was sprawled on the ground like a starfish, chest heaving.

"Baby, are you okay?"

"Yeah." D looked down at his chest and the vest that had taken the brunt of the bullet. "Wish I had one of these on the first time around."

Thank fuck. Caiden bent over, his hands on his knees as he tried to catch his breath, his nerves trying to get the better of him at the thought of D getting shot in the chest, *again*. When he could get enough air into his lungs to speak, he tapped his earpiece. "Target down."

"Affirmative. We're on our way," Zed replied.

Caiden helped D to his feet and looked him over. He cupped his face, running a thumb over his jaw. "Are you sure you're okay?"

"I am now," D said, smile warm and dark eyes filled with so much love. "You came."

"Did you really think I wouldn't?"

D shook his head. "I knew you would." His smile was ridiculous. "Because you love me."

"Don't let it go to your head." Caiden's heart did somersaults, but D didn't need to know that.

"Too late. You love me, and you came to rescue me."

Caiden snorted. "Like you needed rescuing."

"It's nice to have backup," D teased. His smile fell away, and Caiden brushed his fingers down D's jaw. "I'm sorry I screwed things up for you." The pain in his eyes was too much, and Caiden kissed him, pouring all his love into his kiss. D's lips were warm, his mouth hot, and he tasted like a thousand Florida sunsets. Actually he tasted a little bit like blood and stank like the Everglades, but Caiden wouldn't change a thing.

"You risked your life to save me. You barely knew me, and you didn't just walk away from a contract, you protected me. Gibson was the one who fucked up. He tried to come between us."

D's smile lit up his face, and Caiden kissed him again, needing to feel him, to know he was alive and safe. When he pulled back, he let his brow rest against D's.

"I love you. I know it's crazy, and things have moved so fast, but… it feels right, doesn't it?" Caiden met D's gaze, those brown eyes warm and fathomless.

"Like you said, baby. I love you, and yeah, it feels right. From the moment I saw you, some part of me knew I'd lose my heart to you. When I realized you were my target, I knew they were wrong about you. I had to do everything in my power to protect you."

Caiden smiled against D's lips. Whoops and catcalls had them breaking apart, and D shook his head. He turned as Zed and the team approached, Harrison with them.

Zed held his hand out to D. "Good to see you alive and causing mischief."

"Come here, asshole." D pulled him into a fierce hug, patting his back. "Thanks, man."

"Of course. We're a family."

"A fucked-up family," Mess chipped in, grin wide. "But a family."

D punched Mess in the shoulder and chuckled. He greeted the rest of the team and stopped in front of Harrison. To Caiden's surprise, D held out his hand.

"Thank you for jumping in there. You're all right, Marine."

"You're one tough son of a bitch," Harrison replied. "Glad I could—"

The punch D landed across Harrison's face was unexpected, and everyone stared dumbstruck.

"Jesus fuck!" Harrison rubbed his jaw. "What the hell was that for?"

D thrust a finger at him, and Harrison took a step back, running into 42, who caught him and steadied him.

"That's for trying to steal my guy."

Harrison threw up his hands. "I didn't even know he was your guy!"

42 took hold of Harrison's chin and inspected his jaw. "You okay, Marine?"

"Yeah," Harrison murmured, blinking at 42. A small smile tugged at the corner of his lips, and it was obvious he liked what he saw. "Thanks."

Judging by the way 42's cheeks flushed, he was okay with Harrison liking what he saw.

Mess leaned in to Harrison, whispering loud enough to be heard in Miami, "You should put some pants on before your little Marine salutes my buddy there."

"Shit." Harrison cupped himself, and the boys laughed. Caiden shook his head at their antics before sidling up close to D.

"To be fair," Caiden murmured, brushing his lips over D's cheek. "I don't think *you* even knew I was your guy."

"Oh, I knew," D said solemnly, turning to bring Caiden into his arms. "Deep in my gut, I knew." He knocked the side of his head. "It just took a little time to get through this thick skull."

"You two are all kinds of fucked-up," Theta offered, slapping them both on the back. He beamed at Caiden. "Welcome to the family."

Caiden opened his mouth to say he wasn't really part of the family, but his heart protested, so he closed his mouth.

"You could be," D said, wrapping an arm around Caiden's waist and pulling him in close. "You could stay."

Would Alpha take him in if he asked? Would D? Was it possible to start a whole new life just like that? "It can't be that easy, can it?"

D's eyes were filled with promise. "What if it is?"

Chapter Sixteen

TALK ABOUT one hell of a night.

"Are you sure you're okay?" Caiden asked, looking him over.

"Yes," D said with a smile. He'd lost track of how many times Caiden had asked him that in the last hour. He'd forgotten how nice it was to be fussed over, to have someone who loved him concerned about his well-being, checking on him, comforting him. Yeah, the comforting was real nice. He liked that. A lot.

"You say that, and yet…." Caiden motioned to D's torso covered in cuts and bruises. "Maybe we need more disinfectant."

D waved his hands. "Oh no. I've suffered enough. I don't need you poking at my wounds with that fiery hell water." His body was in pain, but no more than when Caiden had wiped each and every one of his cuts with those damned little devil pads. If he didn't know any better, he'd say Theta made sure to find the ones that stung the most, on purpose.

With Gibson tied up in the back of Mrs. Brady—who the fuck named their van after a TV mom other than the lunatics he worked with?—and sound asleep, thanks to Theta's nighty-night cocktail, Zed and the team went to secure the rest of Gibson's men for the cleanup crew Alpha had dispatched half an hour ago. D and Caiden stayed to guard Gibson. It was a gorgeous night, all things considered.

Caiden couldn't seem to stop himself from touching D. "I can't believe you just rushed in there like that. What if you hadn't been wearing the vest?"

"Then I wouldn't have rushed in there like that," D said, kissing his cheek. He still would have run in there like that, but Caiden didn't need to know that. When he'd seen Caiden on the floor, Gibson pulling that gun, D had thought of nothing else except saving Caiden. Alpha would have his ass if they found out. D wasn't one to throw caution to the wind like that, but drawing Gibson's attention away from Caiden had been his only thought.

Caiden huffed, and D turned into him, moving his folded arms away from his chest. "You're so cute when you're indignant."

"D," Caiden sighed, his brow creased with worry. "I thought I'd lost you. Again."

D shook his head. "I'm like a cockroach. Not so easy to kill."

"That's… disgusting, and in no way reassuring. Awful. That was awful."

D laughed, bringing Caiden into his arms. "Aw, now who's the grump?"

"Promise me you won't ever do something so rash or stupid again."

"I can't promise you that," D said truthfully. "I can't promise I won't do everything in my power to keep you safe. I'll be careful, think things through better, but don't ask me to lie to you and tell you that I won't do whatever it takes to save you if some asshole like Gibson tries to take you out. I love you, Cade. Is it so unreasonable that I'd want to keep you at my side as long as possible?"

Caiden sighed. "I get it."

Headlights appeared ahead, and D moved away from Caiden to check the car. The driver's window lowered, and D smiled brightly at the driver.

"Hey, Pixie." D held out his hand to the tiny slip of a woman who'd been given the nickname on account of her looking like a sweet little pixie. She was also one hell of a getaway driver and could drive circles around any of them there, including Zed and his guys.

"Hey, D. Staying out of trouble?" She winked at him, and he chuckled. "You got my passengers?"

"Yep." D whistled back at Caiden, who opened the side door of the van. Harrison stepped out, wearing clothes he'd borrowed from Iota, since he was the only one with extra clothes big enough to fit the Marine. He helped Isabella out, one of the guys' jackets wrapped tight around her. They stopped by D, who opened the door for Isabella. "Pixie's going to take you somewhere safe until you can go home." He leaned in to Pixie. "Can I have a card?"

Pixie handed him a tiny black business card with ten blue numbers printed on it. After thanking her, he handed it to Isabella. "If you need anything or don't feel safe at any point, you call that number and my people will answer." He gave her a pointed look, and she nodded, catching him by surprise when she hugged him. He returned her embrace and helped her into the back of the "taxi."

Harrison nodded to D before getting ready to climb in beside her, but then Caiden stopped him.

"Harrison, wait."

Harrison faced Caiden, and D turned away, pretending he wasn't listening to every. Single. Word.

"I'm sorry I had to lead you on. I didn't mean to hurt you."

Harrison sounded tired but not upset. "I understand why you did what you did. I'm just sorry we don't get a second chance. If you ever get tired of the vigilante over there, you look me up."

"Vigilante?" D growled, spinning on his heels.

Harrison chuckled. "See you around, *Lorenzo*." He shut the door behind him, and Pixie gave D a salute, popping her gum before hitting the accelerator. D grabbed Caiden and jerked him behind him, getting out of Pixie's way as she swung the car in the opposite direction, wheels kicking up dust and dirt. She gunned it out of there, taillights fading off into the distance.

Caiden shook his head from beside D. "Alpha sure does recruit some interesting people."

"Amen, brother." D chuckled, heading back to the van as Zed and his boys made their way over.

"Alpha's cleanup crew should be here any minute," Zed called out. "We should get ready to head out."

D walked toward the van, but then he did something drastic—no, *insane*. There was a very real possibility Caiden would tell him to fuck off or even turn and run for the hills, away from the crazy that was D, but he'd take the chance. Whirling around, in the middle of fucking nowhere, dressed in some other dude's combat pants, boots, and T-shirt, he dropped down onto one knee in front of Caiden.

Caiden's eyes all but bugged out of his head as he gaped at D. "What are you doing?"

"Probably the craziest thing I've ever done, and let me tell you, that's saying something. You might not be ready, now or ever, but we almost lost each other, more than once. I have no idea what tomorrow will bring, but if you're by my side, I know I'll survive it. Marry me, Caiden." He took Caiden's hand in his and smiled up at that beautiful face. "I don't have a name to offer you, but I have a slightly bruised heart filled with nothing but respect, admiration, and love for you. Let's brave this wild, wild ride together."

Caiden pulled D up, searched his gaze, then threw his arms around him before slamming his mouth against D's to the shouts and catcalls of Zed and the guys. D really did love those asshats. Caiden kissed D within an inch of his life. When they pulled back, gasping for breath, Caiden cupped D's face, tears in his eyes.

"Yes. I'll marry you, D. Who else is going to keep you out of trouble?"

"I know I can be—wait, what?" D blinked at him. "Did you say yes?" A part of him had been bracing for the gentle rejection. His eyes widened. "Holy shit, you said yes!" He whooped loud, wrapped Caiden in his arms, and kissed him.

"Okay, lovebirds, time to go," Zed announced, forcing D and Caiden to come up for air.

Holy shit. D still couldn't believe it, but judging by the dopey grin on Caiden's face and his dreamy sigh, D hadn't imagined it. They climbed into the van, the rest of the guys shoving and tripping one another to get in, leaving Mess out.

"Oh, fuck you all. I gotta ride with the bad guy? What the hell. That's so not safe, Zed!"

"There's a seat belt," Theta said helpfully.

Mess flipped him off and stormed off to the rear of the van, the guys mercilessly taunting him. As soon as everyone had their seat belts on, they were off. D sat by the window with Caiden tucked beside him, his arm around Caiden. They were ridiculous on the ride back, kissing, murmuring at each other. D had never had that before. The intimacy, the lightheartedness, the way he could drown out everyone and everything around him, it was only them. D was so comfortable, surrounded by men he knew would have his back and the man he loved at his side, that he eventually fell asleep without a second thought. He hadn't even tried to stay awake. He gave in to the exhaustion and let himself go.

When he woke, they were outside the Locke and Keyes Agency. Apparently while he'd been asleep, they'd dropped Gibson off at the designated safe house before heading home to St. Pete's. They'd stopped at a few safe places along the way, and apparently D had even gotten out of the van with Caiden to pee and stretch his legs. He recalled jack shit, but knowing Caiden was at his side, he didn't care.

Upstairs, he and Caiden showered, and for the first time in forty-eight hours, he felt human again. They changed into some clean clothes, but not before Caiden fussed over him some more and tried to burn him alive with those damned wipes. Dressed and comfortable, they headed for the meeting room for a debriefing.

"Have you thought about Alpha's job offer?" Something else D had missed while asleep in the van.

They made a good team, a great one, according to Alpha. Not long after the idea of having Caiden brought in as a permanent member of Locke and Keyes formed in his head, Alpha had made the offer on the drive from Homestead.

Had it been Alpha's intention all along? Alpha was pretty sneaky that way. In fact, there was a whole lot D didn't know about Alpha. Hell, Zed had been working with Alpha far longer than D, and even he didn't know much about Alpha. D had no idea how long this op had been running before he was saved two years ago, but in that time, they had slowly been growing. First Zed and his team, then Si, D, and soon Caiden.

D turned to Caiden, walking him back to the large table until Caiden was against it. He positioned himself between Caiden's legs, his hands on Caiden's waist. The rest of the crew would be along shortly, but they had a few minutes before the crazy that was their little makeshift family showed up. The last forty-eight hours had been a whirlwind of activity and life-altering moments. The most important of those moments stood in his arms, pretending to give considerable thought to D's question.

"Hm, let me see." Caiden put a finger to his lips. "Do I want to become a permanent member of the Locke and Keyes Agency, which is really a black op where I get to be out in the field exposing scumbags like Gibson, and move to sunny Florida to live with my sexy new fiancé? Or do I want to return to my dinky apartment, otherwise known as 'the place where technology goes to die,' and spend my days stuck behind a desk monitoring endless media feeds?"

D sighed, loving the mischief in Caiden's green eyes. "Yeah, tough choice. I can see that."

"I mean, I'd be giving up my 401K."

"There is that," D said with a husky chuckle. He kissed a trail up Caiden's neck.

"There's the hazard pay, which would make up for it."

D nipped at Caiden's jaw, his stubble sending a shiver through D. So fucking sexy. "Maybe I can help you weigh your options?"

"What did you have in mind?"

"How about a list," D murmured, kissing his way up Caiden's jaw to his ear. "Con. I snore."

"Pro. They're cute little snores." Caiden slipped his hands under the hem of D's shirt. "I also get to wake up in your arms every morning."

"Con. I'm going to be all clingy and possessive on account of never being able to get enough of you." He nipped at Caiden's earlobe, his hands roaming across Caiden's lean torso, over the muscles of his abs, his skin soft beneath D's rough fingers.

"Pro. You can cook."

D smiled at that. He loved cooking for Caiden. "Con. I have an insatiable appetite when it comes to you. It's going to be sex, sex, sex all the time."

Caiden's groan went straight to D's dick. "Pro. You have an insatiable appetite when it comes to me, and it's going to be sex, sex, sex all the time."

D chuckled. "Con. Gators."

"Pro. I'll have someone to throw in front of me should I come across a gator."

"Wow. I see where our love stands."

"Yep, between me and the gator." Caiden motioned to D where he stood, and where the imaginary gator behind D would be.

D barked out a laugh. God, he loved this man. Loved everything about him. His sense of humor, the way he mumbled whole conversations to himself when he didn't think anyone was watching, how he looked at D as if he were the most amazing, precious man he'd ever known, like he was *lucky* to have D, when it was the other way around.

Caiden wrapped his arms around D, brushing his lips over D's. "Pro. I love you and will go wherever you go. Even if there are prehistoric reptiles."

"So that's a yes?" D asked, not leaving anything to chance.

"On one condition," Caiden said, putting a finger to D's lips to stop him from kissing Caiden. "From this moment on, no secrets. We'll be dealing with enough of those on the job. I want complete transparency between us. No one gets kept in the dark."

D smiled, and Caiden eyed him. With a chuckle, he kissed Caiden's finger before gently moving it away. "Deal. Kiss on it?"

"Deal." Caiden pressed his lips to D's, and D opened up for him, moaning at the taste of Caiden on his tongue. He couldn't wait to have Caiden in his bed every night, to wake up to his man curled around him like he was afraid D might slip away if he didn't. To have Caiden at his side while on a job.

"Ugh, don't you two ever come up for air?"

D flipped off the snarky little shit as he pulled away from Caiden. "Cade, this pain in the ass is Si, short for Epsilon, but you already knew that. Si, this is Caiden Cardosa."

"I know who he is," Si said, taking Caiden's hand in his for a shake. His smile reached his big gray eyes. "I'm the guy who vetted him for Alpha."

Caiden frowned. "Vetted me?"

Si nodded. "Alpha wanted you on the team. It was my job to see whether you'd be a good fit for Locke and Keyes. Once my research was concluded, I deduced you guys would either kill each other or fuck." He leaned into Caiden. "Considering D was supposed to have put a bullet in you in Vienna and sacrificed himself to protect you, I was betting on the latter."

"So this mission was what? A test?" Caiden asked.

"Call it an interview," Si replied, shoving his hands into his pockets.

Caiden eyed Si, and D chuckled. "Don't let his size fool you. He's a whole lot of trouble in a pocket-size package, with a mouth to match."

Si flipped him off, and D laughed. Epsilon was the youngest of their trio, and the smallest. He looked like a preppy college kid rather than the thirty-something-year-old he was, with a mess of dirty-blond hair, big gray eyes, trendy glasses, pouty lips, and soft features.

"Aw, but he looks like a kitten," Caiden teased.

Si narrowed his eyes, and D stepped in front of Caiden, his hands up in front of him. "Give him a break. He's new around here. Please."

With a grunt, Si pushed his glasses up his nose. "Fine. He gets *one*." Si spun on his heels and headed for the fridge. D turned to Caiden, who looked amused.

"Crisis averted."

"What was that about?"

"Like I said, don't let his size fool you. He might look like a kitten, but the guy is an evil mastermind. He was recruited by the NSA straight out of college."

Caiden cocked his head to one side. "Analyst, right?"

"Yeah, but he is the snarkiest, most evil motherfucker you will ever meet. He never forgets, and he *will* make you pay. Bitch will tear you to pieces, I'm not kidding. Just ask Mess. He made the mistake of telling Si he didn't want to spar with him during one session because he didn't want to hurt him. It did not go well." D's eyes widened at the memory. "When Mess next went out on a mission, he had no bullets. Like, none. Si had taken them all. Mess only discovered it when he went to fire his rifle and nothing happened."

Caiden stared at him. "Holy shit. He could have gotten killed. I bet Zed was pissed."

"Yeah, he was. At Mess. They're supposed to check their gear before and after every mission. As far as Zed was concerned, Mess fucked up. Don't worry, the guy can improvise like no one you've ever known, and Si knew that. He'd never do anything that would result in one of us getting killed." He pursed his lips. "Hurt, maybe. In pain, definitely, but not killed."

"Don't piss off the kitten. Got it."

D chuckled. "Come on. The guys will be here any minute." He pulled Caiden's chair out for him.

Si put a hand to his heart from across the table where he sat. "Aw, look at you being all chivalrous instead of grunting and pounding your chest. It's like watching Jane Porter trying to teach Tarzan how to be more civilized."

"Fuck off," D grumbled, taking his seat and ignoring Si's cackle.

The door opened, and in walked Becky with her bouncing ponytail and pink cashmere sweater. Today's nail polish was white with pink sparkles. D inhaled a deep breath, groaning at the trays of freshly baked pastries sitting neatly on the shelves of the dessert cart

Becky wheeled in. No matter what the meeting was about, D always looked forward to it because of the food. They said the way to a man's heart was through his stomach. Truer words could not have been spoken about the Locke and Keyes crew, and Alpha seemed to know it, because every meeting was catered with delicious, mouthwatering treats.

"That smells so good," Caiden said, leaning so far forward he would have fallen over had D not caught his chair.

"Thanks, babe."

D chuckled. "Don't blame you."

Becky lined the trays of pastries—everything from bear claws to pastelitos—on the meeting table. She'd just finished placing the last one when David wheeled in a second trolley.

"That's a lot of baked goods," Caiden said.

"You won't think so when Zed and his horde descend," Si said with a snicker.

"Thanks, Becky," Caiden said, smiling.

"You're welcome." She winked at him as she headed for the door with her husband. "And welcome to the family."

The noise level suddenly increased outside, and Si rolled his eyes. "Here comes the horde."

Just as he said the words, the door opened and the team flooded in, Zed at the head of the group like always, the rest of his rowdy crew close behind. They greeted Caiden, with Mess darting over to fist-bump him. Caiden chuckled and shook his head at his antics. The team sat around the large table, 42 sitting next to Si. The two were close, banding together in a unified short-guy front.

Mess walked by Si, ruffling his hair on the way.

"I haven't had nearly enough coffee to deal with your shit, Mess," Si grumbled, getting up. He looked over at Caiden. "Do you want me to get you a coffee—"

Zed and his team jumped from their chairs, startling poor Caiden.

"No." Mess shook his head fervently. "Do not let the coffee jinx near the machine. If he touches it, it'll die."

Si flipped Mess off. "Shut up."

"It's true," Zed said, eyes wide. "Anytime Si touches a coffee machine, he sentences it to death."

Caiden smiled up at Si. "Oh, so like me and printers."

"It's okay, buddy," 42 told Si, taking his arm and patting his shoulder as he guided Si back down into his chair. "I'll grab you and Caiden some coffee." He stood and grinned at Caiden. "How do you take your coffee?"

Caiden put in his order, along with everyone else before 42 told the others to get their own damn coffees.

"Hey, do you think I'll get a cool nickname?" Caiden asked D.

"You can be Alpha's Omega," Theta teased.

D barked out a laugh at Caiden's scandalized expression.

"What? Omega? I'm not an omega."

Everyone laughed at Caiden's pout, and he flipped them all off. "What about the other three Orion stars?"

"Those are taken," Alpha said, the black screen coming to life and the familiar blue sound wave moving with their voice. "I'm certain we can come up with something appropriate. In the meantime, I'm sure you've all been wondering why I asked that Ryan Gibson be brought in alive. I've been gathering intel on Gibson's operation for years but had been unsuccessful in discovering his identity until now. Without knowing it was Gibson, the intel I'd collected simply provided pieces of a puzzle. Now that we know who he is, I can confirm that Gibson is part of a much bigger conspiracy.

"The evidence on Graves's main drive didn't merely prove Gibson's guilt on countless cases of wrongdoing across the globe against a number of governments, but contained a very important piece of information: the address to a secret black site containing vital intel that could lead us to whoever was pulling Gibson's string. Whoever this person is—now referred to in communications as M87—they're high up in the food chain, and much like the black hole they're named after, they seem to suck in and destroy everything around them. This conspiracy is one of our greatest missions yet, but it will take time. Si, I'll be bringing you in on this. Are you up to it?"

"You bet," Si replied, his eyes twinkling with glee like they did anytime Alpha brought him in on some nerdy intel job.

"As you can imagine, with Graves losing both the key and the catalog, it was necessary for him to disappear before his clients got wind of what happened. Isabella did not take the news of her husband's side career well. She wanted out of the criminal life, and discovering Kenneth was leading the exact kind of double life she'd left her family to avoid, she is filing for divorce. She is on a plane headed to Hawaii. We know Graves flew to Spain, and that's the last intel we have on him."

"What happened to the catalog?" Caiden asked.

"Those who are innocent of wrongdoing will have their files deleted permanently. Those who've committed heinous crimes will have the evidence turned in to the police. The courts can take it from there. In other news, I'm adding an independent contractor."

The screen flashed to a profile with the image of an all-too-familiar face.

"You've got to be fucking kidding," D said, staring at the man's stupid, handsome face.

"Is that… Harrison?" Zed asked.

"Yes," Alpha confirmed. "I've had 42 doing recon work on Harrison for months now."

Everyone turned their gazes to 42, D frowning at him. "Wait, you knew about Harrison?"

42 side-eyed him. "Like Alpha said, he was a recon mission."

D didn't bother asking why he hadn't known. Alpha had their reasons for everything, picking up puzzle pieces with every mission and fitting them into place, but D had no idea what the bigger picture was. His guess was it had to do with M87.

"Harrison Caveley has been apprised of his previous employer's double life, and to say Harrison was not happy would be an understatement. He'd been hired under false pretenses, his confidence betrayed. Harrison had no idea he was working for a criminal. After much intel gathering and a discussion with Mr. Caveley, I've decided to bring him in, so expect to see more of him."

"Fuck me," D groaned as the guys laughed and teased. Caiden patted D's knee with a chuckle while D promptly told the rest of them to go fuck themselves. *Jerks.*

"I know he's not your favorite person, D," Alpha said.

Was that amusement in Alpha's tone? D could have sworn it was amusement.

"Harrison Caveley has a host of skills that would be beneficial to Operation Alpha Orion. The man did not leave the military on good terms; however, his story is not mine to tell. Mr. Caveley—Harrison—has been wronged. He's eager to get started with Locke and Keyes and prove his worth. I believe he'll make a valuable asset to this team. However, I know trust must be earned, so 42 will be Harrison's handler until that trust happens."

Everyone turned their gazes to 42.

"What?"

Mess waggled his eyebrows. "Didn't know you had a daddy kink."

"Fuck you," 42 spat out, folding his arms over his chest.

They all burst into laughter, and D slipped his hand into Caiden's. The look he received was one he would never forget. No matter where they were or what happened, no matter the darkness they fell into, the pain, or heartache, D knew he would think back to this moment and the look of sheer adoration in Caiden's bright green eyes. The look of a man who trusted him completely, with his life, and more importantly, his heart.

Chapter Seventeen

Six months later.

PARADISE.

In his travels across the globe, D had experienced all manner of luxury and finery, but nothing ever truly felt like paradise the way this moment did right here, and certainly nothing had stolen his breath away like the stunning blond emerging from the turquoise waters of the private beach. The summer breeze ruffled D's open white linen shirt as he stood in the doorway of the bungalow, and his heart beat wildly. He removed his hand from his pants and held it up to shield his eyes from the sun as he lifted his face to the cloudless sky, smiling at the black band on his ring finger.

How had he gone from being on his own, working solo and finding pleasure in any sexy person willing and able, to this? The secluded island offered warm clear waters, a wooden deck behind a bungalow hidden among lush greenery and swaying palms, and nothing but ocean for miles and miles. It would have been easy to pretend they were in some faraway tropical hideout and not still in Florida.

Soft music floated up from the speakers inside the bungalow as Caiden wiped the water from his face and pushed back his hair. He stopped to lift his face to the sky, his eyes closed, and D drank his fill of all that sleek muscle glistening in the hot sun, Caiden's blue boxer-briefs with pink palm trees molding to his beautiful body. His skin had tanned from days spent outside, sipping cocktails, swimming, and making love beneath the Florida sun. As if feeling D's gaze on him, Caiden shielded his eyes from the light and gave D that open, wide smile that stole D's breath away each and every time.

"Hey, gorgeous," Caiden said, reaching him and stepping inside. He hummed when D brought him into his arms.

"Me?" D shook his head. "No, sir." He ran his fingers up Caiden's spine, loving the way Caiden shivered in his embrace. "Not when you're around."

"Such a charmer," Caiden murmured, leaning in for a kiss. When they came up for air, Caiden turned in his arms so they could gaze out at the breathtaking view. D let his chin rest on Caiden's shoulder. They swayed with the music, slow and peaceful.

"What do you think? It's no Vienna, but on the plus side, less chance of someone trying to kill us."

"It's perfect," Caiden said softly. "I had no idea you were such a romantic."

"That's me, all fucking romantic and shit."

Caiden threw his head back and laughed. "I wouldn't change a thing." He turned around, slipping his hands beneath D's open shirt around to his back before moving low to his ass.

D moaned, bucking his hips instinctively. He murmured in Caiden's ear, "I want to feel you inside me."

Caiden pulled away enough to meet his gaze. "Yeah?"

"Yes."

D laughed at Caiden's enthusiasm as he darted off, sprinted over to the king-size bed, and bounced off to land by the nightstand, where he grabbed the bottle of lube. He turned and waggled his eyebrows. "I'm ready."

With a chuckle, D rounded the bed, plucked the lube from him, and tossed it onto the mattress. He took hold of the waistband of Caiden's bathing suit and brought it down his legs, then lowered himself to his knees. He inhaled deeply, closing his eyes as the scent of beach, coconut lotion, and Caiden filled his senses.

Caiden stepped out of his wet bathing shorts, and D tossed them out of the way before reverently running his hands up Caiden's legs, appreciating every inch of him, worshipping, because Caiden deserved no less. Replacing his roaming hands with his lips, D kissed his way across Caiden's hipbone, one hand coming to rest on Caiden's slender waist as D brought Caiden's leaking cock to his mouth. He darted his tongue out, lapping up the pearls of precome, loving the way Caiden bucked his hips in response, a low hiss escaping him.

D worked his tongue in Caiden's slit, smiling when Caiden slipped his fingers into D's hair, taking hold of it like he always did when they had sex. He swallowed Caiden down to the root, enjoying Caiden's soft expletives as D worked him over, hollowing his cheeks and sucking hard. Caiden's grip on his hair tightened, and

D's dick strained against his slacks as he twirled his tongue around the head of Caiden's cock.

"Stop. Baby, stop," Caiden pleaded.

D popped off him and lifted his face, his heart skipping a beat at the inferno of want in Caiden's green eyes. He traced D's bottom lip with his thumb. "Get on the bed," Caiden ordered quietly.

D scrambled to do as he was told, climbing onto the mattress and lying on his back, his hands behind his head, fingers laced, and ankles crossed as he winked at Caiden. "I'm all yours, baby. Come get me."

With a playful growl, Caiden climbed the bed, making quick work of tugging D's pants off. D had been going commando since their first day in their private paradise.

"Sit up," Caiden said. D obliged as Caiden straddled his hips and pushed the shirt off D's shoulders, his mouth on D's, tongue pushing for entrance that D quickly gave. Tossing D's shirt somewhere behind him, Caiden continued to maul D's mouth, his hands on D's face. Tasting the ocean on Caiden's tongue, D slipped his hands over Caiden's waist to his ass, the cool breeze caressing their skin.

Coming up for air, D groaned as Caiden slid down his body until he was on his stomach in between D's legs. "Spread your legs for me, baby."

Fuck, Caiden was going to kill him. D spread his legs wide and brought his knees up.

"Mm, there's that pretty hole."

Oh, he was a dead man. D let his head fall back against the pillow, his chest rising and falling in rapid pants as Caiden ran his hands up D's inner thighs, teasing, taunting. Caiden flicked out a tongue, and D shivered from head to toe. He grabbed fistfuls of the bedsheets as Caiden licked, nipped, and swirled his tongue around D's entrance before a wet finger slipped inside. D cursed and forced himself to look down at Caiden, his breath hitching at the love and need in Caiden's eyes.

"I don't know if I ever thanked you for what you did," Caiden said. "But thank you. For saving my life."

D swallowed hard, his lips lifting in a teasing smile. "How about thanking me with your fingers."

Caiden's grin was sinful. He used D's precome to ease the friction as he pumped D's cock while fucking him with his finger. The scene was glorious and had D writhing on the bed, his entire body buzzing with jolts of pleasure. Sweat beaded his brow, and he groaned.

"Baby, please."

Caiden pulled out, and D immediately mourned the loss, but Caiden didn't make him wait long. He placed a pillow under D's hips, then knelt between his legs, and brought D's legs up and over his shoulders. He lined himself up with D's hole, his thick rosy-tipped cock dripping. Slowly, carefully, Caiden pushed inside him, past the ring of muscles. D gasped and gritted his teeth against the pain until it gave way to pure pleasure.

"Oh God, Cade." D threw his head back against the pillow, his body arching up off the bed. He was so full. Having Caiden inside him was amazing, perfect.

Then Caiden started to move. A growl rumbled up through his chest and out of his mouth.

"Yes!"

Caiden rolled his hips, his hands on D's thighs as he pulled almost all the way out before slowly burying himself balls-deep again. Needing his mouth on Caiden's, D reached for him, and Caiden bent over him, pressing his body to D's as he kissed his way up D's neck to his jaw. The scent of the ocean swirled around them along with the tropical breeze, and the rustling leaves of the palm trees mixed with the sound of their panting breaths as they moved together.

Caiden laced their fingers together and brought D's hands up by his head. He pressed his lips to D's, his tongue seeking entrance. Their tongues tangled, breath mingling as their bodies moved as one, limbs tangled, holding on to each other, the cool breeze feeling delicious across their sweat-slicked skin.

"Fuck, you feel so good," Caiden murmured against D's lips.

D wrapped his arms around Caiden, holding him close, legs around Caiden's waist as Caiden plunged into him.

"Yes. Please, Cade."

Caiden pushed himself onto his hands so he could look into D's eyes as he thrust into D over and over, D's leaking cock trapped between their bodies. Caiden alternated between rocking into him and snapping his hips.

"Fuck, baby." Caiden picked up his pace, the deep hard thrusts curling D's toes. D urged Caiden on, whispering filthy words of encouragement, his body on fire as Caiden thrust wildly, the bed moving beneath them, the sound of flesh hitting flesh mixed with their pleas and curses. D slipped his hand between them, palming his cock, his strokes matching Caiden's pace.

"I'm gonna come," Caiden said with a gasp, and D nodded fervently.

"Please. Come inside me, Cade. I want to feel your come dripping down my thighs."

"Oh fuck!" Caiden drove himself in and out, his teeth gritted, muscles tense as he sucked in a sharp breath. “Oh God, D!” Caiden plunged deep inside him, heat filling D and sending him over the edge, D’s orgasm plowing through him, sending him spiraling into an abyss of pleasure. He roared out Caiden’s name as he milked every last drop out of his cock, Caiden thrusting in short, quick movements until he was too sensitive, then gently pulled out. Come dripped out of D, and Caiden groaned, slipping his fingers between D’s crease. “You’re so damned sexy.”

D could only hum his response. He was too blissed-out to do anything other than breathe and smile as Caiden collapsed onto the bed beside him. D hadn’t known what came over him when he’d proposed.

“What are you thinking about?” Caiden hummed.

“I’m thinking I can’t believe we’re on our honeymoon. It’s crazy, isn’t it?”

Caiden’s smile was radiant. “Which is why it makes perfect sense. Nothing about who we are, what we are together, is ordinary, D, and I wouldn’t want it any other way.”

D had worried about the marriage license and how the name on it wasn’t his but a legend Alpha had created for him—an unassuming guy who Caiden had met while on vacation in Florida. With one sentence, Caiden had blown all of D’s misgivings out of the water.

“It doesn’t matter what name was on there before. What matters is what that name becomes.”

Álvaro Cardosa had a certain ring to it.

“I’ve had more sex in the past week than I’ve had my whole life. I’m surprised my dick hasn’t fallen off.” Caiden smiled contentedly.

“The more you use it, the stronger it becomes,” D said. “True fact.”

Caiden turned to blink at him before bursting into laughter.

"What? It's true."

"You're such a dork." Caiden snickered. He forced himself off the bed, and D groaned. "Come on."

"Can't we nap?" D asked, his body feeling heavy, like he could sink into the mattress.

"Nap later. Let's go."

"Fine." D rolled out of bed, grabbed Caiden, and lifted him off his feet, laughing at his flailing limbs and curses.

"What are you doing!"

"Walking you over the threshold." D carried Caiden outside the bungalow.

"Aren't you supposed to do that in your home?"

"This is better," D said, crossing the deck and down the walkway that led to their little slice of private beach. He walked into the water, and Caiden eyed him.

"D, if you're thinking what I think you're thinking, you—" The rest of Caiden's words turned into a shriek as D hurled him into the water. He laughed when Caiden came up sputtering, hair plastered over his face.

"Mm, so sexy," D teased. "I particularly liked your starfish impression before you hit the water."

Caiden laughed. "You're such a dick."

D waded out to Caiden and popped a kiss on his lips. "Yeah, but I'm your dick."

Caiden cupped D beneath the water. "No, *this* is my dick."

"So possessive," D growled, nipping at his chin. "So very much mine." His smile faltered for a moment, and he ran his thumb over Caiden's bottom lip. "Are you sure this is what you wanted?"

"This, you, it's everything I didn't know I wanted." Something seemed to occur to Caiden, and D cocked his head.

"What is it?"

"I was just thinking about what Alpha said to me when they called me that day in Virginia. They said they were someone who could give me what I wanted. At the time, I thought it was answers about my career. For so long, that had been my only dream. Now I have to wonder if it was you. If Alpha had been offering me what I hadn't even known I wanted."

D pulled Caiden in close, unable to get enough of touching him, of having him in his arms. "It's possible," he said. And it was. They trusted Alpha but still knew very little about the person behind the voice, what their motivation was. Alpha took care of D, Caiden, Zed, Si, and the team. They had a fierce sense of justice, never taking anything from any of the criminals they exposed. The only payment Alpha seemed interested in was the one that came with a swift court ruling. Justice wasn't carried out by Locke and Keyes, not directly. They exposed secrets, made sure those who thought themselves above the law, above decency and humanity, paid for their crimes, made certain they faced the consequences of their actions. Sometimes the guilty chose to take their own way out, unwilling to face prison, but that was on them.

D believed in what he was doing. Gibson had tried to kill Caiden to further his agenda. He'd almost killed D in the process as well. How many more Gibsons were out there hurting innocent people? The list of crimes committed by Gibson and those he worked for was extensive, the casualty list overwhelming. D wasn't about to let monsters like Gibson, Jerry, and anyone else who came along get away with it. They'd gotten away with it long enough. No amount of money or government power was going to protect these people from them.

"You have your serious face on," Caiden teased, easing the worry lines from D's brow. "How about we shower, take a little stroll, and then come back for some dinner and a little more newlywed shenanigans."

D laughed. "God, I love you."

"I love you too."

They headed inside, took a quick shower, and dressed in their tuxedos for the charity dinner they were attending. D tucked his gun with suppressor into the holster inside his tuxedo jacket.

"Ready to go to work?"

Caiden laced his fingers with D's, the hand holding his SIG suppressor raised, and his loving smile on D.

"With you? Always."

KEEP READING FOR AN EXCERPT FROM

THIRDS: Book One

When homicide detective Dexter J. Daley's testimony helps send his partner away for murder, the consequences—and the media frenzy—aren't far behind. He soon finds himself sans boyfriend, sans friends, and, after an unpleasant encounter in a parking garage after the trial, he's lucky he doesn't find himself sans teeth. Dex fears he'll get transferred from the Human Police Force's Sixth Precinct, or worse, get dismissed. Instead, his adoptive father—a sergeant at the Therian-Human Intelligence Recon Defense Squadron otherwise known as the THIRDS—pulls a few strings, and Dex gets recruited as a Defense Agent.

Dex is determined to get his life back on track and eager to get started in his new job. But his first meeting with Team Leader Sloane Brodie, who also happens to be his new jaguar Therian partner, turns disastrous. When the team is called to investigate the murders of three HumaniTherian activists, it soon becomes clear to Dex that getting his partner and the rest of the tightknit team to accept him will be a lot harder than catching the killer—and every bit as dangerous.

Chapter 1

FUCK. MY. Life.

Dex closed his eyes, wishing this was nothing more than some freakishly vivid dream where any moment now he would wake up and everything would go back to the way it was. Of course, when he opened his eyes, nothing changed. He splashed more water on his face in an effort to ease the tension, but it didn't help. Not that he'd been expecting it to. After wiping the excess water from his face, he paused to glare at the man in the mirror. The guy staring back at him looked like shit, pale with reddish-brown circles under his eyes that made him look as if he'd either been crying or using crack. There were definitely a hell of a lot of sleepless nights involved. Dex didn't like the guy in the mirror. What an asshole.

"Are they out there?" His voice came out rough, as if waking from sleep—deep or otherwise—had been out of his reach for some time.

A hand landed on his shoulder, offering a sympathetic squeeze. "Yes. Remember what we talked about? As soon as you've had enough, you walk away."

Dex let out a snort. It was way too late to walk away. Had been about six months ago. He straightened and snatched a paper towel from the automated dispenser. It was like drying off with newspaper, the same newspapers that had his image plastered all over their pages. Images that had been run through some Photoshop douchebag filter to make him look like even more of a prick. He chucked the paper into the wastebasket and stood there, finding it difficult to face his lawyer.

"Hey, look at me." Littman stepped up to him and patted his cheek. "You did the right thing."

Dex looked up then, searching for something, anything that might help the pain go away, even for a little while. "Then why do I feel like shit?"

"Because he was your friend, Dex."

"Exactly. And I fucked him over. Some friend." He went back to leaning over the sink, his fingers gripping the porcelain so tightly his knuckles hurt. "Goddamn it!" That son of a bitch! What the hell had Walsh been thinking? Obviously he hadn't been, or neither of them would be in this mess. Or worse, maybe Walsh *had* thought it through. Maybe he'd been so certain Dex would have his back that he thought *fuck it*.

Dex closed his eyes, trying to get the man's face out of his mind, but he could still see it clearly. That face was going to haunt his dreams for a long time coming. The mixture of anger and pain when the verdict had been given—anger directed at Dex, and pain brought about by what he'd done—had been there for the world to see, especially Dex.

"No," Littman insisted. "He fucked himself over. All you did was tell the truth."

The truth. How could doing the right thing turn out so goddamn bad? Had it even been the right thing? It had seemed like it at the time. Now he wasn't so sure. Regardless, he couldn't hide out in the restroom all his life.

"Let's get this over with." A few deep breaths and he followed Littman out into the corridor. The moment he stepped foot out there, the locusts swarmed him, microphones buzzing, recorders and smartphones at the ready, flashes going off, cameras rolling, a litany of questions flying at him from every direction. It was as if he were underwater, hearing everyone outside the pool yelling and screaming as he sank to the bottom like a stone, no discernible words, only muffled sounds. Littman stepped up beside him, one hand behind Dex's back in assurance, the other held up to the crowd in a vain attempt to bring order to chaos.

"Detective Daley will do his best to answer your questions, but one at a time, please!"

A tall gray-haired man in an expensive suit pushed through his gathered comrades, ignoring their murmured grunts of displeasure, to place a microphone in front of Dex. A half a dozen more swiftly joined it.

"Detective Daley, what would you say to all the Humans who believe you betrayed your own kind?"

At least he'd been prepared for that one. Dex buttoned up his suit jacket, the gesture allowing him a few seconds to calm his nerves and collect his thoughts. Smoothing it down, he met the reporter's gaze. "I joined the Human Police Force to make a difference, and sometimes that requires making tough calls. I chose to tell the truth. No one is above the law, and my job is to enforce it."

A blonde woman in a tailored navy blue pantsuit swiftly jumped in. "Is it because your brother is Therian? Are you a LiberTherian sympathizer?"

It was hardly the first time he'd been accused of such. Having a Therian brother was the sole reason the Human Police Force had taken longer than necessary to consider him when he'd applied ten years ago. If his father hadn't been a respected detective on the force, Dex was certain he never would've been considered, much less hired. Knowing what they thought of his brother should have been enough to make him walk away, but it was those same close-minded individuals Dex had wanted to reach. That was why he'd joined the HPF, to continue making a difference from the inside, like his dad once had. It turned out to be a whole lot harder than he'd imagined, but that only succeeded in strengthening his resolve.

"My brother and I share the same beliefs when it comes to justice. Our fathers taught us to treat both Therians and Humans as equals. I may be liberal-minded, but my strong belief in justice for both species hardly makes me a sympathizer."

An auburn-haired man with a shit-eating grin shoved his smartphone in Dex's face, almost hitting him in the teeth. His expression told Dex he didn't much care if he had. Dex calmly pulled back, his jaw muscles tightening. "Detective Daley, why haven't you joined your father and brother over at the THIRDS? Is it because you didn't qualify?"

Dex returned the asshole's grin. "Whatever you're paying your sources, it's too much. I never applied to the THIRDS."

"But you did go through their training."

"I was offered the opportunity to take the three-week training course in the hopes I might reconsider becoming a candidate. I complied as a courtesy to my family, and I admit, a part of me wanted to know if I was up to the challenge." And damn, had it been one hell of a challenge! Three weeks of intense physical training and skill-building exercises, rappelling, fast roping, room entry procedures, building searches, close-quarter combat, and tactical weapons training. Dex had been pushed to his limits, and when he thought he couldn't give any more, he was forced to reach deep down and give an additional 10 percent. It had been the most grueling, demanding, psychologically stressful three weeks of his life. Nothing he'd ever done had come close to what he'd been put through in those three weeks, not even the HPF training academy.

The THIRDS were the toughest sons of bitches around, and Dex had wanted to prove to himself that he could hack it. But join them? That was something else altogether.

"Did you pass?"

Dex couldn't help his pride from showing. "Top of the class."

"Will you be applying now?" another journalist asked.

"I intend to continue offering my services to the HPF."

"What if they don't want you? Do you think they've lost their trust in you, knowing you helped send a good man, one of their own brothers, to prison?"

And there it was.

Dex turned his head to whisper Littman's name. His lawyer smiled broadly and held a hand up. "Thank you all for coming. I'm afraid that's all Detective Daley has time for. Please respect him and his family during this difficult time."

"What about Detective Walsh and his family? Have you spoken to them? How does his family feel about what you did?"

Dex waded through the toxic pool of newspersons, refusing to think about the hurtful and hateful phone calls, texts, and messages from Walsh's family. People he'd once had barbecues with, whose Little League games he'd attended. He'd never wanted to bring them so much pain, to take away their son, husband, father. Being on the receiving end of their anger was the least Dex deserved.

"Detective Daley! Detective!"

He ignored the onslaught of questions, from what his boyfriend thought about the whole thing to whether his career with the HPF was unofficially over, and everything in between. He wasn't going to think about any of that now. All he wanted was to get home to said boyfriend and maybe cry a little.

Dex walked as fast, but calmly, as he could, with Littman at his side, making a beeline for the north entrance of the Supreme Court Criminal Branch. Outside, the news teams tried to crowd him in, and officers did their best to control the growing mob. The railings on either side of the exit only proved to be a nuisance, corralling him as he tried to push his way through. The steps were blocked, so Dex grabbed Littman's elbow and hurried him down the makeshift ramp to the sidewalk. Thank God they had a car waiting for them.

Dex tried to be nice about getting the journalists to step back so he could get into the back seat. When a couple of jerks tried to cram in, Dex was left with no choice. He grabbed their smartphones and tossed them into the crowd behind them.

"You're going to pay for that!" one of them called out as he scrambled to retrieve his device.

"Bill me!" Dex climbed into the car and slammed the door behind him. The town car pulled away from the curb, and he slumped back against the pristine leather, letting out a long audible breath. Finally, it was over. For the time being anyway.

"You sure you don't want to be dropped off at home?" Littman looked nearly as haggard as Dex felt.

"Nah, the parking garage is fine. I need to drop off the rental anyway."

"You know I would've been happy to pick you up at your home and drop you off."

"I know." Dex stared out the window as they drove up Centre Street, made a left on White, and then drove down Lafayette. When they made a right onto Worth, the Starbucks on the corner had him pining for some frothy caffeine goodness. "I needed to drive around a while before court. Listen to some music, try to relax a little." He'd made sure to rent a car with the darkest tinted windows on the lot and a slamming sound system. Music was probably the only thing that had kept him from going crazy through this whole ordeal, what with his boyfriend's busy schedule. It would have been nice to have Lou there with him, but he understood the man couldn't drop everything for him. They both had demanding careers and sometimes sacrifices had to be made. Still….

"I understand. You should lay low for a while until this blows over. There's talk of that heiress—the one who's been having a not-so-secret affair with her Therian personal trainer—being pregnant, and Daddy's not taking it well. That should keep the vultures busy for a while. I suggest you take some vacation time, maybe surprise Lou with a nice little penthouse suite in the Bahamas or something."

In no time, the car pulled up to the curb in front of the deli next to the parking garage, and Dex mustered up a smile, holding his hand out to his father's old friend. "Thanks. I appreciate everything you've done for me."

"You know I'm always here if you need me." Littman took his hand in his and gave it a pat. "Dex?"

"Yeah?"

"He would have been proud of you."

The thought brought a lump to his throat. "You think so?"

Littman nodded, the conviction in his words going a long way to assure Dex. "I knew your dad a long time. Believe me. He would have been proud. And so is Tony. He's left me about ten messages asking about how you are. Your brother's probably worried sick as well."

Dex pulled his hand away to remove his smartphone from his pocket and chuckled at the fifteen missed calls from his family. He held it up. "You think?"

"Call your family before Tony hunts you down."

"I'll give them both a call soon as I get in. Thanks." After saying goodbye to Littman, Dex once again thanked him for helping him keep his sanity throughout all this and what was surely to come. Dex headed toward the rental in the parking garage. He wasn't stupid enough to drive his precious baby to the courthouse. It was hard to lose the media in an Orange Pearl Dodge Challenger. If they weren't in the city, he'd leave them eating his dust, but since he was in the city, it would make him a sitting duck.

As soon as he walked around to the rental's driver's side, he was doubly grateful he hadn't brought his car, though he was no less pissed. Someone had slashed his back tire.

"You've got to be fucking kidding me."

He kicked the tire, as if doing so might magically repair it. Goddamn it, he should have let Littman drive him home. All he wanted was to get indoors, get something to eat, and vegetate on the couch. Thank God for auto clubs. He reached into his pocket for his phone when someone across the lot called out.

"Detective Daley!"

Instinctively he looked up. A split second later, the air rushed out of his lungs when something solid struck him between his shoulder blades. He stumbled forward, a blow to his thigh forcing him onto his hands and knees with a painful growl. Around him, three large Humans in black ski masks and black gloves crowded him. Damn it, where had they come from? Dex moved, intent on pushing himself to his feet, when someone kicked him in the stomach, leaving him once again winded. He landed roughly on his side, holding on to his bruised ribs and stomach, his teeth gritted as he breathed heavily through his nose.

"You fucked up, Daley. You shouldn't have testified against your partner."

"Fuck you," Dex spat out. Another kick confirmed mouthing off wasn't appreciated. They obviously didn't know him. With a groan, he leaned slightly to take in the sight of their neat attire. Maybe they did know him. "Who sent you?" He didn't need to know. What's more, he didn't care. All he needed was enough time to figure out who he was up against.

"The Human race," one of them snarled.

Dex let out a laugh. What an ass. It hadn't taken him long to piece things together after noticing the gang's black dress slacks and shiny black shoes. With a curse, he rolled forward to press his forehead against the asphalt. The only surprising part of this whole encounter was the fact it hadn't come sooner. At least they weren't going to kill him, just make him bleed a little. "Well, I got the message, so you can all go home now. You did your duty." He received a blow to the arm with the shiny steel baton; most likely the same object they'd used to hit him in the back. Man, he was going to be sore tomorrow.

They dragged him to his feet, one holding on to each of his arms as the third came to stand before him. Dex closed his eyes and braced himself, his mind chastising him for being such a coward. The punch landed square across his jaw, snapping his head to one side and splitting his lip. *Fuuuck, that hurt.* He ran a tongue over his teeth to make sure nothing was loose. Nope, nothing there but the tangy taste of his own blood.

"Hey! HPF! Hands where I can see them!"

The Humans bolted and Dex's knees buckled beneath him. Strong hands caught him, helping him stay on his feet. His back stung, his arm, thigh, and face throbbed from the blows, and his stomach reeled at the knowledge he'd done nothing.

"Daley, you okay?"

Dex recognized that voice. He looked up, puzzled to find fellow Homicide Detective Isaac Pearce holding him up, concern etched on his face.

"Pearce?"

Pearce helped him to the rental and propped him up against it, performing a quick assessment. Seeming confident Dex could stand, he surveyed the parking garage, but the perpetrators were long gone. His attention landed back on Dex. "You all right?"

"Yeah. Wish I could say the same about my suit." Dex straightened, wincing at the sharp pain that shot through his body. "What are you doing here?"

"The usual summons, but my guy never showed. It was a nice day, so I figured I'd walk it. Glad I left when I did."

"Yeah, me too." Dex let out a small laugh, then winced at the sharp sting it brought his lip. Tony was going to lose his shit over this.

"Any idea who they were?" Pearce asked worriedly.

Yep. "Nope." Dex shook his head, wiping his hands on his slacks. "Just some pissed-off Humans." He had enough on his hands without bringing a whole new level of crap down on himself. "To be honest, right now I just want to get home."

"Don't blame you." Pearce motioned toward the slashed tire. "Need a lift?"

If he called the auto club now, Dex would have to wait for someone to come out—because he sure as hell didn't have the strength or will to change the tire himself, wait for them to swap it out, then drive the rental back to the lot. Or he could accept Pearce's offer and worry about the rental later.

"A lift would be greatly appreciated."

"Great." Pearce beamed at him. "I'm around the corner."

With a murmured "Thanks," Dex accompanied Pearce to his car, a silver Lexus that was more befitting a homicide detective. At least that's what his old partner, Walsh, would have thought. The guy never did approve of Dex's tastes. Come to think of it, Walsh was always making snide comments about what a "special snowflake" Dex was. He'd never paid much attention to the remarks, but in light of recent events, it was possible Walsh had always been a judgmental prick. Had Dex simply turned a blind eye to all of it? What if Dex had called him out on it sooner? Could they both have been spared all this?

"You okay?" Pearce asked again as soon as Dex was settled into the passenger seat beside him.

"Yeah, sorry. I'm still trying to wrap my head around all of this."

"Why don't you put on some music? Relax a bit. I'll even let you choose the station."

Dex gave a low whistle as he slipped on his seat belt. "You're going to regret giving me that kind of power." He turned on the radio and navigated through the touchscreen to *Retro Radio*. Dex grinned broadly at Pearce, wiggling his eyebrows when Billy Ocean's "Get Outta My Dreams, Get Into My Car" came blaring through the speakers. Pearce stared at him as if he'd lost his mind and Dex laughed. "I told you, you'd regret it."

With a chuckle, Pearce drove out of the parking garage. "Where to?"

"West Village, Barrow Street."

Despite Bobby McFerrin advising Dex a few minutes later not to worry and be happy, Dex was finding it difficult. *If it were only that easy, Bobby. If only.*

The ride down Sixth Avenue was quiet, filled mostly with power ballads and electro pop from the era of neon spandex, mullets, and shoulder pads with a wingspan to rival that of a Boeing 747. Dex appreciated Pearce letting him zone out instead of trying to make idle conversation. It was odd, being in Pearce's car with him. They'd never offered more than the usual office greetings, despite both working homicide from the HPF's Sixth Precinct. Then again, Pearce had retreated into himself after losing his brother over a year ago, and no one at the Sixth could blame him. Having a younger brother of his own, Dex could imagine how hard it must have been on the poor guy.

Traffic wasn't too bad this time of day, slowing down mainly near Tribeca Park and a few pockets down Sixth Avenue. Less than ten minutes later, they were driving onto busy Bleecker Street. Maybe he could convince Lou to pick him up a burger and fries from Five Guys on the corner. It was dangerous, having that place so close to his house. They pulled up in front of Dex's brownstone, and Pearce turned to him with a smile. "Well, here we are."

"Thanks for not kicking me out of your car," Dex said, shutting off the radio.

"I'll admit I came close when Jefferson Starship came on, but then I saw you tapping your hand in time to the music, and you had this sappy smile on your face… I didn't have the heart." Dex gave a snort and leaned back in his seat, smiling when Pearce started laughing. "You are one weird guy." Pearce's smile faded, and he suddenly looked a little embarrassed. "Want to get a coffee sometime?"

"Sure." Dex tried not to let the surprise show in his voice.

"I know we've never said more than a few words to each other, but you're a cool guy, Daley." His brows drew together in worry, making him appear older than he was. Dex wasn't more than a couple years younger than Pearce, but their job didn't exactly allow for aging gracefully. "Be careful. I'd hate—" Pearce's voice broke and he cleared his throat. "I'd hate for you to get hurt over all this. My brother, Gabe, believed in what he was doing, and look where it got him."

Dex frowned, trying to drum up what he remembered from the incident. He remembered it had been especially hard on Pearce, not having access to the case. But since Gabe had been a THIRDS agent, the HPF had no jurisdiction. "I thought the guy involved had been a Human informant?"

Pearce shook his head. "He was an HPF informant, but he wasn't Human. He was Therian. A kid."

Shit. Pearce's brother had been killed by a Therian informant and here he was, coming to rescue a guy who'd testified against his Human partner in favor of a young Therian punk. "So why aren't you kicking the shit out of me too?"

A deep frown came onto Pearce's face. "If your partner was stupid enough to let his personal prejudice affect his judgment, he deserves what he got. The truth is I admire you. Not everyone would've had the balls to do what you did. What happened to Gabe… was different." He sighed, his expression troubled. "I'm just saying to watch your back. There are a lot of zealots out there looking for any excuse to carry out their own justice, and things have been getting worse since that second HumaniTherian was found dead a few months ago. Some of these Humans are out for blood."

Pearce wasn't wrong on that. Two HumaniTherian activists had been murdered in the last six months, and the evidence was pointing toward a Therian perpetrator, which meant jurisdiction fell to the THIRDS. Although the organization was doing its best to reassure the public, a storm was brewing between Humans and Therians, especially if they didn't catch whoever was behind it soon. Dex's testimony against his partner couldn't have come at a worse time.

"Thanks for the warning, Pearce." Dex stepped out of the car and closed the door behind him, taking a step to the side to wave at Pearce as he drove off. As soon as the guy was gone, Dex let out a sigh of relief. He loved his quiet little tree-lined street. With a smile, he painfully climbed up the steps to his front door. Finally he was home. He stuck the key into the lock, turned it, and pushed the door open, baffled when it went *thump* halfway. Christ, now what? Something heavy was wedged up against it. With a frustrated grunt, he forced it open and carefully stuck his head in, frowning when he saw the large open cardboard box filled with DVDs, CDs, and a host of other things that should have been in his living room. His initial thought went to burglary, except he'd never run into thieves who stopped to bubble wrap their stolen merchandise.

"Lou?"

Dex locked the door behind him and wandered into the living room, his jaw all but hitting the floor at the near-empty state of it, along with the many cardboard boxes littered about in various stages of completeness. Something banged against the floor upstairs, and Dex took the stairs two at a time.

"Babe?" Dex found his boyfriend of four years upstairs in their bedroom, throwing shoes into empty boxes. "What's going on?"

"I'm moving out."

The words hit Dex like a punch to the gut, a feeling he was growing all too familiar with these days. "What?" He quickly maneuvered through the obstacle course of boxes and scattered manbags to take hold of his boyfriend's arms, turning him to face him.

"Sweetheart, stop for a second. Please, talk to me." He went to cup Lou's cheek, only to have Lou move his face away. Ouch. Double sucker punch. Tucking the rejection away for later, he focused on getting to the bottom of this. "Lou, please."

"The nonstop phone calls, the reporters knocking on the door, the news reports on TV calling you a disgrace to your species. I can't take it anymore, Dex."

Guilt washed over him, and he released Lou. How many more casualties would there be as a result of his doing "the right thing"? "Give it some time. This will all blow over. What if we go somewhere far away from this, the two of us, huh?"

Lou shook his head and went back to packing. "I have a life to think about. I've already lost half a dozen clients. I can't afford to lose any more."

"This is New York, Lou. One thing you won't run out of is parties to cater. It's almost September; next thing you know it'll be Halloween and you'll be knee-deep in white chocolate ghosts and tombstone ice sculptures, telling your clients how throwing a party in a real graveyard is a bad idea." When his lighthearted approach failed, Dex knew this was serious. Of course, to most people, the packed boxes would have been a dead giveaway, but Dex wasn't most people. He refused to believe Lou would walk out on him when he needed him the most. "What about me? Aren't I a part of your life?" Dex was taken aback when Lou rounded on him, anger flashing in his hazel eyes.

"You sent your partner to prison, Dex!"

Unbelievable. It wasn't bad enough he was getting it from everyone else, now he was getting it at home too? Dex was growing mighty tired of being treated like a criminal. "*I* didn't send him to prison. The evidence against him did. He shot an unarmed kid in the back and killed him, for fuck's sake! How am I the asshole in this?" He searched Lou's eyes for any signs of the man who'd wake him up in the middle of the night simply to tell him how glad he was to be there with him.

"It wasn't like you'd be able to bring the kid back. Not to mention he was a delinquent *and* a Therian!"

Dex's anger turned into shock. "Whoa, what the hell, Lou? So that makes it okay? What about Cael? He's a Therian. You've never had a problem with him." At least Lou had the decency to look ashamed.

"He's your family. I had no choice."

This was all news to him. Dex loved Cael. He would never push his brother out for anyone. He'd been upfront about his Therian brother when he and Lou had first started dating. If his date couldn't accept Cael, he couldn't accept Dex. "Where is all this coming from? Since when do you have a problem with Therians?"

"Since one ruined my fucking life!" Lou chucked a pair of sneakers at one of the boxes with such force the box toppled over.

"*Your* life?" This conversation grew more astounding by the minute. Dex thrust a finger at himself. "Have you seen my face? I got the shit kicked out of me in the parking garage, thanks for noticing. If a fellow detective hadn't come along, I'd probably be in the hospital right now. And you know what the most fucked-up part of that is? They weren't even street thugs. They were fucking cops!" Dex had known the moment he'd seen their attire and the telltale signs of an ankle holster on one of them. The bastards had probably been at the trial.

Lou threw his arms up in frustration. "Your own cop friends don't want to have anything to do with you, and you expect me to pretend like nothing's happened?

To ignore everyone staring at me, saying, 'Oh, there goes that prick's boyfriend. He's probably a LiberTherian sympathizer too.' I don't want to get the shit kicked out me, Dex."

"Oh my God, seriously?" Humans loved throwing words like HumaniTherian and LiberTherian around as if they were insults. His strong belief that Therians and Humans deserved to be treated equally made him a HumaniTherian, even if he wasn't out picketing on the White House lawn, and he was fine with that. But that didn't make him a LiberTherian. He was hardly an anarchist, and considering he was in law enforcement, he'd never had a problem with authority, though he didn't follow it blindly either. He hated when someone tried to stick him in a little box with a label slapped on his ass. Like everything was black-and-white. Doing his best to summon patience despite his reservoir being nearly depleted, he took hold of Lou's hand and pulled him to their king-sized bed. Lou allowed himself to be led but refused to sit or even look him in the eye. "Do you care that much about what people think?"

No reply. Dex supposed he couldn't blame him. Things were so screwed up, he didn't know which way was up anymore.

"It's not just the trial."

Dex swallowed hard, wondering what new surprises Lou had for him. Sure, they argued sometimes, but no more than any other couple. They had fun together when their jobs allowed it, though now that he thought about it, it had been a while since they'd had a day off together. Lou had been as busy these days with his career as Dex had been with his own, but neither of them ever complained about not spending enough time together. Maybe that was the problem. He could fix that, though. He could take some time off work and take Lou somewhere nice, with sandy white beaches and cocktails. At least that's what he thought until he saw Lou's face.

It was over.

"I'm sorry. I can't do this anymore. I can't keep getting left behind; sitting here on my own until sun-up while you throw yourself into the line of fire every chance you get." The hurt in Lou's eyes only added to Dex's guilt.

"It's my job," Dex replied quietly, exhausted from the day's events, and quite frankly, the whole of his life at the moment.

"Saving the world is not your job. It's your obsession. An unhealthy one that will get you killed. You told me you became an HPF officer so you could make a difference there, like your dad, but if you keep this up, you're going to end up like him."

Dex's chest tightened. "Don't."

"That's why they're the *Human* Police Force. They don't want to see things your way. Okay, so some of them might change their minds, some probably already feel the way you do, but not enough of them to change the way things are. Why do you think the government opened the THIRDS?"

"What do you want from me, Lou? Do you want me to change? Is that it?" Dex leaned toward him, pleading. "I can do that."

Lou shook his head. "You are the job, Dex. I couldn't ask you to change who you are. What I want is for you to take care of yourself, and please, don't call me or come to my job." Lou tugged at his hand, and Dex reluctantly let go. "I'll send the movers for the rest of my stuff tomorrow while you're at work."

"That's pretty much the entire house," Dex murmured, taking stock of the near-empty room. He was also pretty sure Lou was leaving some stuff behind for him, like the bedding.

"Why do you think that is, Dex? You were never here. I was the one who made this a home."

The words made Dex's heart ache and when he spoke, his voice was quiet. "Was I that bad?"

Lou stepped up to him and placed a gentle kiss on his cheek. "You're a great guy, Dex. We had fun, and you were good to me, but we weren't right for each other. If it hadn't happened now, it would have happened eventually." He ran his fingers through Dex's hair, the tender gesture bringing a lump to his throat. Shifting forward, Dex wrapped his arms around Lou's waist and squeezed, his cheek pressed against Lou's chest.

"Please don't go."

"I'm sorry," Lou replied hoarsely, pulling away. "I'll leave the key in the mailbox."

Dex nodded and fell back onto the bed, his body feeling heavy and in pain, inside and out. He was so exhausted he couldn't find the will to do anything but lie there and wish his bed would swallow him up.

"I'm sorry, Dex. I really am."

"Me too," Dex murmured softly. A few minutes later, he heard the front door close, making him cringe. He rubbed his stinging eyes for a moment before his hand flopped back down to the bed. He should get up and shower. Instead, he lay there staring up at the white ceiling. In his pocket, his cell phone went off. He ignored it and closed his eyes. The landline started shrilling, and he let out a low groan. It was probably his dad. The answering machine beeped and a saccharine voice that was definitely not his dad's chirped, "Mr. Daley, this is a friendly reminder that your rental is due back at the lot before 6:00 p.m. Failure to do so will result in an additional day's charge being added to your credit card. We appreciate you using Aisa Rentals and hope you have a pleasant evening."

Dex checked his watch.

5:59 p.m.

Fuck. My. Life.

DEX WAS well on his way to having yet another spectacular clusterfuck of a week, despite feeling pretty confident things couldn't possibly get any worse than they'd been recently. After all, the last month had been pretty epic in the "screw you" department. It had been so bad, he'd actually been looking forward to the end of his two weeks' paid leave in order to get back to work. *Oh, Dex, you silly boy.*

Things can only get better.

Isn't that what Dex had been told this morning? Well, more like that's what the song on the radio had been harping about on his way to work. That's the last time he allowed himself to be reassured by an eighties song. *Retro Radio* was going to be deleted from his playlist first chance he got. That's if his head cleared up enough by the end of his shift to let him make sense of all the shiny glowing buttons on the dash of his car. *Nothing like a good old-fashioned shitkicking to start your morning on your first day back at work.*

It was true he'd been expecting some anger and hostility to come his way after what he'd done. The dirty looks and shoves into lockers or various similarly occupied spaces, his paperwork doubling as toilet paper in the restroom, his desk drawers filled with everything from doggie chew toys to rubber mice. All of it had been expected. Unpleasant, but expected. The friendly beatings? Not so much.

"Tissue?"

With a nod of thanks, Dex took the little paper hankie offered by Captain McGrier and dabbed his split lip. He resumed his slouch, tonguing the sore spot inside his mouth where he'd bitten himself after the first punch hit. His body was aching and his head was killing him, but at least he was pretty sure he wasn't concussed.

"Where'd they get you this time?" McGrier's bushy white brows drew together in an expression that could have meant anything from "I hope Anne's not making meatloaf again," to "I'm seriously considering punching you myself." For a man who only had one facial expression, he was sure tough to get a read on.

"Evidence," Dex replied. Knowing what McGrier was going to ask next, Dex didn't bother waiting. "And no, I didn't see who it was."

Peterson, Johnson, Malone, Rodriguez, and the IT guy with the mohawk and face full of shrapnel. What the hell was his name? Nick? Ned? Ned. Dick Ned.

Of course Dex had seen who it was. They both knew he'd seen who it was. Or more specifically, who *they* had been, but Dex wasn't about to rat out his own brethren, even if his brethren had happily worked him over moments ago in the isolated evidence locker. Damn. How had he become the most hated guy in the precinct? Even Bill—the guy who ate other people's lunches from the fridge—was less hated than him.

McGrier sighed heavily, his chair letting out a screeching protest as he leaned his heavy mass back. "You're one hell of a detective, Daley, but the fact remains, this can't go on."

"No kidding," Dex grumbled. "My dry cleaning bill's tripled in the last month."

"You're the only detective I know who comes to work looking like he stepped out of a goddamn men's fashion magazine. What the fuck is that in your hair?"

Dex instinctively touched his tousled locks. "Forming cream."

McGrier leaned forward and sniffed. "And what's that smell?"

"Citrus mint," Dex muttered, leaning away from him. "FYI, that was kind of creepy."

"FYI, you realize you're a homicide detective, right?"

"What are you trying to say?" Just because he felt like crap didn't mean he had to look it. Judging by the state of his captain's office, it was a pretty safe bet McGrier didn't agree. It was as if the man had an aversion to tidiness. Whenever McGrier called him in, Dex always managed to hover by the door and not step foot inside the Den of Disorder. It was a clean freak's worst nightmare. *Dex's* worst nightmare.

The leaves of the fake potted fern on top of the beat-up filing cabinet were drooping from the thick layers of dust. There were stacks of files—crookedly stacked files—with sheets sticking out every which way on every available surface. On file boxes along the side of the room. On McGrier's desk underneath three coffee mugs—one of which deserved nothing short of incineration, though the tar-like remnants of what had once been a thin layer of coffee might cause it to explode. How did the man work in this? The whole place was in need of a hazmat team.

"You eat Cheesy Doodles at your desk," McGrier informed him.

How'd they go from hair gel to cheese snacks? "Hey, don't knock the crunchy cheesy goodness. You're always eating pistachios—which, by the way, are messier—and you don't hear me bitching about it." Dex nodded toward the war zone of tiny shells on the desk in front of McGrier.

"Kids eat Cheesy Doodles. Grown men eat nuts."

Dex arched an eyebrow and opened his mouth, only to have McGrier jab a finger at him. "Don't you even think about it, wiseass."

"I was only going to say that grown men eat Cheesy Doodles too. That's why they put *extreme* on the packaging. And explosions. What's manlier than explosions?" McGrier's lips pressed together in what Dex translated to be some form of disapproval, so Dex decided to be serious for a moment. "All right, sir, you didn't call me into your office to talk about my wardrobe, Cheesy Doodles, or my love of nuts." Well, he'd tried. Judging by McGrier's scowl, he'd failed. "Fine, I'm sorry. Tell me what this is about."

"I think you know what this is about."

Dex couldn't even come up with a smartass remark. "Yeah, I know. What was I supposed to have done?" No way McGrier would answer that, but Dex liked to play the "what if" game with himself every now and then.

"You did what you believed was right. You need to stop beating yourself up over it."

He would have thought McGrier was trying to be funny if he suspected for even a moment the man had a sense of humor. "Why would I beat myself up when I've got plenty of other people to do that for me?" McGrier was unsurprisingly not impressed with his reply.

"I know you feel like shit right now, and I'm afraid what I have to say isn't going to make things any better."

That got Dex's attention and he sat upright, getting a sick twisting feeling in his gut. In the back of his mind, he'd been waiting for it, but now that it was happening, he wasn't as prepared as he thought he'd be. "What?"

"The commissioner isn't happy about finding the HPF in the middle of this shitstorm, especially with those unsolved HumaniTherian murders. I've been informed to advise you that it's time for you to move on."

"Move on? Move on to what?" The suits were pushing him out? Dex propelled out of his chair so fast it toppled backward. "That's what this is about, isn't it? Votes? Ten years I've been busting my ass here, giving you blood, sweat, and tears, and they're going to push me out for doing my goddamn job?" He slammed his hands on the desk, turning the tiny pistachio shells into launched projectiles. "This is bullshit, Cap!"

"Daley," McGrier said with quiet emphasis, his brows set in a straight line as if he couldn't fathom the reason for Dex's hissy fit. Dex didn't give a damn what his captain thought this was. They were talking about his career, a career that was being dismissed without so much as batting an eyelash, all so a bunch of bureaucratic assholes could bullshit their way through another election.

"There's no way I'm taking this lying down. You hear me? I've seen some pretty fucked-up shit in my time, but this—"

"You're not being pushed out. You're being promoted. Sort of."

"I—what?" Dex blinked a few times as he tried to decipher the words that had come out of McGrier's wobbly mouth. "What do you mean I'm being promoted? *Sort of.*" Now he was really confused.

"What I said. So, why don't you sit back down and relax before you have a stroke or something."

After setting his chair back on its legs, Dex resumed his seat. Not because he had been told to do so, but because he was afraid if he didn't, he might just have that stroke. "I'm being promoted to…."

Fill in the blank.

"It's more like you've been recruited." McGrier studied him closely. What kind of response was his captain expecting from him other than *Huh?*

"Huh?"

"As of this afternoon, you are a Defense agent for the THIRDS." The man grew quiet, and Dex couldn't help but wait for him to throw his arms out and shout "Ta-da!" with a show of jazz hands.

What was happening here? If he'd been told he was getting transferred, he would've understood. If he'd been told he was getting demoted, he would've understood. Hell, he would've understood being let go, but being recruited by the THIRDS? Nope. He couldn't say he understood. Especially since he'd never applied for a position in the first place, as he'd recently found himself stating repeatedly.

"But… how? *Why?* Maybe you can, I don't know, explain? I'm feeling a little slow today. One too many kicks to the head."

McGrier stood and started pacing. "Daley, whatever you may think, I like you. You're an honest young man with a good head on your shoulders. You were a damned good cop and became an even better detective. Things may die down around here, they might not, but I think your skills would be better suited to an organization with a different way of doing things. We both know if they tried to push you out or demote you, they'd lose the Therian vote, but if they promoted you to an organization with a reputation for supporting both Humans and Therians, it'd be a win/win situation for everyone."

"Yeah, if I'd been trying to get in, which I hadn't been. Right now it's a win/what the hell situation."

McGrier continued as if Dex hadn't spoken. "I had a meeting with Lieutenant Sparks while you were on leave, and she happens to have a position open on her team. The fact that you scored top of your class during the training and have Sergeant Maddock to put in a good word for you has made you a key candidate. You know Maddock has always wanted you over there with him and your brother. The THIRDS is the only organization I know of that allows family members to work together, so why not take advantage?"

Dex's mouth moved but nothing came out, so he decided it was best to shut it. Maybe he *was* concussed. Maybe he was in a hospital somewhere hopped up on meds and dreaming about getting recruited by the Therian Human Intelligence Recon Defense Squadron. Jesus Christ, the government loved their acronyms. Somewhere some government suit had jizzed his pants coming up with that one.

The Sixth Precinct had been Dex's home for the last ten years. They were like family. Then again, his "family" had pretty much disowned him in the last few months. Should he fight to stick around where he wasn't wanted? He'd already been beat up twice. If that wasn't their way of flipping him off, he didn't know what was.

McGrier was right, things might die down, or they might get worse. As it was, his presence alone had everyone on edge, and those same dickbags who'd cast him out were forcing everyone else to pick sides. He could spare a lot of good people a whole lot of grief if he took this position, not that he was being given much of a choice.

It all came down to whether he left quietly. He should be grateful for the opportunity. There were officers out there who'd clean toilets if it meant getting their foot through the THIRDS' door. Plus, Dex would get to work with his real family. That didn't make leaving his job behind any easier. It was the only familiar thing he had left. He was—had been—one of the Sixth's top homicide detectives, and he'd worked damn hard to get there. Of course, sitting in McGrier's office with a tissue to his bleeding lip made it pretty obvious he didn't have much of a career left to get back to. With a resigned sigh, he nodded.

"Okay. When do I start?"

With a grim nod, his captain resumed his seat. "September 23. They're giving you a week to catch up on all the new policies and codes before your introduction."

A knock sounded on the door, and Dex tilted his head back to get a better look at the fair-haired detective hovering outside. Ah, Pearce, his knight in tarnished armor. One of the selective few who didn't feel the need to share his opinions about Dex's so-called betrayal. When Pearce noticed him sitting there, he smiled widely.

"Hey, Daley."

"Pearce." Dex returned his smile. It's a shame he was leaving. He could see himself hanging out with Pearce, shooting the breeze over a couple slices of pizza, sharing a few beers on a lazy Sunday afternoon.

"You wanted to see me, sir?"

"Yeah. Daley's leaving us. He's been recruited to the THIRDS."

The air was vacuum-sucked out of the room, and Dex looked from Pearce to the captain and back, hoping someone could shed a little light on the unscheduled loss of atmosphere.

"What team?" Pearce asked quietly.

McGrier actually squirmed in his seat before clearing his throat. "Destructive Delta."

Pearce went tense all over, his jaw clenched so tight, he looked as if he might crack something. Dex suddenly remembered Pearce's brother, and he prayed his luck wasn't that bad. The THIRDS was huge. What were the chances he'd end up on the same team Agent Gabe Pearce had been on? *Shit.* He was Gabe's replacement, wasn't he?

Dex looked up at Pearce. "Same team?"

Pearce merely nodded, his lips pressed together in a thin line.

This wasn't awkward at all. Just great. No one wanted to be the guy who came in after a dead partner. Dex hated baggage, and now he was about to walk into a partnership with enough to fill an airport terminal. His new partner probably had all sorts of expectations, and they hadn't even met yet. Howard Jones had lied to him. Things were not getting better. They were getting worse by the minute.

"Congratulations." The word just about managed to squeeze past Pearce's lips.

"Thanks," Dex muttered.

"Do you know who your partner is?" Pearce sounded a lot more casual than he was probably feeling. Dex couldn't knock the guy for trying.

"No, uh, it's all kind of caught me by surprise."

Pearce nodded and turned his attention back to the captain.

"Pearce, you're going to take Dex's place until we get people shuffled around here. Why don't you walk him to his car? Dex, we'll send your stuff to THIRDS Headquarters, along with any paperwork."

In other words, the cap didn't want Dex getting roughed up now that he was part of a shiny new elite force, and if Pearce was with him, Dex would make it out of the building in one piece. Good times.

Dex got up, removed his Glock from his holster and placed it on McGrier's desk, along with his badge. He exchanged the whole "it was a pleasure working with you" bull with the cap, knowing neither one of them had anything else to say. They didn't bother with the whole "keep in touch" thing because they both knew it wasn't going to happen unless it was in an official capacity.

Pearce walked silently beside him through the old precinct, shoulder to shoulder, lost in his own thoughts. Dex couldn't tell if the look on his face was due to grief or antipathy, but he felt for the guy. He wanted to apologize to Pearce for his loss, for the promotion that reminded him of his loss, for the actions that led to his promotion that in turn reminded him of his loss. Dex would have apologized for his whole damn existence if he thought it would make a difference, but it wouldn't, so he didn't.

Dex had opted for parking his baby in the private parking garage across the street instead of the precinct lot, just in case. The amount of money paid for parking would be far less than what he'd have to shell out for a new windshield or paint job.

When they reached his car, Dex turned to Pearce, figuring this was probably the last he'd see of him. No chance Pearce was going to want to share that coffee with him now.

"Nice car."

"Thanks." Dex patted the hood of his baby with a dopey grin. Sometimes he liked to pretend he was John McClane in a *Die Hard* movie, except with more speed limits, fewer explosions, and generally a lot less action going on. He really needed to start daydreaming a little bigger. As he suspected, Pearce gave him a curt nod and turned to walk away, but to Dex's surprise, stopped.

"Watch your back over there, Daley, and don't expect a warm welcome."

Well, that didn't bode well. "Why do you say that?"

Pearce seemed to mull it over before turning back, his hands shoved into his jacket pockets. "Destructive Delta is in Unit Alpha, and those positions are the highest, most dangerous, most sought after in the THIRDS, yet Gabe's position is still open, has been on and off for over a year. What does that tell you?"

"I don't know, but I can imagine losing Gabe was probably tough for the team."

Pearce nodded, his lips pursed. "I'm sure it was, but the THIRDS don't mourn, they keep moving. They're not like the rest of us. Rumor is the team leader, Agent Brodie, has run off over half a dozen agents. I've met him, and believe me when I say he's the biggest asshole to walk this earth. As far as he's concerned, no one is good enough to replace Gabe. I would have found his loyalty admirable if he hadn't been the one to send Gabe to meet that Therian informant on his own the night he was killed."

"You think it was Agent Brodie's fault Gabe got killed?" Dex was concerned for Pearce. Maybe this team leader *was* an asshole, but if the THIRDS were as good as everyone claimed them to be, surely they wouldn't have sent in their own teammate knowing he couldn't handle himself. "You don't want to go down that path." Dex put a hand on Pearce's shoulder. "It doesn't lead anywhere good. I didn't know Gabe, but I get the feeling he wouldn't want you thinking like that either." Dex understood what it felt like to lose family at the hands of criminals. He also understood firsthand how dangerous it could be to fall into despair. Lucky for him, he'd had his adoptive dad—Anthony Maddock—at the time to pull him out before he'd lost himself.

"You're right." Pearce's scowl gave way to a sad smile. "Gabe wouldn't have wanted that. At least he died defending what he loved. Take care of yourself, Daley. I'll call you about that coffee."

With that, Pearce walked away, his footsteps resonating through the empty, cavernous garage until he disappeared into the shadows, leaving Dex standing by his lonesome facing an undiscernible future.

Damn you, Howard Jones!

CHARLIE COCHET is the international bestselling author of the THIRDS series. Born in Cuba and raised in the US, Charlie enjoys the best of both worlds, from her daily Cuban latte to her passion for classic rock.

Currently residing in Central Florida, Charlie is at the beck and call of a rascally Doxiepoo bent on world domination. When she isn't writing, she can usually be found devouring a book, releasing her creativity through art, or binge-watching a new TV series. She runs on coffee, thrives on music, and loves to hear from readers.

Website: www.charliecochet.com

Blog: www.charliecochet.com/blog

Email: charlie@charliecochet.com

Facebook: www.facebook.com/charliecochet

Facebook Reader Group: www.facebook.com/groups/charliecochet/

Twitter: @charliecochet

Pinterest: www.pinterest.com/charliecochet

Goodreads: www.goodreads.com/CharlieCochet

Instagram: www.instagram.com/charliecochet

THIRDS HQ: www.thirdshq.com

Would you like to receive news on Charlie Cochet's upcoming books, exclusive content, giveaways, first access to extras, and more? Sign up for Charlie's newsletter: bit.ly/CharlieCochetNews

Follow me on BookBub (www.bookbub.com/authors/charlie-cochet)!

CHARLIE
COCHET

THIRDS

THIRDS

BLOOD
&
THUNDER

Sequel to *Hell & High Water*
THIRDS: Book Two

When a series of bombs go off in a Therian youth center, injuring members of THIRDS Team Destructive Delta and causing a rift between agents Dexter J. Daley and Sloane Brodie, peace seems unattainable. Especially when a new and frightening group, the Order of Adrasteia, appears to always be a step ahead. With panic and intolerance spreading and streets becoming littered with the Order's propaganda, hostility between Humans and Therians grows daily. Dex and Sloane, along with the rest of the team, are determined to take down the Order and restore peace, not to mention settle a personal score. But the deeper the team investigates the bombings, the more they believe there's a more sinister motive than a desire to shed blood and spread chaos.

Discovering the frightful truth behind the Order's intent forces Sloane to confront secrets from a past he thought he'd left behind for good, a past that could not only destroy him and his career, but also the reputation of the organization that made him all he is today. Now more than ever, Dex and Sloane need each other, and, along with trust, the strength of their bond will mean the difference between justice and all-out war.

Sequel to *Blood & Thunder*
THIRDS: Book Three

New York City's streets are more dangerous than ever with the leaderless Order of Adrasteia and the Ikelos Coalition, a newly emerged Therian group, at war. Innocent civilians are caught in the crossfire, and although the THIRDS round up more and more members of the Order in the hopes of keeping the volatile group from reorganizing, the members of the Coalition continue to escape and wreak havoc in the name of vigilante justice.

Worse yet, someone inside the THIRDS has been feeding the Coalition information. It's up to Destructive Delta to draw out the mole and put an end to the war before anyone else gets hurt. But to get the job done, the team will have to work through the aftereffects of the Therian Youth Center bombing. A skirmish with Coalition members leads Agent Dexter J. Daley to a shocking discovery, and suddenly it becomes clear that the random violence isn't so random. There's more going on than Dex and Sloane originally believed, and their fiery partnership is put to the test. As the case takes an explosive turn, Dex and Sloane are in danger of losing more than their relationship.

www.dreamspinnerpress.com